Choose your Lane to love!
Readers love the
Romantic Suspense from AMY LANE

By Amy Lane

Published by DREAMSPINNER PRESS
www.dreamspinnerpress.com

By Amy Lane

Published by DREAMSPINNER PRESS
www.dreamspinnerpress.com

SLOW PITCH

AMY LANE

DREAMSPINNER
PRESS

Published by
DREAMSPINNER PRESS

5032 Capital Circle SW, Suite 2, PMB# 279, Tallahassee, FL 32305-7886 USA
www.dreamspinnerpress.com

Trade Paperback ISBN: 978-1-64108-245-7
Digital ISBN: 978-1-64080-546-0
Library of Congress Control Number: 2019957860
Trade Paperback published May 2020
v. 1.0

Printed in the United States of America

This paper meets the requirements of
ANSI/NISO Z39.48-1992 (Permanence of Paper).

Calling, the usual suspects. Mate—you think I don't pay attention, but I get why you love sports. Mary, Tenner is yours.

HATESEX AND BASEBALL

"HEY, BATTER batter, *sha-wing*, batter!"

Tenner Gibson rolled his eyes. God, that guy was annoying, but Tenner needed to get his head in the game. He eyed the pitcher across from him and hefted the bat, choking up a little for control.

Slow-pitch softball—the ball went up, up, up in an arc and came down, down, and Tenner waited for it to come just right—

"Sha-*wing, batter!*"

And he swung too early and whiffed.

"St-er-ike!" the umpire called, and Tenner lost his patience.

"Goddammit, Pat, could you make that asshole shut up!"

"C'mon, Ten-Spot!" the catcher chided. "What's up your craw? It's just a little trash-talking."

Pat Caldwell, Tenner's friend and the asshole who had drafted him into this league, grinned from behind his catcher's mask and chewed his bubblegum fiercely. Tenner could still hear their conversation....

"C'mon, Ten-Spot, the other team has to forfeit if they don't get one more player. If you play for them for the rest of this season, we can grab you for next season!"

"So I'm playing with a bunch of strangers for this season?" Tenner had rubbed the back of his neck and pulled his attention away from his computer.

Pat, ginger-haired, fortyish, handsome, and very, very married to his wife and three adorable children, held up his hands in supplication. "Please, Tenner. Next season is *this summer*. There's spring season, then summer, and then fall. C'mon, do me a favor, will you? I need to play. My daughters hate baseball—they want to play soccer. And my son's in love with ballet. If this team doesn't come up with another guy, we won't have enough teams in the league. And I worked my ass off scraping together a team of my own. We had to grab my wife's little brother to play for us. He's only here for two months *and* he's a self-professed asshole, and still, playing with him is better than not playing at all!"

"I don't have cleats!" Tenner protested. "Or pants or—"

Pat had three children under thirteen. He could sense a rare but important victory a mile away. "There's a sports store two blocks from here. Let's go!"

"But I have to call Nina." His ex-wife did *not* like her plans changed.

It didn't matter. Pat was dragging Tenner out of the office and into the bright spring day to his car—predictably a minivan—and taking him to the store for cleats, baseball socks, and those nylon pants you could slide in without taking off skin.

And a bright yellow shirt, because who didn't like the way they looked in bright bumblebee-wet-dream gold?

Besides Tenner, of course. He looked like he had jaundice. Even his eyeballs looked yellow.

But now he was a member of the CompuCo Sunspots, whether he liked it or not.

He had to admit, part of him was secretly thrilled. He hadn't played sports since college, and while he worked out daily—and was looking forward to coaching Under 8 soccer in the fall—there was something about playing competitively that just added to the joy of the whole thing.

And he'd always loved baseball.

He'd texted his ex-wife and told her he'd be picking Piper up later, if that was okay. Nina had not been pleased. *I have a date, Tenner. We agreed that you'd be punctual.*

He'd sighed. *Please, Nina. I'm at a softball game. I haven't played since college.*

He waited for a moment, knowing their layers of anger and guilt went both ways. *Fine. Remember she has gymnastics tomorrow.*

Thank you. I'll be there as soon as the game's over.

And so, here they were, bottom of the ninth, bases loaded, tied, two outs. All he needed was a base hit—a sad, soggy little base hit—and they could win the game and he could get to Nina's house before she even remembered she'd told him he could be late.

All he had to do was pretend the ball was this asshole's head.

Holy crap, the entire game this player on Pat's team had been nothing but a pain in Tenner's ass. For fuck's sake, had he never heard of moderation? The guy was cute—six-feet plus, blond hair that waved, stunning blue eyes—but damn, was he loud. Loud, obnoxious, and constantly taunting the other team, especially Tenner. He'd hooted and hollered when the other guys were up, sure, but with Tenner, he seemed to get a thousand times louder.

"Hey, batter batter, sha-*wing*, batter!"

Tenner used to be able to blow these guys off in college—and the shit talk had gotten pretty nasty then. It wasn't just "sha-*wing*, batter!" eight years ago. It had been "Come suck my fat johnson, faggot!" And that had been the pretty stuff.

It hadn't made Tenner's life particularly easy, because he'd never wanted to be a trailblazer. He'd wanted to have a perfectly normal life—wife, kids, job, the works. Enter Nina, who'd been a baseball groupie and had a fast-and-loose definition of the truth.

Particularly the truth of whether or not she was on birth control.

And here came the ball. The big, soft grapefruit-sized ball that Tenner wasn't quite used to yet. *Slow, Tenner. It's slow. Wait for it. Wait for it. Wait for—*

"Sha-*wing*, batter!"

Whiff!

"Strike three! You're out!"

"I swear to Christ, Pat, I'm going to rip off his skull and use it for a soccer ball!"

And Tenner's friend—his best friend, the only one with a front-seat view to Tenner and Nina and why they'd really gotten a divorce—laughed so hard, he sat down in the dirt.

"Ten-Spot, dude! That was the best swing! It's a good thing you didn't catch a piece of it or someone on the freeway would be dead!" The freeway was a good mile away. It was clearly an effort on Pat's part to not make Tenner quit in a fit of pique.

Tenner let go of some of his anger and held his hand out to help Pat up. "I'm gonna kill that asshole," he said as his team, with lots of groans and resentful looks at Tenner, made ready to take the outfield. Extra innings. He cast a glare over his shoulder at the guy—Ross Something Or Other—and seriously wished he could use his head for batting practice.

But it would sort of be a waste of a handsome bastard, Tenner could admit that. Well over six feet tall to Ten's five-eleven, Ross had that sort of rangy body that didn't seem capable of sinuous motion and was so much more beautiful because of it. Yeah, Tenner hated the guy—and his cocky Jake Busey smile in a leaner, prettier face—but he sure could admire his lazy blue eyes in tanned skin, with hair that was probably more brown in the winter but was bleached yellow by the sun.

God, before Nina, when Tenner had given in to his libido in college, Ross "I'm Gonna Fuckin' Kill Him" had been right up his alley.

Sadly, for the past few years, nothing had been up Tenner's alley but a fine assortment of medically safe novelty items with the appropriate washable lubricant, in controlled and very, very private circumstances.

He pulled his gaze away from Ross "I'm Gonna Fuckin' Kill That Guy" to watch Pat dust himself off, his good humor unshakable.

"Oh, dude! You can't kill him! That's my wife's brother, Ross McTierney."

"Nice whiff, man!" Ross said, smirking his way toward them. "You gonna go out to right field and see if you can smell that one sailing by?"

"You wanna make a bet," Tenner muttered to Patrick. "I could slit his throat in a church."

Pat rolled his eyes. "Go get your glove, Hamlet. We've got another inning to go."

Tenner turned on his heel so he didn't have to even look at Ross McTierney's grinning face and snagged his glove from the dugout. He was getting his team back to bat if he had to make every damned out himself.

HE LITERALLY had to make every damned out himself.

Their captain—a little, rather quiet guy in his twenties named Hanford Birmingham—had taken one look at Tenner lacing up his new cleats and been transported with glee.

"You can catch the ball?" he'd asked. "Like, if it comes at you? Our last first baseman used to just sort of scream and drop it. I think that's why he quit after one game."

Tenner tried not to sigh and reminded himself that he would get to be on Pat's team in eight weeks. And at least those guys appeared to know what they were doing.

"Yeah," he said gamely. "Catch, throw, hit occasionally. I can do it all."

He'd thought that Hanford was being... well, *unassuming* was the word that came to mind. But then he'd played the first inning and had seen firsthand how bad it was. The team's only real asset was Kipp

Harding, the pitcher, who could lob a softball up at a perfect rate of slowness. A guy could wear himself out swinging at the damned thing and right when they thought they could connect with the ball, it would crash the last four feet to the ground.

Uncanny.

Between Kipp striking guys out, Danny, who was about twenty years old and could run like the wind and maybe catch, playing center field, and Tenner on first, they were almost not awful. Unfortunately, Tenner was the only one who could hit, and thanks to Ross "Whose Head Would Make A Good Soccer Ball," he'd just blown the chance to win, five to four.

Tenner was late to pick up his daughter, he'd left a project on his desk that could get him a healthy raise, and he was stuck in the outfield or his team would forfeit when they were that close to a win.

"Piss in His Dead Skull" Ross McTierney was *not* going to fuck this up.

Fortunately, he wasn't hitting first.

The first guy—a fiftyish, semi-in-shape engineer—nailed the ball right toward Tenner's face. Tenner would have taken exception to that if he hadn't been able to block the ball and make the out.

The second guy lobbed a pop fly up, up, up, until Kipp—in a stunning burst of honesty in the heat of the game—had blurted, "Dude, I'm not catching that. Tenner, get over here."

And he had.

And then Ross Fuckin' McTierney got up to bat. He took a few practice swings, spat on the plate, and then, oh God, winked right at Tenner before sizing up Kipp's thirtysomething runner's body with a few lazy sweeps of those blue eyes.

And then he swung at the ball and tried to knock it clear to the freeway.

But Tenner was pissed, and he held a grudge, and dammit, he was due. He ignored poor Hanford, looking like a light-struck deer in right field, and hauled his ass toward the back fence and leaped, just as the ball arced down.

And he caught it, his glove raised in triumph, shouting, "Motherfucker, whiff *this*!"

"No!" Ross screamed, although he sounded more impressed than mad. "No! Oh my God, who *does* that!"

"I do," Tenner called back, grinning fiercely as he ran to the dugout. "I do."

He figured that was it. All they had to do was make one run. One lousy run. He hadn't made the other four. He'd batted them in, sure, but he was the ninth batter up this time. What were the odds they would fill the bases and get sent to the outfield—twice—without either team scoring?

What were the odds?

What *were* the odds?

What were the goddamned motherfuckin' odds?

Nina was texting him the entire time he sat in the dugout. He was only about a half-hour late; he knew that. He knew that picking Piper up in his baseball clothes wasn't the worst thing in the world. He even knew Piper's favorite TV show was on right now, so she wasn't going to wonder where he was.

But every ten seconds his phone buzzed, and by the time he got up to bat, he'd sent Nina a picture of the guys on the field so she could know he wasn't missing their daughter's future because he was lazy or lying or in a bar picking up a guy just so he could break the three-year-long dry streak he had going.

One more run, he texted. *And I'm on my way.*

They can't make it without you?

They'll have to forfeit the game. For all her flaws, Nina had a vicious competitive streak. He knew this.

Fine. You owe me.

He wanted to ask her, what else? Alimony? Child support? He paid double, on time, every month. The lost years he could have been happy? She had those too. His solemn promise not to go out and be gay? Well, he couldn't make it, but he'd promised not to let the worst parts of his "lifestyle" affect Piper, and he assumed that meant dating. Because whatever.

But he didn't ask her what else, because he had *this*. He had lights on a warm spring night, and a bunch of guys gamely trying to hit the ball, and he'd made four hits out of five at bats and one helluva play in the outfield.

Sitting there, hoping at least one of these guys could make a run before the final out, he allowed a little peace to seep into his soul.

God, he'd missed this.

And then Hanford made the second out of the inning, and Kipp went up and made it to third base, and it was Tenner's turn to hit the ball again.

"Hey, batter batter, sha-*wing*, batter!"

But Tenner had that peace in his soul this time. This time when Ross "Fuck You" McTierney shouted "sha-*wing*, batter!" he paused a breath, just a breath, before he swung.

The ball never fucking landed.

TEN MINUTES later, he was *still* trying to pack up his bag to leave, after dealing with congratulations and thank-yous from his team. And, he had to admit, they felt pretty damned good.

Man, sometimes when life was stressful and you were getting homicidal, it was good to nail the crap out of that grapefruit-sized white ball and relieve some frustration! His shoulders and chest still rang with the force of the swing that had sent the ball out into the stratosphere, and he was going to take the win.

"Thanks so much for playing with us," Hanford said, extending his hand tentatively. Now that he'd shown the damned ball who was boss, Tenner could relax enough to appreciate Hanford for trying to coach a disparate bunch of nonathletes in a game he wanted to play for fun.

"Thank you for letting me," he said sincerely. "I look forward to playing for you the rest of the season."

Hanford's face—small, sort of plain, round with a pointed chin— lit up like a Christmas tree. "Until June? Oh, that's wonderful." He bit his lip. "You wouldn't want to...." His eyes darted to the parking lot. "We don't have a budget or anything. It's just, you know, recreational. But I would love it if you could practice with me and the guys on Sunday. Like, give us some pointers?" His eyes, big and limpid and brown, were his best feature, and they sent a faint tingle to Tenner's gut. "Please?"

Sunday. "Can I bring my daughter?" he asked, thinking there was a playground he could see from any of the four diamonds at the park. There was even a fountain mat for water play.

"Absolutely." Hanford really was sort of adorable when he smiled. "My sister's bringing her kids. They can play together."

"Your sister?" Tenner asked.

Hanford shrugged. "We all have dinner at my parents' Sunday night. We're kind of a tight family." He gave another one of those puppy-dog looks from those big brown eyes. "I can't wait to see you Sunday. Bye!"

"Bye," Tenner called a little wistfully. Sweet kid. Tenner was getting a definite playing-for-Tenner's team crush vibe from him, and man, didn't some admiration feel good?

He turned back to put on his regular tennis shoes and shove his cleats in his new equipment bag, shucking his hitting gloves off with them. He still smelled like sweat and dust, but man, had he missed that stench in the last eight or so years.

He'd missed a lot of things.

But at the moment, baseball was the only thing he could have, so he was going to enjoy it.

The last five minutes with Hanford had given the rest of the players time to clear out. He stood up and swung the bag over his shoulder, looking for his car beyond the field in the empty parking lot, when a deep voice behind him almost made him trip.

"Nice fucking catch."

Oh God. Not this asshole. "Nice fucking chatter," Tenner told him, coming out of the dugout and barely squeezing by Ross "Stealthy As A Cheetah" McTierney.

"Chatter's part of the game. Being a superhero is just showing off."

Tenner was relaxed enough with victory to not mind when McTierney came up alongside him and matched his pace. The sidewalk that ran between the four now-vacant fields also ran behind the snack bar and the restrooms before passing three playgrounds and feeding into the parking lot. Somewhere behind them, the guy who umped the game was walking toward the big pole with the circuit breaker on it to turn off the lights. But other than that, they were alone.

"Oh, and nailing that sucker over the fence in my direction wasn't showing off?" Tenner retorted. "I watched you set up that hit. You could have sent it over Hanford's head, like you'd been doing all night, or you could have sent it over mine and… and… that poor kid in right field, bless his heart."

"You don't even know his name?" McTierney guffawed.

"No, I don't know his name! I've known this team exactly as long as I've known you, but I like them better."

"Well, then, that's because you don't really know me, do you?" McTierney sallied with a cheerful wink. Tenner resisted a hard swallow, because when he wasn't being an asshole on the field, this guy was actually sort of fun. A slug to the gut, and not a faint tingle, a cocky, strutting asshole with a charming smile.

"Look, just because you're Patrick's brother-in-law, that doesn't mean we're going to be besties. Wait, what are you—"

They were nearing the bathrooms, and McTierney sped up enough to cut Tenner off, leaning his arm up on the cinderblock wall that provided cover for the entrance of the ladies' room and grinning directly into Tenner's face.

"Not talking about Pat," he said, eyes hooded, lower lip bitten suggestively. "And we don't need to be besties. But I do think you want to get to know me a little better."

Oh wow. He was right there. Close enough Tenner could smell the same grass and sweat and dust on Ross McTierney's body that he could smell on his own.

"I, uh...." It came out as a squeak, and Tenner had to stop and clear his throat. "I don't have time for this," he said. It came out a little stronger this time.

Ross's smirk cranked up to eleven. "We don't need much time," he purred, and Tenner was unprepared—so woefully unprepared—for the sucker punch of libido that woke up his cock, balls, nipples, taint, asshole, and all of his skin in one glorious breath.

He could swear his swallow echoed to the parking lot. "You, uhm...."

Ross leaned closer, and he must have spit out his gum, but Tenner could still smell the pop of mint on his breath. "I have wanted that tight little ass since you stepped out on the field, and your snotty little attitude hasn't changed my mind."

Time stopped, and Tenner was aware of the width of that long body, the faint twist of that upper lip, and the dare in those sky-blue eyes.

With an audible click, the vast intrusive banks of overhead lights that blessed the field went dark, leaving only the sunspots behind their eyes remaining.

And then it was just him, him and this devastating man, sweaty and alone in the spring dark.

Ross might have advanced first, leaning a little more until Tenner could smell the remnants of aftershave, but Tenner moved the hardest, sealing their mouths together in an explosion of adrenaline and frustration and lust.

UP AGAINST THE WALL

DAMN BUT Ross wanted him. No-holds-barred wanted him. He'd worked to piss him off during the game, had practically strained something in his back trying to send that ball over the guy's head in right field, had been itching to grab that tight little ass from the moment this guy had stalked onto the field with his smoldering brown eyes and "Got better shit to do!" expression.

Ross was going to give him better shit to do, and Tenner was going to by God *like* it.

And the way he sprang into the kiss, all tongue and teeth and hands rucking up the back of Ross's shirt—Ross couldn't see his profile in the dark, but he could feel the guy, his compact frame, his wound-up energy—he wanted to fuck that tight into loose, that power into compliance, that stalk into sprawl.

He reached down and cupped Tenner's ass, gratified when Tenner hopped up and wrapped his legs around Ross's waist. Oh God, his cock was erect through his baseball pants and rubbing against Ross's abdomen, and Ross couldn't wait to even get to the car.

Without breaking the kiss, he carried Tenner around the corner, into the alcove over the ladies' restroom. He held one hand up behind Tenner's head as they hit the back wall, and he heard Tenner grunt as Ross's knuckles scraped the cinderblock.

"Sorry," he mumbled. "Okay?"

"It's nothing." Tenner pulled away to kiss down Ross's jaw and nibble on his neck, and Ross's knees got a little wobbly. Oooh… wow. He loved a good neck nibble. He let go of Tenner's ass, and Tenner took the hint, putting his feet on the ground and shoving his hands under Ross's shirt.

He actively kneaded everything—abs, pecs, *holy hell, nipples!*—and Ross fumbled with Tenner's belt so he could get to the good stuff. He shoved down everything, pants and jock, and fell to his knees.

Oh wow, this guy was primed. Erect, dripping, thick, Ross devoured him, tasting the bitter tang of precome. He had to use two hands to wrap around it, and he pulled back long enough to look into Tenner's eyes in the moonlight to show his appreciation.

"Fucking monster," he breathed. "Gorgeous cock."

Ross went back to sucking, and Tenner mumbled something and then moaned.

"Am I hurting you?" Ross asked, because even if he was about to fuck against a cinderblock wall, that was the last thing on his mind.

"I'm gonna come and my health screen is clear," Tenner said, and Ross tightened his fist, because what a good guy.

"Good, come quick, let me swallow!" He went to suck again. It had been a while and he loved the feel of that monster stretching his lips, pushing back into his throat, but he had a thought. He paused for a moment, still stroking, his breath brushing Tenner's head. "But I wanna fuck you too. Do you tighten up too much?"

"I don't remember," Tenner said, and Ross frowned before moving one of his hands and rooting through his back pocket. He ignored the two foil packets he'd put there right after the game and managed the little ampoule of lube. He handed the lubricant off to Tenner.

"I'm going to go slow for a bit," he said, shuddering in anticipation. "Use that and stretch yourself out. We're gonna have some fun."

His own cock was ripe and wet in his jock, the ache exquisite. Slowing down enough to let Tenner move, seeing his hand go back, shiny with slickness, knowing what he was doing with his two fingers, made Ross need.

Tenner relaxed, a hum of happiness filling the little alcove. "Ah...." *Yes! A man who loved to bottom!* Ross enjoyed bottoming too, but this was his sexual fantasy, and it involved taking this guy's tight ass until he melted.

And judging by the amount of precome he was leaking into Ross's mouth, Ross was well on his way.

"How's your ass, Ten?" Ross asked, the diminutive slipping out. "Slack? Loose? Begging for more?"

His response was a moan and—*oh yes!*—a thrust into Ross's fist. Lovely. Ross took a breath and swallowed as much of that glorious cock as he could, giving Tenner's balls a gentle roll as he did.

Tenner moved his free hand to his mouth to muffle his cry, and his cock spurted hard, and again, dumping come down Ross's throat as if he hadn't come in years.

Ross swallowed it greedily. So long. It had been so long since Ross had wanted a guy like this. Tenner, stalking onto the field, taking that happy bullshit game as serious as nuclear physics, lightening up at the end and smiling at that sweet little puppy with the crush—all of it had made Ross want him more.

Tenner made a sound of discomfort, and Ross pulled off immediately, standing up as quick as he could, given that he'd hit thirty that year and his knees weren't fifteen anymore. He leaned in for a kiss, gratified when Tenner responded, opening his mouth, accepting his own taste, the kiss growing passionate and urgent once more.

While they kissed, Ross worked his own belt, pushing the works down and enjoying the feel of the breeze on his sweaty bits.

His cock bobbed painfully, though, and unless he wanted to just blow his cool by rutting against this guy's hip until he came, they needed to get a move on.

"Turn around," he whispered, and Tenner's compliance was one of the most gratifying things he'd ever witnessed.

Ross slid the condom on with fingers nimble from want, if not recent practice.

"It's been a while," Tenner panted, and Ross dropped his hand, testing the stretch, stretching some more.

"That's a shame," he rasped in Tenner's ear, spreading his two fingers. "That's the sweetest, tightest ass I've felt in a long time."

Tenner moaned into his own shoulder, and the sound sent sparks of excitement dancing up Ross's spine. Tenner wanted this as much as Ross did, and that was so damned sexy.

He pulled his fingers out, gratified by the little whimper of loss Tenner made, and then replaced the fingers with his cock.

"Ahhhh...."

The sigh came from both of them. Tenner's ass gripped him like a vise, but as Tenner pushed out eagerly, accepting, Ross glided in, the extra lubricant doing its job. *Oh... oh....*

"Oh wow," Tenner whispered, resting his head against the cinderblock wall. "So good."

Ross paused to kiss the back of his neck, behind his ear, the corner of his jaw. To his surprise, Tenner reached back over his shoulder and cupped Ross's head.

"Should I move?" he asked, his lips brushing Tenner's ear.

"Please?"

"I love to hear you beg."

Slow at first—for Ross, so he could savor, and for Tenner, because he was so tight—Ross began to thrust.

Tenner was muffling the most amazing noises behind his fist, and Ross spent a moment wishing they could linger, that he could torment this tight-assed sexual powerhouse by going slow until he screamed. But he knew that eventually a patrolman would be by to make sure there weren't deviants in the park doing pretty much what he and Tenner were doing right now, so he began to move faster.

Tenner's moans grew too loud to muffle.

"Shhhh…," Ross soothed, pulling that thick dark hair back from Tenner's face. "Sh… I'm gonna go for it, okay? I'm gonna do us both right."

"God, yes!" It came out as a whispered shout, and Ross had just enough humor left to chuckle before everything became his cock in Tenner's ass and the two of them pumping, a hot red ball of lust in the dark.

Ross started fucking like he'd never fucked before.

Tenner grunted softly, once, twice. "Am I hurting you?" Ross demanded, praying he wasn't, because God, he didn't want to stop.

"Don't you dare stop!"

And thank you, Big Guy, for the license to fuck!

Faster and faster, and heavens to betsy, Tenner was so tight, so soft, so sweet, so—

"Mmmmmmffffff!" Tenner howled into his shoulder, his ass tightening so hard on Ross's cock he couldn't move, and Ross buried his face against Tenner's neck and came.

For a moment, his eyes closed in the dark. All he could smell was Tenner's sweat, all he could feel was Tenner's skin against his cheek, Tenner's grip around his cock, and all he could hear was Tenner's harsh breathing against the cinderblock wall.

Tenner's come saturated his taste buds, and his entire world was this moment, bound together with this surprising man.

Ross had to do this again.

"Oh shit," Tenner mumbled. "Hell. I've got to go."

"That's disappointing," Ross said, taking a deep breath before grabbing his condom at the base of his cock and pulling out. "I was sort of hoping for a beer or something afterwards."

"Oh my God." Tenner leaned his head against the cinderblock. "I have a daughter!"

"That's so cool! Where's she at?"

"Oh shit oh shit oh shit." Ross had stepped back to tie off the condom and throw it in the trash can right by the closed door, while Tenner was using the space to scramble into his pants. He adjusted himself very carefully and then tucked in his shirt, like the tightass he was, and zipped up.

"You okay there, Tenner?"

"I have to go pick her up!" Tenner practically wailed. "I'm sorry—" He paused in the act of grabbing his equipment bag and slinging it over his shoulder. "I... I don't usually do this sort of thing. Is there... is there, like, protocol or—"

"Buddy, hold up," Ross said gently. He turned Tenner toward him and wiped his lips off and straightened his hair. Keeping one hand on Tenner's stomach, he did a quick squat and scoop and came back with Tenner's hat, which he placed on his head at the exact angle Tenner had worn it all night. "You're not too late. That took us, what? Eight minutes? Nobody will ever know."

Tenner's mouth parted a little as Ross straightened him up, and the look in his eyes was so yearning, so vulnerable, Ross wanted him all over again.

But not against a cinderblock bathroom alcove—in a real bed, like grown-ups, with sunlight and everything. Tenner's stomach tightened under his hand, and Ross grimaced.

"Wait a minute. We gotta do that again." He took off Tenner's hat in spite of Tenner's protests.

"We can't do that again. I've got to—"

"You've got jizz on your shirt, Ten. Here." He yanked his own shirt out of his pants and jerked it over his head. Tenner's was bright Sunspot yellow, but Pat's team was in a reasonably dignified indigo. Ross pulled the yellow one off, over Tenner's head, before hauling the blue one on. Then he let Tenner tuck himself in while Ross dealt with the hat again. "There. No jizz. No one will ever know."

Well, someone observant might, because Ross would bet that in the light, Tenner's mouth was swollen from Ross's kisses. But here in the dark, all Ross could see were the limpid brown eyes.

"You are… surprisingly sweet," Tenner said with dignity. "I'm sorry. I've got to—" He started off down the baseball path, but Ross kept pace. "What are you doing?"

"I'm parked out this way too. Besides, I couldn't just let you walk out here in the dark."

He heard Tenner's snort. "I am a grown-assed man."

"And you are a tight-assed one too," Ross said with a smirk. "But it's not safe for anyone. See?" he said as they rounded the corner. Two vehicles were there—Ross's Tahoe and Tenner's little CR-V. Ross's was fire-engine red, special order, because when he was in the States, he worked a lot of job sites off-road, and Tenner's car was a more sedate white, but Ross had sort of figured that.

As they approached their cars, a security vehicle turned in and started a loop around the parking lot. They both trotted a little faster, and Tenner called out to him, "Hey, how will I get you your shirt back?"

Ross was still bare-chested, but he held Tenner's yellow shirt in his hand.

"Don't worry. I'll find you!"

And then Tenner was taking off, Ross not far behind him.

Ross hadn't missed the fact that Tenner and Ross's brother-in-law were friends. It was time to have a little heart-to-heart with Patrick about the buddy he'd dragged to the game.

NEVER TOO LATE

"OH MY God, Tenner, how many games did you play?"

Tenner had a lot of practice keeping his temper. "I'm so sorry, Nina. The game went into extra innings. I promise, next time you'll have more warning."

Nina—petite and brunette with the angular features of a fashion model—rolled her green eyes. "Did you at least win?"

And Tenner couldn't have stopped the smile if he'd tried. "Yes, yes, we did." *And I got an extra play for my pay.*

"Well, you don't need to come in. She's been waiting."

"Thank you again for letting me play. It's been a while, and I had a blast." He smiled again tentatively, hoping as he always did for some sort of truce. Détente. Peace. They'd survived the hard years together, hadn't they? Piper in diapers, with colic, Nina still in school getting her business degree. Tenner remembered playing tag team, coming home from work and taking baby duty while Nina worked on papers. They'd both been sleep deprived in the 7-Eleven, on their last diaper. All this hostility now just seemed so... pointless.

"Well, I'm glad *you're* happy," she snapped. "I'll be lucky if I can get to the restaurant on time."

"Don't let me stop you," he said. "Piper, honey, you have all your stuff?"

"Coming, Daddy!" Piper charged through the door with two backpacks on her shoulder. "Sorry, I had to pack my dolls."

Tenner caught her on her way out and hefted her up in his arms. She was almost too big, but not yet. "Look at you!" He grinned. "Did you grow?"

She grinned back, showcasing a missing tooth. "No, but look what happened!"

"The tooth monster came and *stole* your tooth!" he said, making his eyes big and wide. "Oh no, how could you let that happen?"

She giggled. "No, Daddy! I *lost* the tooth. My whole class is losing their front teeth. I'm the third to the last one."

"Well, it's a good thing it fell out, because that would have been horrible right there. How will we ever show our faces if you're the last kid in the class without a hole in her mouth?"

Piper threw her head back, lost in a cloud of dark hair, and giggled. "It's a *tooth*!" she squealed. "Not a hole!"

He winked. "Sure, sure, that's what they tell you because they don't want you to worry. Now go hop in your jump seat, and I'll check your belt in a minute, okay?"

"Yes, Daddy."

He rubbed noses with her and set her down, smiling tiredly as she ran. "She's a great kid, Nina. I love her little outfit." It was pink and frilly, and super expensive. He didn't mind any of those things, but he didn't tell Nina about the drawer full of basic shorts and jeans and T-shirts that Piper had picked out with him so they could do things like go on walks or go fishing or play in the dirt while she was with him. He dropped her off at school clean, in her mom-approved clothes, with her hair braided neatly, and Nina never had to know.

"So glad you approve," Nina said, sounding surprised and a little pleased. "Don't forget gymnastics."

"Have I ever?" Usually he could take her baiting, but gah! Tonight he'd felt wanted. Was that it? After two and a half years of dealing with someone who hated his guts, someone had literally stopped him dead, grinned at him, and said, "I want you." Or, well, something along those lines. Tenner had been wanted. Someone had put hands all over his body and tried to please him.

And Ten had to admit—even in the midst of all that adrenaline and testosterone, Ross McTierney had worked hard to please him.

Tenner wouldn't mind taking his turn, actually, but... but hookups like that didn't happen twice, did they? Was there like a call-back process for a hot angry screw against a wall?

"There's always a first time," she said. "I mean, you pretended to be straight once."

God. This. "I tried to be straight because this really fun girl I knew in college wanted to hang out with me. And then we were having a baby, and I didn't want to leave her alone. Nina, I'm sorry. I am, but some of this was on you. And now we both have a great kid and an obligation to at least be civil to each other. I mean, you're going out on a date, and you look fantastic. Go, have a good time. I'm planning to play with the best thing that's ever happened to me. Have a nice weekend, okay?"

She looked away. "You too," she muttered. "Email me your schedule. I... you know I hate last-minute stuff."

It was true, and while it wasn't "I'm sorry for being a bitch," it was as close as she'd come in almost three years.

"I do." He grinned. "But hey, if nothing else, this guarantees her Sunday in the park while we practice."

"Better you than me," Nina said in complete sincerity. "She does love to play." Nina had loved sitting in the stands, with a beer and vendors who would sell her water and frozen ices, but actually being out in a field had never been her thing.

"You know it. Have a good weekend." He took the win then and turned toward where Piper was waiting for him in the car.

Piper chattered on the way to his house like she'd been let off a leash. He heard everything—from what she'd learned in school to how much she liked doing summersaults in gymnastics, to how much she really wanted an I-Spy toy so she could look at bugs.

Especially that last one.

He got her to his three-bedroom, two-and-a-half-bath house in Empire Hills in Folsom, loving it more as he pulled in. Nina had chosen something larger—but then, her job paid better—in a more upscale neighborhood, but Tenner's place had... well, Tenner.

It had rich furniture with hardwood floors and deeply colored area rugs and a giant floor-to-ceiling condominium for the cat he'd adopted pretty much the minute the ink was dry on the sale.

He'd loved pets, had grown up with several of them, and while Nina was very frank about hating the cleaning and the mess that came with them, Tenner had vowed he wasn't going to deprive himself of a creature that would love him, just because he had to clean a litter box. The result was Joe, the big long-haired black cat with one white sock, who ran up to Piper as soon as she walked in, rubbing his face against her legs hard enough to knock her off balance. After they said their hellos, he shooed her upstairs to take her bath while he fed the big furry food vacuum on the enclosed porch that overlooked the backyard. He listened to her singing in the bathtub wistfully—she was almost too old for baths now, she told him, and someday she'd take a shower like Mom.

In another twenty minutes, she came downstairs in her cartoon-themed pajamas, and he sat her down for dessert.

As she ate her two-cookie allotment with a glass of almond milk, because it made her tummy feel better, she began to wind down, her eyes going half-mast, her chatter stalling.

"How come you were late, Daddy?"

"I got to play softball," he said, and the happiness radiating on her face almost undid him.

"Like the pictures you used to have over the fire?"

Nina had put up their wedding picture, Piper's most current picture, and one picture of Tenner, a candid one of him crouching at first base and looking young and fit and happy.

"Yeah," Tenner told her. He didn't tell her that Nina had thrown the picture across the room so the frame shattered on the wall the day he'd told her he wanted a divorce, but he did miss that picture.

"I liked that picture," Piper said, yawning. "You look like a hero in it."

Tenner laughed softly. "I sure did love to play," he conceded. Then he booped her nose. "But not as much as I love you. You ready to go to bed, champ?"

She yawned. "I need a story."

She really didn't. She was reading chapter books already. She'd told him so. But he loved to read to her. "Go brush your teeth, and I will be up in a minute."

While she was in the bathroom, he ran into his bedroom to change. It wasn't until he was pulling the blue shirt over his head that that entire interlude—that eight-minute breathless fuck in the dark—rushed back behind his eyes.

He paused, taking a deep breath, and assessed.

His ass was a little sore, a little used, but that was almost pleasant. He went into the other bathroom to splash some water on his face and groaned. Oh, wow. It's a good thing he'd hung out on Nina's porch, because in the brighter light of her foyer, nobody could have missed the beard burn on his neck, his cheeks, even his temple.

Or maybe some of those scrapes were from having his face mashed up against the cinderblock.

Ross's hand on his forehead, cushioning him from the roughness. His lips on Tenner's temple, turning this blatantly carnal act into something more.

He swallowed. Wow. It would be great—*great*—if he could blame that entire interlude on the irritating asshole who'd been yanking his chain during the entire game. But what had happened in that alcove had been between two consenting adults, and one of them had been... considerate. Tender. Mindful of sex and the fragile humans having it.

As much as Tenner would love to hate the guy for making him face— He flailed his arms at the mirror. *This.* Making him face *this* sex-blossomed, relaxed, fairly satisfied version of himself, the fact was, Ross "Blows Like a God" McTierney hadn't been the bad guy here.

And Tenner hadn't either, really. Besides being late to pick Piper up—and he'd communicated as much as he could—he'd been... well, at the very least, a guy having a good time.

"Daddy!" Piper called, and Tenner forsook any thoughts of taking a shower before he read to her and trotted to her bedroom.

He'd seen Piper's room at Nina's house, but even when they'd lived together, he'd understood the importance of canopy beds and stencils on pink walls. He and Piper had decorated her room. She'd picked furniture of pale wood, without the canopy, so she could look out the second-story window and see the people on the street. She'd asked for her walls to be done in simple cream colors, with little rainbow appliques of ponies and butterflies and caterpillars all over, and a shelf that she kept her two soccer medals on, as well as her certificates for mastering units in school. She saved those throughout the week, because that side of the wall was papered with them, and he wanted her to be proud.

He'd put a stuffed chair in there, adult-sized, so she could sit on his lap when he read to her, but she'd gotten into bed and had an assortment of large, brightly illustrated books on her blankets.

Old favorites. Comfort books. He knew most of them by heart.

A few of them were even the cardboard books that she'd loved as a toddler, and he picked one of those up and gave it to her.

"You ready?" he asked, and she nodded excitedly. They had a rhythm here, and they read it together, pausing at some points, squealing in delight at others. So much fun. The next thing she picked was a book of poetry. He read four of those, with all the voices and the enthusiasm and the theatrics that he could muster, and Piper yawned at the end.

"One more," she slurred.

He kissed her forehead. "Tomorrow night. We have to be up in the morning for gymnastics."

"Okay, Daddy. Can I watch you play baseball?"

"I'm practicing on Sunday. I thought you'd want to play in the park."

"I'll watch you. I want to see you look like the picture."

"Night, pumpkin."

"Night, Daddy."

He got up and turned off the light, making sure the caterpillar nightlight was still on. He didn't even want to think about how his own daughter wanted to see him happy again.

It felt like too much of a lie.

THE THING about being a dad on the weekend was you spent a lot of time trying to make every moment count. But in real life, kids had their downtime just like adults did, and as Tenner hit Kipp's gamely pitched balls into the outfield to give the rest of the team fielding practice, he had to admit this was a good compromise. Piper had spent the day before at gymnastics and at a local park, flying a kite Tenner had picked up from the grocery store. She'd fallen asleep in the car on the way home without their milk-and-cookie ritual, and had slept long that morning. After running around the backyard while Tenner cleaned up the house, she was perfectly happy sitting in the sandpit and playing with Hanford's sister's kids, building sandcastles while she paused every so often to wave to him.

He'd usually wave back.

Hanford's sister, a tall woman with faint ocher tones to her skin and eyes as wide and brown as her brother's, had assessed Tenner boldly, and then shaken her head a little at Hanford.

Tenner could swear she mouthed "Too old," at him, and Hanford had looked a little crushed. A part of Tenner wanted to roll his eyes and cock his hip and give her some attitude for that. Too old? He wasn't even thirty yet! Too goddamned old for Hanford Birmingham? Was she kidding?

But looking at Hanford holding his nephew's hand with a sort of dewy expression on his face brought Tenner up short. Even if Hanford was *exactly* Tenner's age, Tenner had a kid and an ex-wife and baggage Hanford didn't know how to deal with yet.

The thought depressed him a little.

Right up until he was sizing up Kipp's gentle lob—up, up, up—and choking up on the bat. Then, from right behind him, came the now familiar chant.

"Hey, batter batter, sha-*wing*, batter!"

He ignored it and hit the ball deep into center, watching in dismay as Hanford and Charlie Saylor and Greg Nemensky all headed for a collision as they tried to catch it.

"Call it!" Tenner yelled. "Goddammit, somebody call—"

Charlie and Greg connected first, bouncing off each other, and Hanford tripped over Charlie's prone body in time to watch the ball drop right in front of him.

"Oh my God!" Kipp looked at Tenner in chagrin. "Are they okay?"

Tenner looked over his shoulder at Ross and narrowed his eyes. "You just had to, didn't you?" he asked.

He didn't even stick around for Ross to hold up his hands in honest confusion. "What'd I do? I swear, Ten, it wasn't me!"

Tenner didn't hang out to listen to the rest of it. He was trotting across the field to see how bad it was.

HANFORD HAD grass stains on his knees and chin, and that was fine, but Charlie had twisted his ankle when he'd stumbled back from the collision. Greg offered to call his wife, then take him to the doctor, and that effectively ended practice.

Greg and Charlie left, and Hanford's sister took her little brother and her kids home with a sniff in Tenner's direction, as though he should have known better, and the rest of the team had begged off. They'd been pretty close to ending practice anyway. Just as Tenner turned to Ross to ask him what in the furry hell he was doing there, Piper wandered over from the playground.

"Daddy, those other kids left. Can we go home and watch TV now? I want mac and cheese for dinner."

Tenner gave Ross a sideways look, not sure what to do with him there. "Sure, baby. Mac and cheese sounds good—"

"And you can bring your friend," she said as though she were the Queen herself, making a huge concession. She yawned. "He can watch TV with me."

Tenner opened his mouth to say, "Oh, honey, this isn't my friend. This is some loser who's here for no discernible reason that I can see," when Ross squatted down in front of Piper and offered his hand.

"Hi, honey. I'm Ross, and I'm a friend of your dad's. Did you say mac and cheese? That sounds *outstanding*. It's the best offer for dinner I've had in *months*. I would *love* to have mac and cheese with you and watch TV." He looked up at Tenner, his eyes direct, without bullshit. "Right, Ten?"

Tenner opened, then closed his mouth, trying to think of a reason, any reason, not to invite this guy over to his house when his daughter was all but begging to go home. It wasn't that Ross wasn't appealing—look at him, treating Piper like a human being and making her smile like that. It was just… God, was it even responsible to talk to the guy he'd banged in the park two nights ago?

"We live at 420 Union Street, Folsom, California," she said wisely, and while Tenner gaped at her and cursed an apparently very effective school system, she threw in their zip code for good measure.

Ross stood up and winked at him. "Smart kid," he said. "I'll follow you there."

"I have to get my equipment bag," Tenner told Piper. "Ross, can you come help me?"

"Sure thing." Ross gave him a big smile and cracked his gum, and Tenner realized he was dressed in baseball gear, same as Ten was.

"Did you come out here to practice with us?" Tenner asked, a little disconcerted.

"Yeah, well, a little bird told me you'd be here today," Ross said blithely. He got to the dugout first and started throwing Tenner's bat and practice balls into the big canvas duffel. "I wanted to stop by and see how you were doing."

Tenner frowned at him. "A little bird…? You listened to us planning this Friday night!" he accused.

Ross gave him a lazy wink. "Guilty as charged. Are you going to use this as an excuse not to have me over for mac and cheese? Because I've got to tell you, I'm developing a craving."

"Why *are* you coming over for mac and cheese?" Tenner asked almost desperately. "I mean, there's so many better things you could be eating."

"My sister's cooking, are you kidding me?"

Tenner rolled his eyes. "I've eaten at Pat and Desi's house many times. If it's not her cooking, it's his, and they're both fantastic."

Ross cracked his gum again. "You got me. I was both lying *and* stereotyping. Are you going to use *that* as an excuse not to invite me to your house?"

"I'm not looking for an excuse not to invite you over!" Tenner exploded, and Ross's grin was wider than Bugs Bunny's ever was.

"Good! Let's get crackin', hoss—your kid's gonna eat her shoes if we don't get a move on."

And with that, Ross swung his way over to where Piper waited patiently for her father. "Okay, sweetheart, you gotta be honest with me. Is there dessert with this mac and cheese, because if there's not, I can pick us up some on the way there."

"Ice cream!" Piper squealed excitedly. "Daddy got us ice cream and fresh strawberries, and I get to mash up the berries and add the sugar and it's going to be a*maz*ing!"

Ross glanced over his shoulder at Tenner and winked. "Did you hear that, Ten? It's gonna be a*maz*ing!"

Tenner shook his head and rolled his eyes. It was going to be a disaster. He wasn't even sure if he was *allowed* to date again. He watched Ross's long legs eating up ground, his tight athlete's body moving with that sinuous hidden power that Tenner had felt when Ross was *pounding away in his ass*.

A disaster, he repeated to himself. A hard-fucking, tender-kissing, sweet-touching considerate and amazing disaster.

His heart was speeding up already.

Amazing Disaster

ROSS WOULD have taken that kid to Disneyland for the invite, but she'd walked into it because she apparently liked his smile.

He was good with that. Pat and Desi's kids adored him. He smiled a lot, played games, took them places—he had lots of years being the fun uncle—and Ross wasn't going to mess with that now.

He followed Tenner to his house, not because he doubted the address—and he could definitely get it from Pat if he got lost—but because he wanted Tenner to see that he meant what he'd said. He was there for a modest dinner of mac and cheese, and he wasn't going to let that little girl down even if, as far as she knew, he was just a new and interesting friend.

He had the yellow shirt in his hand and a duffel over his shoulder, containing cargo shorts and a T-shirt, when he knocked on the door.

"Don't let the cat out, Daddy!" Piper called, and Tenner grimaced apologetically.

"Joe—no!" Tenner opened the door and scooped up a cat nearly as large as his daughter, holding the indignant furry black thing looped over his arm like a furious dishtowel. "Hurry in, man. Sorry about the cat. He likes to greet people he doesn't know."

Ross grinned and dropped his duffel so he could hold out his hands. "Okay, so hand him over. If he likes to greet people, I'm here to be greeted. Hello, Joe."

He held Joe up to face level and wrinkled his nose, inviting the cat for a whisker rub. Joe took the bait, rubbing his handsome white whiskers against Ross's nose again and again, until Ross cuddled him up against his chest.

"Joe?" Ross asked, checking out Joe's one white sock and white whiskers.

"As in Shoeless," Tenner explained, pointing to the sock. "How else do you explain the one white foot."

Ross snorted and kept loving until the cat was practically comatose with happiness. He grinned. "That's a kitty. You're a big furry pushover, you are." He winked at Tenner. "I think he likes me."

Tenner's expression remained unimpressed. "He probably thinks you have food."

"Me? Naw. I'm charming. Face it. I just charmed the whiskers off your kitty here. I'm a genius."

"Why are you here?" Tenner asked, his eyes darting behind him, probably checking for his daughter. "With clothes!"

Oh, yeah—that probably looked presumptuous. "Don't get your knickers in a knot. I was going to change out of my baseball clothes." Ross gestured to Tenner, who had probably changed as soon as he walked through the door. "Like you did."

Tenner's expression softened. "That's fine. The downstairs bathroom is down the hall by the staircase."

Ross took an assessing look around, liking the dark hardwood floors and the light coming in from skylights in the vaulted living room ceiling. "Nice digs! Three bedrooms? That's sweet. Pat's place is in this same neighborhood, but, like, way bigger. Pat's got the mansion on the hill, you know?"

"Pat's got a law degree and an MBA," Tenner said dryly. "Pat can afford the mansion on the hill."

Ross winked at him. "Yeah. My sister caught herself a good one, but the McMansion isn't everything."

"I'll settle for my McCottage," Tenner said, pursing his lips. "And I'd better go start the McFeast. Would you like some salad with your mac and cheese with hot dogs?"

"The luxury never ends," Ross said, chuckling at his own joke. "Be out in a sec."

Once he'd changed, he set his duffel down by the door and sauntered into the kitchen. On his way, he passed Piper, coloring quietly on the couch, Joe purring on her lap, SpongeBob on for background noise. She gave Ross an absent smile and wave, but was so obviously content, Ross returned the gesture without a word. When he got into the kitchen, water was set to boil and Tenner was pulling stuff out of the refrigerator.

"Here," Ross said. "Hand me the lettuce and carrots. I mean, if you're going to spoil me with greens, I might as well help."

Tenner pulled out of the fridge long enough to do exactly that, asking, "Beer?"

"Domestic or imported?"

Tenner wrinkled his nose. "Does it matter?"

And Ross had to laugh. "Only when it's noteworthy. Like, if you're a beer connoisseur or something. I could ask for a beer, and you'd go, 'Here, have a Reeking Fish—it's apparently brewed with real tuna!' And I'd be like, 'I'd rather drink warm Michelob, thank you,' and then we'd never speak again. But if you have standard beers, microbrewery that doesn't suck, or regular old domestic, then it's just a beer."

And finally—*finally*—he got a laugh out of the guy. "Fat Tire. It's supposed to be microbrew, but it's practically old-school in Folsom."

Ross felt a happy feeling start at his toes. "Pale ale? Lager? Dark? Never mind. I don't care. Surprise me. It's all good."

"Oh my God, you're easy," Tenner said, handing him something blond.

"I thought we'd already established that Friday night," Ross said, and he was unprepared for the utter look of shutdown and shame crossing Tenner's face.

"About Friday night…," he said, dropping his voice, and Ross held out a hand.

"We don't have to talk about it right now," he said kindly. Poor Tenner. He looked like a kid who'd been caught peeing in the bushes— not only embarrassed but ashamed. "I get it. It wasn't your usual MO. Not mine, either, to be honest, but don't worry. We can pretend it didn't happen until you're ready for it to happen again."

Some of Tenner's usual uptightness cranked his expression to maximum disapproval. "My God, you're arrogant. Seriously, you think that's going to happen again?"

Ross used the bottle opener built into the side of the counter, highly satisfied by the hiss as the cap popped off. "God, I hope so." He took a drink and swallowed before Tenner could stop sputtering in outrage. "Not tonight, of course. You're taking care of your kid. You don't want her to get attached—I get it. I'm a baseball friend and that's all. But if you're picking her up on Friday night, there's got to be some nights you're all by yourself, right?"

Tenner opened his mouth and closed it again. "I drop her off at school Monday morning. Depending on her school schedule and Nina's travel schedule, I get her for a half week sometimes, but most weekends, she's here."

"Then what are you doing Monday night?" Ross asked hopefully, but he kind of figured it wouldn't be that simple.

Popping the top off Tenner's obvious reluctance would be a lot harder than popping the top off his beer, but possibly a lot more satisfying.

"Bringing home my work, as usual," Tenner said, his understated sarcasm sending a shiver up Ross's spine. He'd suspected as much, that Tenner didn't have much of a social life, but Tenner had just confirmed it. He set his beer down on the counter and started chopping up lettuce. Ross noticed the salad ingredients included crushed pita chips, green olives, and feta cheese.

"Does Piper eat that?" Ross asked, distracted.

"No." The backs of Tenner's ears turned red.

"No?" Oh, how fascinating.

"There is another grown-up in the house. I like Mediterranean salad. Usually I chop chicken into mine and make it a meal, but…." He gestured to the water, which wasn't quite boiling yet.

"Mac and cheese and hot dogs. I understand. Now, about work. You're in Pat's department?"

Tenner shrugged. "I work with video chip components and help clean up the code so the chip can give the computer better instructions. Sounds boring, but I get to play video games early, so that's exciting."

He sounded like he meant it.

"What's your current favorite?" Ross asked, enchanted.

Tenner named one of the newest ones, and Ross let out a low whistle.

"I haven't even had a chance to play that one yet," he said.

Tenner swallowed, and Ross saw the exact moment he decided to make the invitation. "After dinner. You know. Piper and I usually play a couple rounds of Mario Kart, but once she's in bed, you and I could play a round or two."

Well, yeah. That game was a little violent for a kid. "I'd like that," Ross said. "Seriously. Thanks for the invite."

And now Tenner's entire neck was red. Oh, this was *really* fascinating. Ross wondered what he could get Tenner to say that would make his nose light up like a spinning cherry!

"Glad to do it," Tenner told him, his eyes totally concentrating on dicing little green olives. His cheeks got blotchy with that one. Damn. So adorable. "So, uh, what do you do? I mean… uh, for work."

And there went his forehead. Oh my God! This was amazing amounts of fun. Still without looking at Ross, Tenner used the back of his chef's knife to expertly scoop the chopped components of the salad into a white glass bowl. Ross waited for him to set the grater on top of the bowl and start grating carrots into it before answering.

"I'm a horticulturist, or at least that's what's on my degree. But I'm more like a horticultural engineer."

The carrot paused on the grater, and Tenner actually looked at him. "Like where to plant what? Really?"

Ross laughed softly. "Now see, I usually lose most potential dates with that. Too many syllables, you know?"

"But plants are so important right now," Tenner said earnestly. "What have you been working on? What brings you here?"

Ross let out a breath. This part was… hard. "Well, I was in the Amazon," he said, his heart hurting. "There's so much devastation. And my government grant ran out, so I came back to lobby for private funding to go back."

"Any luck?" Tenner asked, and Ross gave a sigh of relief. He obviously didn't have to explain how important this work was.

"Well, I did get a couple of companies to fund my team, but first, I had to offer my services in trade."

"So…." Tenner was regarding him seriously, and Ross was surged with an entirely different form of gratification.

Respect.

Not just a pretty face or a good fuck—this guy was listening to Ross as a person, and Ross usually only got that kind of attention in the field.

"Well, besides helping with environmental impact assessments on a local level, I'm giving seminars to a bunch of different companies in the area—yours included—where I talk about the importance of, say, solar panels over the parking lot, or drought-resistant landscaping, and why it's important to choose indigenous and noninvasive species when to plant. I like the idea, honestly, it's important work too. So much can be done with education and a little bit of resource allocation. And Pat and Des are the greatest. I'm living in their basement playroom right now, but I've got my own bathroom, and Desi set up an actual bed that doesn't wreck my back. The kids don't go down there much—they're getting old enough to not need all those big bulky toys, you know?"

"Yeah," Tenner said, and to Ross's disappointment, that marvelous red flush began to recede. Bummer. Ross had been hoping it would flood to Tenner's almost delicate little nose.

"What's wrong?" he asked. "Did all that talk about environmentalism turn you off?"

"Oh, no, not at all!" Tenner finished up with the carrots and added a couple of slices of radish and then put the grater in the sink. "It's fascinating. And you're right, it's really important work."

"So…?"

"Could you pass me the feta please?" Tenner inquired politely, pointing to the counter on Ross's other side.

"Sure." Ross picked up the little plastic container and held it, just out of Tenner's reach.

Tenner looked at him sideways. "Can I have it, please?"

"Sure," Ross said again.

"But you're not giving it—"

Ross kissed him.

It was sort of a ballsy move, but he figured he'd only need one little kiss. He'd forgotten how sweet Tenner's lips were, how that combination of aggression and shyness made his balls ache. Ross pulled back first, his face hot, and put the cheese in Tenner's hand.

"Why did you do that?" Tenner asked, his eyes darting predictably to the living room, where they could both see the back of Piper's elbow as she leaned on the side of the couch to color.

"Why'd you go all white and quiet?" Ross asked, equally as intense.

"I was wondering when you'd be leaving to go out in the field again," Tenner said with dignity, and Ross caught his breath.

Not stupid. Tenner Gibson was not stupid.

"Does it matter?" Ross asked, playing for time.

Tenner met his eyes, and Ross thought a little wistfully about how he'd been waiting for that. Big brown eyes…. When they weren't narrowed in concentration or irritation, they were really damned pretty.

"I don't know, Ross," Tenner said evenly. "Why *are* you here?"

Well, shit. "Because Friday night was totally awesome," Ross said. "But it wasn't perfect, and I'd like to know you better."

Tenner went back to his salad again, dumping feta crumbles in before sealing the container again. "Beans or no beans?"

"No beans," Ross said automatically. "They give me gas."

Tenner rolled his eyes. "Me too. Maybe we should have beans for sure."

"No, please." Ross took the salad bowl off the cutting board and gave Tenner the package of hot dogs sitting in front of him. "No beans."

Tenner took the hot dogs and checked the water again. Boiling. "Okay, here's the big question. Blue box mac and cheese or my homemade mac and cheese?"

"Which one does Piper like best?" Ross asked carefully.

"She says it's mine, but I think that's because I let her wear jeans and get dirty in the backyard."

"I like that reason. She sounds like a bright and gifted child, and I will side with her," Ross said gravely.

"Good answer." Tenner's lips—mostly lean but with a little tender pout on the bottom—twisted. "Unlike the one you gave me for how long you're here."

"Two months," Ross said, conceding. "I'm raising enough money to be gone another two months, and then I've promised to come back again and make sure the programs I start up are being run right."

"And after that?" Tenner asked mildly.

"After that, we'll see." Ross shrugged. "The Amazon is going to need years and years of restoration, and fundraising is important too."

"Have you worked in a lot of places?" Tenner was moving now, reaching into a pantry to pull out a bag of whole-grain egg noodles. As Ross spoke, he came back to the stove to dump them into the boiling water.

"I've moved around ever since I got out of college," Ross told him cheerfully. "It's been great—helped me see the world and learn more about the ecosystem. And it's like every new place I go, the more in demand I am. I mean, when I finally decide to settle down, I'll be able to pick and choose my jobs."

Tenner snorted.

"What?"

"Damn, son. Must be great not to ever get knocked down."

Wow. Yeah. That *had* sounded pretty conceited, hadn't it? "That's not true," he said. "I've had my share of rejection. This Amazon thing?

The first time I ran it by a government agency, I was given a giant folder talking about why climate change was a myth."

Tenner groaned. "Oh, for God's sake—"

"Right? I had to approach three different agencies before I found one that was actually on my side, and more importantly, had the funds to help. I got knocked down plenty. I just... you know. Found a way."

"Wow." Tenner gave the noodles a couple of swipes with a wooden spoon to break up any clumps before rinsing off his chef's knife and moving on to the hot dogs.

"Wow what? What is that sound?" For a moment, Ross was uncertain, and he hated that. He wasn't always on top, and had learned to pick himself up plenty after setbacks, but he usually knew what he was dealing with. It was disconcerting that he couldn't read this man.

Tenner shook his head and shrugged. "Just... that's a lot of optimism." He gave Ross a rather broken smile. "That's really admirable, that's all."

And now Ross's neck was on fire. He took a hasty sip of his beer. "Thank you. That's, uh, nice of you to say. But what... what makes you say that?"

"No reason."

Oh, there was most obviously a reason—something had obviously killed Tenner Gibson's optimism dead.

"Could you get the bag of shredded cheddar out of the refrigerator? And that strainer from the top of the fridge? It's about time to get this show on the road."

TENNER KEPT him busy for the next few minutes, setting the table and dishing up food. He called Piper to have her wash her hands, and she bobbed in a few minutes later, looking tired but content.

Dinner was a surprisingly fun affair. Piper chattered happily, and they all had a contest to see who had the most hot dog pieces in their mac and cheese. Ross dared her to eat some salad, and she dared him to eat some applesauce, and Ross got to watch from under his eyelashes as Tenner laughed without inhibition.

The difference between Tenner in front of his daughter, and Tenner on a baseball field or in Ross's arms was like the difference between a raging tiger and a newborn kitten.

Tenner in front of Piper laughed a lot.

Tenner on the softball field would take your head off as soon as smile.

Ross couldn't decide which guy he liked most—the guy on the softball field had promised that sexual ferocity they'd shared in that dark little corner. But this guy, laughing at his daughter, playing games with her food, talking about all the desserts they could eat together—this guy was all of the good dads Ross had ever known. His father, his grandfather, his sister's husband. Tenner was like part of the Good Dad Task Force, out to make the world a better place.

Ross washed dishes while Tenner and Piper cut up and mashed strawberries, adding a little bit of sugar for the perfect ice cream topping. When dessert was done, Piper wiped her mouth carefully with a napkin, then sat back against her chair.

"Bath time?" she asked.

"Bath time," Tenner confirmed, using his own napkin to pat where she missed a spot. "I'll be up in a minute to help you wash your hair."

She beamed at him. "You'll braid it nice and tight tomorrow, right? Because when *you* braid it, it stays for two days and Mom doesn't have to do it on Tuesday."

Right now, it was back in a ponytail. Ross wondered at how long it must take, Piper sitting between Tenner's thighs, while he carefully wove the fine strands of dark hair into a perfect french braid.

"I always do," Tenner promised. "Now go get clean and not stinky at all."

She laughed and ran up the stairs, leaving Ross charmed, and, face it, just a bit gooey.

"God, she's fun," Ross said into the silence.

"She's perfect." Tenner shook himself then, like maybe he'd shown his soft center *with that sentence* and not with the entire last hour, where he'd been a charming father and everything that was right with the world. "I understand she'll be a teenager tomorrow and there will be much hatred and rolling of the eyes."

Ross chuckled. "Not if you stay in contact," he said soberly. "I mean, there will be mood swings and some boundary pushing. I won't lie. But most of the time, if you're kind and generous and embrace the person they're becoming, you can get through the rough spots."

Tenner's eyebrows went up. "Oh my God. Did you read a manual?"

Ross chuckled, feeling a little self-conscious, which was fairly new for him. "No! Empirical evidence, based on my own parents and watching my sisters raise their own kids. Pat and Desi are great examples, right?"

Tenner shrugged, conceding. "Well, Pat got me and Nina through the diaper years, so I'll have to give you that. He got me through the divorce too. It was his idea to have Piper pick furniture for my house so she'd feel comfortable."

"That's sweet. So, uh…." And just like that, Ross was back to feeling self-conscious. "About that divorce…."

Tenner let out a breath. "It was my fault. I… I never should have told her I was gay."

Ross's eyebrows went up to his hairline. "When was that?"

"About a year and a half before the divorce. I… she wanted passion and excitement. I mean, we're not even thirty yet. She deserved some. And I was not…." He made motions with his hands. "You know."

Well, this was embarrassing. "Alas, no. Very bisexual. But I've been with guys who've been all or nothing, so let's say I do."

Tenner rolled his eyes. "I should be so lucky. Anyway, I thought it would make her feel better—it wasn't *her* issue—she's beautiful and smart. And she used to be funny. It was a *me* thing, and she shouldn't have to live with that."

"What happened?"

"She stopped touching me, period," Tenner muttered as if he was ashamed.

And Ross, who had shown up for the mac and cheese and the adorable single father, found his chest becoming very, very tight. "Like, no hugs or…."

"Or holding hands or kisses on the cheek or hanging out in front of the television. No smiles over jokes or telling each other about our day or… none of the good parts. It was like I killed everything between us, even our friendship. And we were really good friends." He shrugged. "I thought."

"Oh, baby—" Ross reached across the table to cover his hand at the very least, but Tenner jerked away.

"I should go check on Piper. She gets lost singing to herself sometimes." And with that, he disappeared up the stairs, leaving Ross to wonder what in the hell he was doing there.

LITTLE BUBBLES OF HOPE

TENNER MOSTLY expected Ross to be gone when he got downstairs with Piper.

He got it—he did.

Tenner had been a hot quick fuck in the dark, and Ross wanted more of that. He'd been human and kind with Piper, and damned seductive as they'd been preparing dinner. But nobody signed on for the long haul when all they'd done was bang someone against a cinderblock wall, right?

And Tenner's long haul was obviously fraught with some damage. There was the kid, the ex-wife, the obvious caveat that Tenner didn't do quick and easy. So why would Ross want to hang around for that?

But Tenner couldn't lie to himself. After those years with Nina, trying to be straight, he'd learned that only led to heartbreak. So he had to admit… he'd sort of liked the guy.

That upper lip curl Ross had when he was being particularly full of himself? Yeah, on the one hand it pissed Tenner off, but on the other?

Dead sexy.

And he'd listened and taken his ration of crap and given back as good as he got.

And he'd been honest about leaving, about the possibility of his return. He'd even seemed to know why it was important.

It wasn't that Tenner was looking for Mr. Right, or even Mr. Right Now, but God, he refused to start another relationship that was out and out doomed from the get-go. He had to have learned something from those loveless years with Nina, right?

So it had been nice having male company—an adult—in his kitchen, someone who knew a side of Tenner that Tenner had barely shared with anyone.

That surprise kiss had been… tremendous. God, so sweet.

But as Tenner set out Piper's PJs and made sure her clothes from Nina's were clean and folded in her backpack, and her "daddy's house" clothes were in the hamper, he had to admit, he kept waiting for the sound of the front door opening and Ross's casual, "Thanks for dinner, Ten, see you around!"

But it never happened.

Piper fell asleep while he was loosely braiding her hair for bed. One minute she was sitting up, talking about how someday *she* would play baseball, and the next minute, her little head had slumped to the side and Tenner had to stretch her out in bed and finish the braid there.

"Night, pumpkin," he whispered, kissing her forehead, but she didn't wake up.

He wandered downstairs dispiritedly, wondering how Ross had managed to leave without making any noise, and was surprised to hear Mario Kart in the background.

"Hey," Ross said from the couch, where he was wielding the remote controller. "You didn't have any passwords enabled, so I got a head start."

Tenner found he was staring at the cocky blond god with hunger in his eyes, so he said, "Not much of one," to cover.

That lip curl, the dead sexy one, made an appearance. "Want to see what I can really do?"

He hadn't left. He was there, crouched in the stuffed chair, ready to play Mario Kart with Piper and Tenner.

"Sure," Tenner said. "Piper's asleep, though. It'll be just me."

Ross slid him a sort of sideways smile. "Not a hardship. Now come sit and pick your character. Let the asskicking begin!"

As. If.

TWO HOURS later, they were still neck and neck, and Ross called a time-out—not a halt. He'd been very careful to say it wasn't over until someone was wiping the floor with someone else, but a pause, while he went to use the bathroom and fetch them both another beer.

It was their third since Piper had gone to bed, and as Ross came back and handed Tenner his, it dawned on Tenner that Ross might not be okay to drive.

"You can stay in the guest bedroom," he said guilelessly. After all, Ross was a friend. A guy friend. Over for some beers and some gaming. "You don't have to drive back to Pat's like this, or take an Uber."

Ross grimaced. "I'm not sure there's an Uber out here this late anyway. Wow. I'm sorry." He sat down on the couch next to Tenner this time, and not in the chair kitty-corner to him. "I honestly didn't mean to get too buzzed to drive."

Tenner shrugged. "Pat's done it a time or two. So have some of the other guys we work with. Piper won't see anything wrong with it."

"Mm." Ross took a hearty swig of his beer as if fortifying himself. "There's not, you know. Even if I didn't sleep in the guest bedroom, there's nothing wrong with me staying the night."

Tenner stiffened. "I am not—"

Ross held up his hand. "No, that's not what I meant. No, of course you can't expose your daughter to every guy you date. I get that. I *really* get why it's important for any guy in your life to be Daddy's friend for a good long time before you tell her anything different, you know?"

Tenner nodded. "It would be the same if I was dating a woman," he said, and Ross shook his head.

"No, it wouldn't."

"Yes, yes, it would—"

"No, no, it wouldn't. I mean, the same rule would apply, Ten, but look at you. If you were dating women, do you think you'd have been so hungry Friday night? Would you have gone—what? How long was it?"

"Two and a half years," Tenner muttered, hardly able to believe that dry spell was over.

"Yeah. If you and Nina had split up and you'd been dating women, do you really think you would have gone so long after the divorce to get you some?"

"That's insufferably crude," Tenner said before taking a sip of his beer. And belching.

Ross laughed softly. "Yeah, that's the problem. I'm being crude. No, fess up. There's something more going on here."

Tenner regarded him with a certain amount of distrust, which was hard, because Ross didn't get any less pretty after three beers.

"It's Nina," he said after a minute. "In the custody settlement, I get fifty percent custody, more or less, because swapping Piper out over the school week seemed unnecessary to both of us. So we try to make that up over the summer. And Nina travels a lot with work, so we do that too. But the legal agreement says, and I quote, because she could afford a truly fancy lawyer, that as soon as I start 'flaunting my lifestyle,' we will have to revisit the agreement. I could lose custody completely."

Ross's eyes were all over the place and so was his expression. It went from disbelief to anger to confusion and back to disbelief again.

"Can she do that?" he asked finally.

"I don't know!" Tenner protested. "I don't. I signed it. Because I wanted it to be as quick and as painless as possible. And as long as I got to see my daughter again, it felt like a fair trade."

"It was *not*!" Ross argued, and apparently, he'd settled on anger. "What does that even *mean*?"

"I assume it means she doesn't want me to date men," Tenner said, shrugging.

"Or maybe it means she doesn't want you to have key parties with a lot of cocaine and a disco ball!" Ross argued. "Because what kind of lifestyle does she think you're going to flaunt? Mediterranean salad and microbrews aren't exactly noteworthy as a lifestyle. Does she have a thing with computer engineers? I mean, most of the time I assume they're sort of boring, but I kind of like you, so you get a pass—"

"Thanks so much."

"Yeah, well, you're sarcastic and that turns my key. But oh my God! No wonder you were uptight! Tenner, that's no way to live!"

"Well, it's certainly no way to date," Tenner muttered, taking another swig of beer.

Ross dropped his chin to his chest and massaged the back of his neck with one hand. "Tenner, man, you deserve more than a quick fuck against a wall. How are you ever going to meet someone if you're afraid to even step a toe out of line?"

Tenner set his mostly empty beer down and straightened, then got up and moved behind the couch. "I have no idea," he said, tired enough to not dodge the question. "But I'm not meeting the perfect guy and getting married tonight." He paused. "Here—put both your hands down by your side. I'm going to show you some neck stretches, okay?"

"Gonna rub one out, I mean rub my neck?" Ross said, and he must have been tired and drunk, because so far he'd been more subtle than that.

"Sure, I'll rub one out on your neck." Tenner giggled a little. "Seriously, you've been resting all your weight on your elbows, and that's not good for your shoulders or your neck. Now straighten up and look straight ahead."

Ross did, and Tenner placed careful fingers on the sides of his neck and his jawline. "Now look over your left shoulder—stretch—no, don't use your fingers. Just look as far as you can for a good ten seconds."

Tenner counted silently to himself, the soft heat of Ross's skin burning through his fingertips.

"Return to neutral. Now, look the other way."

And again. Tenner's palms itched with the desire to cup Ross's jaw, to lean his head in and nuzzle the back of his neck. God, the alcohol was part of it, but the warmth, the closeness, the permission—the *intimacy*—all of it was making Tenner's skin throb with the promise of heat.

He must have paused too long since that last exercise, because Ross's voice came as a surprise. "Whatever you're thinking about, go ahead."

Tenner took a step forward, surreptitiously checking the staircase with his eyes to make sure there was no small person there to see things she shouldn't.

Then, very carefully, he ran his lips along the back of Ross's neck. Ross hummed in his throat and leaned back against the couch, tilting his head and exposing his jawline.

Tenner leaned a little more and nibbled up the side, to his jaw, to his ear. He sucked on the lobe for a moment and watched as Ross arched his hips off the couch.

"You like that," Tenner whispered, and Ross arched again.

"I'm a total freak for my neck and ears," Ross admitted. "How far do you want this to go?"

Tenner started to withdraw, but Ross turned his head and caught his lips first. A quiet kiss, lingering just enough for tongue, for a gentle gasp of acceptance, and then ending.

"Not tonight," Tenner rasped.

Ross's slow grin made him regret those words almost instantly. "I'll be back," Ross promised. "Maybe not tomorrow—I gotta work late. But Tuesday. You doing anything Tuesday?"

Tenner thought but it was hard, because he was still leaning over the couch and he could still smell Ross's grass and earth and sun smell, which apparently didn't go away when he was indoors, and ah, God.

"Dance. Piper has dance class, and she likes it when both Nina and I watch her."

"Aw, man! I've got softball practice with Pat Wednesday night!" Ross's face lit up. "You could come too! We don't even have to... I mean I'd like to... but come! Maybe we can figure out how to help your team limp forward a little."

"Into the T-Ball leagues?" Tenner asked dryly. Well, Ross had been there. He'd seen what a disaster they'd been.

Ross raised his ringers to Tenner's cheek, rubbing a little against the rasp. "Yeah," Ross said. "Do that. We can have all Thursday after work together, and I'll leave Friday morning. I'll bring clothes Wednesday night...." He paused and his eyes searched Tenner's. "A sleepover. If that's okay."

Tenner bit his lip, suddenly embarrassed. On the one hand, cow and barn were never destined to meet again. But on the other... oh, had this been like a first date?

"Sure," he graveled. "Sure." All his reservations about Ross leaving, about Piper getting attached—they could deal with that, right? Ross could come over Wednesday, and people could assume he was spending the night in the guest room, the way he'd be doing tonight, right? It's not like *Tenner* would get attached to this gorgeous roller coaster of a man who liked to laugh and play Mario Kart and who cut a hot dog piece in half on Piper's plate so she could win the game of who had the most hot dogs.

Right?

"It'll be all right, Ten," Ross said gently, brushing their lips together again. "All the things you're thinking, making you frown like that— they're gonna be okay."

Tenner kissed him one more time and pulled away. "Wednesday and Thursday sound good," he said, carefully not addressing anything else. "Are you up for one more game, or are you ready to crash?"

"One more game," Ross said. "C'mere, sit next to me. We can pretend we're straight."

But when Tenner sat down, Ross scooted over until their thighs were touching, and whenever it was Tenner's turn to play, Ross rested his hand on Tenner's knee. And before Ross took his turn at the controls, he snuck his head in for a quick kiss.

Fun—yes. And a little juvenile, considering what they'd done in that alcove. But it was, in its way, wholesome. Innocent. It was two kids who'd never had sex before enjoying all the excitement of finding other things to do.

And every time Ross touched him, that insistent throb of arousal under his skin grew in power and proportion until it became a massive, waiting monster in his groin and his chest.

Wednesday and Thursday, he thought.

It was like waiting for prom, except he was going with a boy this time.

THE MOONS IN OUR ORBIT

THE BRIGHTLY blocked comforter and matching area rug over the hardwood floor certainly made Ross feel welcome in the guest room.

"The shower is fully stocked," Tenner said, lingering in the doorway. "We get up around six thirty. I mean, you don't have to be out by then, but—"

"I'll be gone by then," Ross said, taking a step forward so they were standing close. "I usually do jeans and a dress shirt for work, so I need to change. Nice room."

"Thanks. I, uh, had my parents in mind when I decorated." He shrugged. "They stay at Nina's when they visit Piper."

Ross's heart wasn't getting less bruised. "Because…?"

"Because I came out to everybody. I was destroying my family. Did you expect my parents to throw me a party?"

"Mine did," Ross argued, stung. "I mean, when I came out as bi. I mean, it was my sixteenth birthday party, but my mom's a total smartass. She made my cake rainbow and had 'Just tell us who's coming home for dinner,' put on the top."

Tenner was regarding him in shock, his mouth opening and closing with no sound coming out, so Ross kept going.

"It was the first time Desi had Pat over for dinner. I remember her looking at him with this sort of challenge, and Patrick sort of rolled his eyes. He said, 'If he brings home a guy, make sure he can play baseball. That is all I ask.'"

Tenner narrowed his eyes. "You lie."

"You know the guy. Tell me if I'm lying!"

Tenner laughed suddenly. "He was begging. He wanted me to play for the Sunspots so bad. I guess if I didn't play for them—"

"Then the team couldn't play, and if the team didn't play, there wouldn't be enough people for the league, blah blah blah. He was lying."

"He was not!"

"He was exaggerating. Trust me. I get that you've known him for what? Six years?"

"Seven," Tenner told him.

"Yeah. You have no idea of the depths that man will sink to play or see a baseball game. It's insane." Ross sobered. "Anyway. I got a cake. You got a raw deal. I'm sorry."

Tenner's shrug almost undid him. "I got Piper. I win."

He made to leave, but Ross stopped him with fingers along his jaw. "A good night kiss," he breathed, not asking.

Tenner opened his mouth, not arguing, and Ross tasted him again. Ah! This wasn't getting any worse. He tasted of beer, of course, but the last few hours had made the taste more Tenner than beer.

And Tenner—fierce competitor, responsible father, upright citizen—had an amazingly wild undertone.

Ross pulled back, breathing hard, and leaned his forehead against Tenner's. "You and me, we're going to have a good time together," he promised rashly. There were so many reasons this couldn't work; he wasn't so cocky he couldn't see them.

He needed more of that taste inside him, more of that complexity, the bitter and the sweet. He wasn't ready for it to end now. He just wasn't.

Tenner made to talk, his expression unhappy, and Ross could hear the question underneath. For how long? For three days? For two months? Every time Ross came to town?

But Ross wasn't ready to answer that one yet. He captured Tenner's lips again and plunged his tongue in, kissing until Tenner pulled back, his best Dad look on his face.

"Sleep well," he muttered, taking a step back and adjusting himself. "I know I won't."

Ross chuckled, but it was a strained sound, needy, and not cocky at all. "Me neither, dammit. Night."

But Tenner gave him a salute from behind his head and trudged up the stairs, clicking the switch at the top so the house fell into darkness.

Ross sighed and undressed to his briefs, then set his phone for six so he could get up.

BY THE time he'd gotten to his sister's place and showered for work, everybody was up and running around in circles doing the school routine. Pat wasn't really a morning crazy person—he huddled in the chaos with his tablet and his coffee and gave terse instructions from time to time.

"Your backpack's in the bathroom. No, I don't know why, but that's where I tripped over it. No, your brother's not trying to kill you. Coffee, Allison. *Cof. Fee.* What's the rule?"

His twelve-year-old tossed her glossy copper curls and flounced off to find the backpack. "No talking to Dad before his coffee. I get it!"

"Coffee…," Pat murmured, falling into himself.

Ross poured himself a cup and parked next to his second-favorite relative and sipped.

Loudly.

Pat looked over his tablet to see who dared intrude on his time, and Ross gave him a toothy grin.

"The fuck do you want?"

Ross held his hand to his heart. "Wounded. Wounded am I, that you, my favorite brother-in-law, would suspect that I, the man who sleeps under his roof, eats the bread from his table, wants anything more than simple scraps of his affection."

Pat managed to maintain his scowl for a whole three seconds before he started to chuckle, sipping at his coffee with relish. "Do you need lunch money or a backpack?"

"I do not," Ross assured him.

"I might not kill you. What *do* you need?"

"Info."

"I can give you a breakdown of CPU speeds using current video technology or baseball scores. Choose wisely."

Ross chuckled and took another sip of his coffee. "Tenner."

Pat set down his coffee. "Gibson? From baseball? The guy you were trying so hard to piss off?"

"That's the one." Ross didn't know what he put in his voice, but Pat's eyes got big, and he bit his lip, uncharacteristically uncertain.

"You, uh… got a crush?"

"Mm… I have an *interest*."

Pat let out a sigh and looked wistfully at his coffee, and then cocked his head toward the morning chaos, which seemed to have moved on to the bathroom. Abner—his boy, the middle child—was possibly in fear for his life, but Desi was insisting he'd earned it, so nothing was pressing.

"Tenner's had a rough go of it," Pat said. "We knew him and Nina together. He looked like the perfect husband."

"Yeah?"

"He was supportive, did all the right things, loves Piper like crazy. But Nina… she never really looked happy, you know?"

"I get that impression," Ross said, his voice gaining an edge, and Pat raised an eyebrow.

"What do you know?"

Ross didn't want to betray a confidence, but God, he wanted to talk. "I know about his custody agreement," he said, and both of Pat's eyebrows shot up.

"Oh, wow. He told you that. Okay. So more than an interest. Yeah. Look, here's the thing. I think Nina really loved him, but he couldn't, you know, be the husband she needed."

"It would make a person bitter," Ross conceded. Tenner had tried not to demonize her as well. Ross needed to follow his lead.

"It would. And Tenner tries hard, but you've seen him. He can be a closed-off bastard with everyone but Piper."

Well, yeah. What had seemed like a fun romantic puzzle to Ross would have been a grim emotional void to someone who didn't have the key to that puzzle. It hadn't been Nina's fault she didn't have the key.

"Complicated," Ross said softly.

"Not the kind of thing you can change overnight," Pat agreed. "But then, I understand you're coming back to live in my basement after this next trip?"

"Your basement is my dream home," Ross told him, sincerity dripping from every syllable, and Pat laughed.

"God, you're an ass. Anyway, I want to tell you to stay away from that sitch because it can get messy…."

"But?" Ross prompted.

"But…." Pat took a wistful sip of coffee. "But Tenner's lonely. And he doesn't deserve to be. He did something dumb in college—don't we all? But he's a good father and a truly good man. And if coming back to him gives you an excuse to come back to us? Settle down a little? I'm all for it too." He paused and darted a surreptitious look toward the sounds of chaos coming from his bathroom. "I'll be honest, I think Abner might be ready to come out in a year or two. And it's nothing we're going to force, of course, but I think it would be great if his awesome Uncle Ross was here to make him feel all okay-fine."

Ross had to swallow a couple of times for that one. "I think his awesome dad would do a pretty good job of that too," he said after a moment. "But I'll think about it."

At that moment, Ross's sister came bustling in, her rich blond hair pulled back in a ponytail, her blue eyes snapping with irritation.

"Patrick, could you help me with this thing?" she muttered, gesturing to the prosthetic she attached to her arm every morning. She'd been born without the lower part, from the elbow down, and had played every sport but baseball growing up. Pat often said that's how he knew he loved her. If he could be with a woman who didn't like baseball, it had to be true love forever, because that was the only explanation.

Pat's love of technology and decent health insurance kept her in the newest and shiniest of prosthetics to help her through her day, but any computer engineer knew that every upgrade had its price.

"Yes, honey," Pat said. "Sorry, honey. We can go back to the old one if it's—"

She rolled her eyes. "You were right. I was wrong. This one works very nicely, thank you. It's much more responsive than the old one." The look she sent it was one of pure disgust. "It just doesn't like me."

Pat put the flesh-colored extension down for a moment and wrapped Desi up in a warm embrace from behind, kissing her cheek. "How could it not like you, sweetheart? You make the angels sing and the heavens weep."

It should have been impossible to roll your eyes, smirk, and blush at the same time, but Ross's sister managed to do all three.

"You're impossible," she mumbled before turning her head for a kiss.

"I'm out of here," Ross said cheerfully. "You guys feel free to gross your kids out while you suck face. I've got a job to do."

"Hey, Ross!" Desi stopped him, breaking away from Pat with obvious reluctance. "Can you take Abner to school? His sisters are making him apeshit, and I need to have a talk with both of them."

"What's Paulina doing?" Pat asked, surprised. "Allison, yes, but Polly?"

"They're badgering him," Desi said. "Asking who his friends are, what his favorite subject is. He gets all family shy and shuts up. And then they get relentless." She sniffed and looked at her brother with knowing eyes. "They haven't learned yet that the best way to get information is to do lots of favors and play on guilt." She gave a smile that was all teeth. "Like I have."

"Going!" Ross set his coffee cup down in the sink, not wanting to get caught there. "Gotta go! Abner! You, me, car, now!"

"You think you're going to just walk out and pretend you were here all night?" Desi demanded, and Pat fumbled with the strap on her prosthetic.

"You weren't here all night?" he asked, horrified.

"I was in a friend's guest room," Ross told them both righteously, but he saw Pat's eyes widen in sudden understanding.

"I wish you'd been getting laid in a bar!" he said. "Desi, *hold still*. Let me help you with this thing today, and I'll figure out a shortcut tonight so you can yell at Ross with both hands tomorrow!"

"Oh, yeah. Sorry, honey." Ross's first-favorite relative relaxed her shoulders and arms, but kept her gimlet glare focused on Ross. "Whose guest room?"

"Uncle Ross!" Abner was running through the house like the hounds of hell were after him. "Uncle Ross, can we go? Like, now? *Now*, Uncle Ross!"

Ross jangled his pockets to make sure he had keys, badge, phone, and wallet, and sighed with relief when he found them all where they should be.

"Now, Abner!" he said, darting for the kitchen door. He paused at the landing to make sure Abner got out first and as his sister—now literally armed—tried to make him stay and answer her question, Ross said, "Tenner Gibson's! Gotta go. Bye!"

Then *he* fled like the hounds of hell were after him.

"Tenner Gibson—that's Piper's Dad. Why were you at his house?" Abner asked as they got into Ross's Tahoe. Ross started the thing up while waiting for ten-year-old Abner to belt himself into the back seat. Ross and Desi were tall and muscular—but Pat was about an inch shorter than Desi and wiry, and Abner looked like he was heading that way too. His hair was a dark auburn color, the kind most women looked for longingly in boxes, and his eyes were green, which meant every time he set foot out of doors, he risked becoming a giant heat blister. His summers in the dry wilds of Folsom, California, were a long misery of zinc oxide, dorky sun hats, and SPF Shade-on-Mars.

And he looked desperately like he wanted to talk about anything but himself.

"I kind of want to date him," Ross said honestly, wondering what kind of trouble that could get him into. "I was over at his place last night, playing video games too late and ended up sleeping in his guest room."

As he made to back out, he caught a glimpse of Abner's suspicious green eyes in the rearview.

"So, no sex."

"No, sir, we hardly know each other." Ross swung the car around and turned to face forward.

"So how do you know if he wants to date you back?"

Ross crossed his eyes, trying to make sense of the logic, and failing. "Look, buddy? All I can tell you is that there are many steps between knowing if he wants to date me back and sex." At least there should have been if you weren't two horndogs on a hot spring night.

And then he had a terrifying thought.

"Abner... do you go to school with Piper?"

"Yeah, but we only see each other at assemblies because she's in the second grade and I'm in the fifth."

"Okay, look. You can't say anything about dating to her. I mean, you can put in a good word for *me*, but she might not know about the dating, and that would be a shi—erm, crappy thing to do to her dad."

"Why?" Abner asked, his tone indicating he very much needed the answer.

"Because who you want to date is a private thing. You can share it with family, but it's always your business and no one else's. This would be... I don't know. Cheating. It's Tenner's job to tell his daughter if he wants to date me."

"Does he?" Abner asked cautiously.

"Vote's still out." But Ross realized unhappily that this was going to be a thing. Their families mingled, their kids knew each other, and everybody worked in the same area. Just telling his family might have repercussions for Tenner that Ross had never anticipated, but he wasn't sure how he could have stopped it. He wouldn't lie to Des and Pat for the world.

"Well, *I'd* want to date you if I was a grown-up."

"And if dating your uncle wasn't icky," Ross completed.

"Yeah, that too. I hope you score."

Ross grunted. He wasn't exactly sure what he'd done to Patrick to deserve this, but it must have been heinous. "It's not about scoring," he said, hoping that if God struck him down as he was driving, the big guy would make sure Abner landed safely. "It's about establishing a relationship with someone you have a connection with."

No lightning. Go figure. He must have been telling the truth.

"So you can't kiss until you have a relationship?" Abner asked, making sure.

"You can't kiss until you know the person well enough to know they're going to want to kiss you back," Ross temporized. There were no clouds, but he still couldn't discount lightning on a bright spring day.

"When can you score?"

Oh, to hell with this noise. "When you're eighteen. And a half."

"Why the half?" Abner asked suspiciously.

"You have to wait until the permit goes through," Ross said with a perfectly straight face. "Here's your school, kid. Do I drop you off in front?"

"Yeah, thanks, Uncle Ross. Nobody at home gives me a straight answer." Abner slid out of the car after it stopped, and Ross banged his head softly against the steering wheel. While he was waiting at the light, he whipped out his phone.

Bad news, Patrick. Your son thinks he's going to need a permit to get laid.

When he got to work, he saw the response.

That's fine. Will he need to fill out paperwork with that?

Sure. I told him he had to wait until he was 18 1/2 before the permit went through.

You're GOOD. I'll pass it on to Desi. We can keep this going for years.

As Ross got out of his SUV to walk through the solar-paneled parking lot of Green's Hill Developing, he kept a wary eye out for lightning.

There just had to be something morally wrong about telling a ten-year-old he had to have government approval for sexual activity.

WORSE THAN PAPERWORK

"HEY, TEN, how goes the project?"

Tenner looked up from what was turning out to be a surprisingly productive day. He'd expected to be logy and baffled—his weekend had been something of an event—but truth to tell, every time he surfaced from being lost in his work, he found himself sort of reveling in feeling that everything would be okay.

When had he started to think that way?

Everything hadn't been okay since he'd had to drop out of college baseball to get married. Everything *really* hadn't been okay since he'd told Nina he was gay.

But now, after one, uhm, not-so-regrettable incident and a super fun evening that had been mostly PG-rated, he found that everything was... sort of okay.

It just made it easier for him to relax, that was all.

Could have been anybody. One good night with some lube and a good toy would get you the same.

But he knew that was bullshit. One night with some lube and a good toy wouldn't get him two hours on the couch playing Mario Kart with an adult, or the nice touches to his knee or the careful, masterful kisses.

Gah! Especially the kisses! Dildos were not great kissers. Lubricant was hard on the lips.

Wednesday, Wednesday, Wednesday....

"Tenner?"

"Wednesday!" Tenner blurted, shocked out of his reverie.

"What's Wednesday?"

Tenner turned around to see Pat had stuck his head into Ten's cubicle. "Uh, I'm coming to practice with you," Tenner said, trying to pull his head out of... well, Ross McTierney.

"Oh! Did, uh, Ross invite you? Because when you get to play on my team next season, it would be great if you knew everybody!"

It was the word "uh" that gave him away.

"Did he, uh, say anything to you?" Tenner asked, not sure if he sounded pathetic or dumb. Maybe both.

Pat slid into the cubicle and stuck his hands into his pockets. "Did you bring lunch? I forgot mine. The house was crazy this morning. Do you want to go out for lunch?"

Tenner looked at that forced casual attitude, and his stomach went cold. "Did I do anything wrong?"

Pat shook his head. "No. I suspect you might be doing something very right. But I want to talk about it. Is that okay?"

"He was in the guest room," Tenner blurted. "You know that, right? I had Piper last night and—"

Pat grabbed his upper arm and hauled him up by it, like he would a recalcitrant three-year-old. "No, Tenner, you're not in trouble, but I really think we need to go somewhere else for this conversation, okay?"

"My keys—"

"I'll drive."

Tenner scrambled for his wallet and work badge even as Pat pulled him out into the hall.

PAT TOOK him to Pat's favorite Indian food restaurant, which Tenner understood was Pat's way of making it seem like his paying for the meal wasn't a favor. It was like baseball. Pat only played baseball with his guys at work—so it was a reward to Pat if they joined him on the field. Pat only ate Indian food when he wanted to talk to someone. He claimed it was his right to pay because his family hated it.

So this day, Pat took Tenner for Indian food. They both sat on cushions and ate tandoori chicken and naan, and Pat rambled on about how much he loved his kids for a solid twenty minutes.

Tenner sort of loved him like this, because he wanted to think that his own excitement at being Piper's parent wasn't an anomaly. His own parents had been fine with him, but not particularly excited or indulgent. Just… fine. He'd produced a grandchild—that had been his best thing. And then he'd gotten a divorce and come out, and he hadn't even existed anymore.

So having Pat talk about things like unconditional love and surviving events like a daughter's first pimples and training bras and buying Kotex and going to every school activity known to man like it was why they were put into this world, made Tenner feel like he'd accomplished one really awesome thing in his life.

And then without changing expression, Pat brought up Ross.

"So, sorry about my brother-in-law the other night," he said, all conversation, zero intent. "I mean, I love the guy—he's great with the kids, you know—but he's like Des. Competition brings out the, uh, more interesting side of the two of them."

Desi had once baked fifteen dozen cupcakes for the school bake sale—ten dozen regular, two dozen gluten-free, two dozen sugar-free, and one dozen completely vegan. Nina had brought store-bought cookies, and while Tenner hadn't seen what the big deal was, Nina assured him there had been one, and that she'd lost. It had been shortly after the divorce, so Tenner had been grateful to Pat's wife. At the time, Desi's showing up Nina had seemed like a gesture of support, but even he could see that level of competition would be tough to live up to.

"Makes things fun," he said lightly, thinking about Ross getting excited about Mario Kart. "I was sort of wound up. Late picking up Piper, you know?"

Pat sobered. "That went okay?"

"Oh, yeah." Tenner shrugged. "Nina doesn't like it when plans change, but once we get a routine established, she's fine. And she knows how much I love playing softball. She's not a monster."

Pat smiled slightly. "No, but she does have you over a barrel, datingwise, doesn't she?"

Tenner couldn't look at him. "It's just so... ambiguous," he said after a moment. "I mean, when I do decide to date, it would be nice to know that it's not going to screw me over."

"Ten, would you like me to have a lawyer look over that custody agreement for you? So you, uh, know exactly what it could mean?"

Tenner swallowed. "What, uh, exactly could it mean?" he asked, uncertain.

Pat gave him one of those looks—one of those patented Dad looks. One of those looks that said, "I know you think you're cute and you have this all handled, Junior, but I don't know who in the hell you think you're fooling."

"It could mean that eventually my brother-in-law won't have to sleep in the guest room."

Tenner choked on his black lentils. "I, uh, I mean, I assume as long as Piper isn't there, it doesn't, uh… I have no idea what you're talking about."

He wasn't sure how Pat did it. He tilted his head, raised one eyebrow, and widened his eyes, and Tenner was suddenly ready to confess everything from the first time he got laid in college to the assassination of Abraham Lincoln, Martin Luther King, and both Kennedys.

"Tenner."

"It was the guest room," Tenner said when he'd had a drink of water and washed down his lentils. "The guest room. He's a, uh…." He couldn't say friend and *really* couldn't say fuckbuddy. "We ate dinner with Piper and played video games. It was perfectly innocent." Aside from that first, uh, thing that was, or the kisses…. Oh dear God, the kisses had caused his head to spin and his body to sing—making the bang behind the bathroom seem more like an amuse-bouche than a cheap hot dog in the car.

"I know my brother-in-law," Pat said, barely blinking. "Innocent, he is not. And you know what? Innocent is over-fucking-rated. Involuntary chastity is boring. You're young, at least chronologically. You're healthy. Why shouldn't it be more than that?"

Tenner breathed in evenly. "You know why. You just said it yourself."

Pat shook his head. "No. I know what you've been using as an excuse since the divorce."

"An excuse?" Tenner fought a flicker of irritation. "Piper is *not* an excuse—"

"No, she's not an excuse for you to be careful with your romantic attachments, Ten. But you have been *celibate* for a year and a—"

"Two and a half. Almost three," Tenner muttered, miserable. Somehow, that hadn't come out in the first horrible months after he'd asked Nina for a divorce.

Pat dropped the piece of naan with tandoori chicken and lentils on it into his lap, and kept staring at Tenner.

"I beg your pardon?"

"I… well, I told her I was gay about a year and a half before the divorce," Tenner muttered. "She… she sort of stopped touching me, period. I was like, 'Honey, this isn't your fault. My body doesn't do that, but I love you as a friend. Can we just keep raising our child together as friends?'" Patrick's expression didn't change, and Tenner gestured rather desperately at his lap. "You… aren't you going to pick that up?"

"Sure," Pat muttered and went about cleanup on automatic. "But first tell me how you haven't been laid in three years. I'm riveted."

"I thought you said involuntary chastity was boring?" Tenner asked bitterly.

"Imagine my fucking surprise!" Pat snapped. "It took you a year and a half to ask for a divorce after that?"

"I thought we could be friends!" God, Ross hadn't gotten this either.

"Well, if she's your friend, talk to her like a friend!" Pat argued. "Tell her you would like to have a relationship with a perfectly nice guy who plays softball and is trying to save the world!"

Oh God. "I'm sorry?"

"Oh, cut the bullshit, Tenner. He stayed the night at your house, and I don't care if he was on the roof, we both know that the entire game, where he was trying to get under your skin, was foreplay."

Tenner tried not to gape. "I, uh, never thought of that," he said weakly.

Pat got rid of the last of the food on the napkin in his lap and gave Tenner another one of those Dad looks. "Sure, sure you haven't. Look, you send me a copy of the custody agreement, and I'll have *my* lawyer look over it, when directed by someone not full of unnecessary guilt and fruitless remorse. *You* talk to your ex-wife and see if you can get her to give you the go-ahead to date quietly, agreeing not to tell Piper until it's something permanent that will impact her life. The world has shifted a lot in two and a half years, and Nina might have thawed a little bit too. Are we agreed?"

"Why?" Tenner asked bitterly, his excitement over Wednesday evaporating like soda bubbles. "Why would I do all this for someone who's leaving in two months anyway?"

Pat's Dad look stayed, but it morphed somehow, gentled. Tenner had seen him wear that look of pure patience when one of his children had done something really stupid… for all the right reasons.

"Because he might come back and stay, Tenner. There's no guarantee you guys will hit it off so well that he'll come back and stay for you, but what if you do? Give him a reason, kid. He's getting old enough to settle down, and God, aren't you old enough to hope again?"

Tenner concentrated on finishing the last of the sauce on his plate. "After I, uhm, come to your guys' practice Wednesday night…. He was going to come over afterwards."

"No Piper?" Pat seemed to know exactly what that meant.

"No Piper," Tenner confirmed. "Aren't you going to say that's moving a little fast?"

Pat snorted. "I am not the person to judge the fast or the slow. I just want to see your train leave the station. Piper's a great kid, Ten-Spot, but she can't be the be-all and end-all of your existence. Maybe it's time to let someone else in?"

Will he be careful? Will he not derail my entire life? Or will he jump around and change things and leave wreckage in his wake?

"Sure."

Pat frowned. "I think I deserve a better answer than that. I'm going to have to go home and change—the stain may never wash out of these pants."

Tenner managed a crooked smile. "I'll see you on practice Wednesday?" he said, some of his earlier hope returning.

Pat let out a long breath through his nose. "I'll take it. I don't like it, but I'll take it. The rest of this we'll have to leave to Ross. That kid better not let me down."

Tenner rolled his eyes, feeling like a teenager. "I have to ask you. What gave you the impression that the two of us couldn't manage our own lives?"

And Pat's eyeroll made Tenner's look pathetic and sad, the forlorn imitation of a child trying to be the parent. "Are you kidding? That kid won't stop playing around, and you won't stop working. Neither one of you can wipe your own asses. You both make me tired. Fix each other, dammit, so I can work on my own kids."

Tenner shrugged. "Nobody's as perfect as you are, Pat."

"Yeah, sure, tell that to my daughters. I'm gonna go get some soda water, then head to the bathroom so it doesn't look like I've got a killer kidney infection. Stay here and think about the error of your ways."

But as Pat bobbed his way back to the hostess stand like the evil little leprechaun he was, Tenner thought about how Pat's children gave him T-shirts about farting every Father's Day, and saved their baseball hats and foam fingers carefully in their room so they could go to a River Cats or Giants game on a moment's notice. Sure, they had their normal problems—a little bit of sass, dragging feet on homework, the occasional

"Oh my God, *Dad*!"—but for the most part, he was pretty sure Pat's kids knew. They all had to know.

When Tenner grew up, he wanted to be just like Patrick.

TO THAT end, Tenner got back to work and attempted to finish enough of his project to let him off early Tuesday so he could watch Piper dance. He was midway through running a test to see if the chip was making its benchmarks when his phone pinged.

I am thinking about you every second of the goddamned day. Please tell me I'm not alone.

His chest buzzed with what he had to admit was excitement.

Not alone.

That's it? I practically wrote you a love sonnet on the phone and I get "Not alone"?

God. Ross. Handsome. Golden. Vain as a lion. Lots of roar and bluster. Of course, Tenner missed him.

Wednesday's a long way off.

Be still my heart. I may die of too much affection.

Yeah. That's likely.

Wow. The schmoop just keeps on coming.

If you got any more pets, you'd get static shock. Tenner smiled a little with that last one. So true.

If you don't give me some goddamned affection, I'm sending you a dick pic!

Tenner's eyes went wide. *No! Piper plays with my phone!*

Thought bubbles appeared, and Tenner stared at the screen with horror. When the picture showed up, though, it was of a middle-aged man with a bright shiny head and a fringe of dark brown hair.

Meet my friend Richard.

You. Dick.

No, he's Dick. I'm Ross. I'm dying to see you again.

And Tenner couldn't help it. He was laughing quietly at his desk, smiling so hard his cheeks hurt.

So am I. You made me feel really special.

He read the text about sixty times before he pressed Send.

Good. I like being that guy. See you Wednesday.

It can't come soon enough.

TENNER WOULD never admit it to his daughter, but he loathed dance class. He liked watching the kids dance—they were cute as hell, even that one kid who'd liked to dangle from the barre when she was four and sing the theme song to *Shrek* at the top of her lungs. He loved that kid, in fact, because as it turned out, she was his.

No, it wasn't watching little girls wander around the stage, get lost, and pick leotards out of their bottoms that bothered him. It was the damned sound system that made it Purgatory. The music was too loud, piped through an ancient speaker, and after a long workday, it reverberated around Tenner's head like a nuclear-powered ping-pong ball, smashing his good mood into bits and making him yearn for a sensory deprivation chamber and long centuries of silence.

It wasn't the greatest venue to talk to Nina, but his date with Ross had been buzzing around his stomach, the thought of practicing together, giving each other shit, then going back to his house to… what?

More banging?

Maybe some Mario Kart afterward?

Ice cream?

Tenner didn't remember how any of this worked. Not at all. He'd dated in *college*. There'd been lots of midnight blowjobs in the dorms, the occasional sleepover, and then that fumbled attempt to come out to his parents over Christmas vacation when he'd finally thought, "Hey, I'm gay, I'm in love, and they keep asking about girls!"

The silence had been… glacial. He'd had to get his own ride to the airport. And as he'd taken a cab from his folks' little white farmhouse in Nebraska back to CSU Sacramento, it had occurred to him that coming out had isolated him from everything he'd ever known.

The next time he'd contacted his parents, he'd been dating Nina.

So he didn't know how to date as a grown-up, and he might very well have wrecked all attempts at dating by launching himself onto Ross McTierney like some sort of spring-loaded stuffed toy. But suddenly, he hungered to know that he *could* date. That appearing in a restaurant with a friend (Ross) who was well-dressed and looking at him like he was important (definitely Ross) and holding his hand and winking (oh my God, could it please be Ross?) seemed like something he'd needed for a long time.

Was it because he was lonely? Or could he have stayed celibate his entire life if he hadn't had that surprising moment of yielding in the dark?

He had no idea. This thing he was about to do outside the dance studio with Nina was a nice way of maybe investigating this new and hidden—or long forbidden—side of him further.

The dance teacher called all the little girls into a huddle to teach them a new skill, and Tenner gave Nina a nod.

Together they walked gratefully into the balmy spring night, and Nina gave an audible sigh of relief. "Oh my God," she muttered. "That sound system. I love this teacher, but for sweet fuck's sake!"

Tenner laughed. "It makes me want to live in a seminary where nobody talks for years."

She nodded enthusiastically. "Right? Yikes. Sorry, Ten, I mean, I'm so sorry."

Tenner chuckled again, a part of him sad. They'd been so good at this once upon a time. Laughing at the funny stuff.

"You're forgiven," he said. "At last year's recital, she was the best one."

It was Nina's turn to laugh. "No, no, she really wasn't. She lost the steps and turned around and danced with her own shadow, but you're very sweet to say so."

He inclined his head, and before he could find a way to bring up the subject, she said, "So what's up? You're not cancelling on Friday, are you?"

"Oh, no!" he said. "I might be there around the same time, though. I hope that's okay."

"Yeah, sure." She sounded so mellow now, but then, having her plans changed at the last moment had always brought out the worst in her. "Piper says watching you practice with the team on Sunday was a lot of fun. I guess one of the guys came home for dinner?"

Tenner rolled his eyes. "She invited him, Nina. I mean, it's a good thing he was a good sport about it, but she practically lassoed him to come eat at our house. But yeah. It's a sweet team."

"Good. Is that what you wanted to talk about?" Anxiously she looked behind his shoulder. He glanced over too and saw the girls were still learning a new move, something with lots of extended hands and bounces.

"No, uh, actually...." He chewed his lip. "Nina, you're dating, right?"

Her relaxed expression disappeared. "Yeah. A couple of nights out, a couple of different guys. Why?"

He swallowed. "I'm glad." He put all the sincerity into his voice that he could manage. "You're a good mom. You don't deserve to be alone."

And suddenly her entire body went still. "Are *you* dating?"

He swallowed. "I'd like to."

"You can't bring any of that crap into your house, Tenner. You know what the settlement says—"

Tenner held out his hand. "No sleepovers while Piper's there—I promise. I... I... need you to think about what the settlement *does* say."

Her eyes began to dart nervously. "What do you mean?"

"What sort of lifestyle are you talking about?"

She opened her mouth and nothing came out, and he realized that she was as lost as he was about that clause in the settlement.

"Look. I'm not going to press you anymore about it," he said softly. "I, you know... I think you deserve to be happy, Nina. I need you to ask yourself why I don't."

"I never said that!" she defended, and he cocked his head.

"Just alone."

She opened her mouth again, and the music started up. They locked eyes for a miserable moment, and then he gestured her back into the dance studio for that eardrum-shattering piano music.

It was a start.

ANTICIPATION

ROSS AND Pat threw the ball in a leisurely way, remembering to include Abner when he looked ready to catch it. Baseball wasn't his game, but his sisters were both at an indoor soccer game, and Pat had offered to take Abner to baseball to save him the boredom.

They were a couple of minutes early, but Ross still kept looking around oh-so-casually to see who would arrive.

"He's got a project he's trying to finish," Pat said as if he could read his mind.

"I didn't say anything," Ross defended.

"Of course not. He'll be a few minutes late. Knowing Tenner, he'll want to have all his loose ends tied up before he gets here."

Ross nodded. "I don't even know who you're talking about."

"Of course not. Are you coming home tonight?"

Ross's eyes darted to where Abner stood, staring wistfully at the bullpen where his backpack sat with a book he'd been reading in the car.

"Abner, fly, be free," Ross said. "We won't torture you anymore."

Abner gave a grand smile. "Thanks, Uncle Ross. You're the *best!*" And with that, he tore off toward the bullpen and whatever sword-and-sorcery tome had captured his attention this week.

"Sure," Pat muttered. "Uncle Ross is the best, and Dad's just some asshole who wanted a game of catch with his kid."

"You really want to bond with him? Find one of those whats-it, role-playing fairs, and let him deck himself out with a toy sword. You wear tights and a doublet or whatever, and you will be the best dad in the world."

Pat grimaced at him sourly. "That is way too much stuff I don't like to do," he said after a moment. "Can we talk about your love life some more?"

"I'm not planning on coming home until after the game Friday," Ross said bluntly. "But Abner sees Piper at school sometimes, and I thought it would be best not to put that out there."

The dawning comprehension on Pat's face made Ross roll his eyes. "Oh my God—here you are, some weirdo Cupid Machiavelli guy, and you forgot that kids talk to each other? The actual fucking hell?"

"I forgot," Pat muttered. "I'm sorry. It just seems like a stupid thing to keep secret from a kid, and I forgot that Tenner has to. And that's even stupider. But you're right. And smart about it. But don't gloat. It's so very unattractive."

Ross grinned lazily and cracked his gum. "Sure, it is."

"God. Such an asshole. I can't believe you get laid ever."

"Heh heh heh heh."

Pat hurled the ball into his mitt with unnecessary force, and Ross kept returning it with almost languid motions, because playing the arrogant dumb jock was easy.

What was hard was keeping his excitement tamped down. God, he wanted to see Tenner. They'd swapped texts the night before, and while their messages said nothing in particular, they seemed to be saying everything at once.

They said Tenner had once possessed all the confidence in the world, and he was trying to rebuild that, brick by brick. They said this guy who had yielded so sweetly in the dark was going to be a prickly, interesting package when they were in bed, with the lights on, and Ross was taking him apart and putting him back together again.

Or that's the way Ross kept imagining it. But he got the feeling Tenner was planning on fucking his own pound of flesh, and he didn't think that was happening. Not that he minded turning over the reins every once in a while, but not this time.

Not when Tenner would sass back and boss back and argue with him every minute of what was promising to be a very awesome weekend in the middle of the week.

If it wasn't for that niggling fear.... *He's got responsibilities, man. You can't fuck up his life.*

Yeah. That. Ross had to leave in seven and a half weeks. His job was important—and tramping through the charred portion of what had once been lush and thriving rainforest, working on reforestation in spite of hostile governments and stifling temperatures wasn't going to be a cakewalk. Usually during his funding hiatuses from fieldwork, he'd troll the bar scene to his heart's content, sometimes pick up a semivacation fling, someone who could tell him goodbye with a fond smile. He tended to do a lot of landscape planning and fundraising for companies that needed a good shove in the right direction, so he interacted with a lot of smart businesspeople who didn't get their hands dirty and didn't understand why he loved digging in their backyards. That's okay—it made him a novel distraction, which meant leaving in a couple of weeks wasn't a hardship. He loved a short romance. Donna, his last fly-by-night had even told him he left right when his flaws as a boyfriend would have started driving her mad.

He was messy, he was obnoxious, and he tended to be cavalier about things like time and rent and dealing with the everyday trivia that made up the lives of people with roots.

But he was really rocking in bed, and that wasn't just vanity talking. That was the absolute knowledge that he brought everything to bed that he tried to bring to ordinary life—passion, consideration, a sense of adventure. He didn't like to leave the bedroom until both parties were drenched in sweat and come and felt like they wouldn't need sex again for a week.

He sort of made it a point of honor. And that way, when he said goodbye, people were like, "Great, hon, it's been real, but there are parts of me that need at least six months before we do this again."

But those people hadn't had kids. Or a prickly ex-wife. Or so much to lose by giving it their all in bed.

Tenner had those things, and Ross had to continually remind himself of that. He didn't want to hurt anybody, and blowing through Tenner Gibson's life like a sexual hurricane could leave wreckage.

But as Ross recognized Tenner's CR-V pulling into the parking lot, he felt a thrill coursing up and down his spine, splitting off and striking all erogenous zones north and south, east and west.

Maybe a very contained hurricane. Maybe a lightning storm.

People survived lightning all the time, right? It zapped through their system and left them with some fried nerve endings and an incredible story.

And as he watched Tenner's wiry, compact body swing out of the car and come trotting toward the field, he ignored the common sense part of him, the voice of reason that he employed at work, fighting for funding, or in the field, wrestling to use limited resources in the most efficient way possible—the part that trekked through forests and witnessed the gift that nature was to man and the blight that man was on nature, and mourned that governments couldn't find a way to worship the fragile ecosystem that bound the world together.

The part of him that chanted repeatedly that yeah, people got hit by lightning all the time and survived to tell the tale.

And the tale was—inevitably—that the lightning changed their lives.

TENNER WAS just as intent during practice as he was during a game. He kept his eye on the ball and the play at all times, and brother, when he snapped his wrist to throw that absurdly large ball, he put enough thunder behind it to take off the receiver's mitt if they weren't careful.

Ross spent most of the practice trying to distract him from that.

"Okay, Kelso, I'm hitting to you!" he called to the third baseman. Dirk Kelso rolled his eyes.

"You've said that three times. But you keep hitting to Gibson on first!"

"Do I?" Ross asked, throwing the ball up. With a lazy swing he sent it right over Tenner's head. "I had no idea."

"You suck!" Tenner snarled, launching himself from his alert semicrouch to run back and field the thing. God, he ran like a jackrabbit on speed. Absolutely focused, he passed his right fielder and damned near climbed the fence to catch the ball before it hit and sank.

"You really fucking do!" Pat complained. "Either hit it to someone else or we'll make you run the bases and have Kelso bat 'em out!"

"I suck at it," Kelso admitted. "But if Ross doesn't stop messing with Gibson's head, I'll do it."

Tenner trotted back to his base, only slightly out of breath, before he launched the ball at Pat, who was pitching.

"Ouch!" Pat complained. "What did I ever do to you?"

"You brought him!" Tenner snapped. "Jesus, McTierney, pick on someone else!"

Ross cracked his gum and grinned. "Sure," he said. "Or actually— Vlad, c'mon on in and hit. I'm gonna run bases!"

Dark-haired, sloe-eyed Vlad Kominski nodded and started in from left field just as Ross smacked the ball right at Tenner again—and then raced him to first base.

Tenner had to step out to get it, but when he saw Ross running, he didn't hesitate to race for the bag.

Ross hadn't been chasing balls all over creation, and he pumped his legs with manic glee as Tenner tried to radically slow down so he wouldn't miss the base. He wasn't going to make it, he wasn't going to make it, until wait, Tenner slipped in the dust, and they were *both* going to make it and—

Ross spun wide, leaped over Tenner's outstretched leg, and tagged the bag from behind.

Tenner turned toward him, ball in hand, and gaped. "You can't do that!" he panted.

"Who says?"

"You're out!"

"It's batting practice. I'm not even in."

"But… but…," Tenner flailed, his mitt on one hand, the ball in the other. "What in the hell was that?"

Ross grinned and cracked his gum while Tenner looked for words, and the rest of the team dissolved where they stood.

"You have got balls," Tenner finally managed to say—his first coherent words in about thirty seconds of the team giggling their asses off.

"No, Ten, you've got the ball. You should probably throw that in." Ross batted his big baby blues for effect, and Tenner turned toward Pat so fast, Pat made ready to duck.

"Patrick, I'm going to kill him," Tenner said with absolute certainty.

"You can't, Ten-Spot. The wife is sort of attached."

"She has a son."

Pat gave him a begging look. "Please? Ross likes baseball. What can I say?"

"Feather pillows and Benadryl. No one would ever know."

Pat held up his mitt. "Throw the ball, Ten. I'll run it by Desi, see what she has to say."

"Can you tell her to wait until it's time for him to leave anyway?" Vlad asked. "We might win this season!"

"Speak for yourself," Tenner grumbled, throwing the ball to Pat. "I'm just here to get dicked with."

"Yeah, you are," Ross added for Tenner's ears only, rewarded when Tenner glared at him.

"Being an asshole will *not* get you into my pants," Tenner muttered.

"No, but it will put that adorable little flush on your cheeks," Ross teased, and Tenner's look of outrage warmed his soul.

The crack of the ball called him back to practice, and Vlad lobbed the ball into center where it was easily caught and fielded.

Tenner gave a huff of exasperation.

"Not going anywhere," Ross practically sang.

"You realize I had plans for tonight," Tenner muttered.

"Am I still part of them?" Oh, Ross had no doubts. Tenner's flush was high on his cheekbones and deep under his neck. They were going to tear each other apart.

"Not if I kick you in the balls for being an ass," Tenner sang back. "Run!"

Oh, shit! Vlad really got hold of that one! Ross paused just long enough to pat Tenner's ass like he would any teammate's and then took off, running the bases with Vlad at his heels.

PRACTICE BROKE up eventually, leaving Ross and Tenner to help Pat pack up the equipment and haul it back to his car.

"Where's your Tahoe?" Tenner asked. His CR-V was the only other thing left in the parking lot.

"Don't need it," Ross said cheerfully. "You pass my work on the way to your work. Hand me that duffel, okay, Pat?"

Pat grabbed Ross's well-worn Army surplus duffel bag from the third seat in the Odyssey and threw it to Ross without batting an eyelash. "When should I send out a search party?"

"I'll come home with you Friday night," Ross said. "We've both got games."

"Mm." Pat cast a look at Tenner, who was standing near his car, pretending he didn't notice Ross had pretty much announced his sleepover. "See you tomorrow, Ten."

"Right." Tenner gave a sort of noncommittal nod and turned toward his CR-V.

"You should run and get in the passenger side before he takes off without you," Pat told Ross, shoving his equipment one last time so the hatch would shut.

"Very probably. I'll call if I need anything."

"A ride, an ambulance—"

"Advice, takeout. Let's not get dramatic. I'm pretty sure he likes me."

They both heard the beep as Tenner unlocked his vehicle and grimaced.

"Run," Pat said. "Be really sure."

Ross couldn't help it—his smile about split his cheeks. But he ran and got to the passenger's side, letting himself in right as Tenner was starting the car.

"I didn't say you could come," Tenner muttered as Ross threw his duffel in the back.

"You didn't say I couldn't."

"Pulling that shit on the field—who told you that was cute?" Oh, he sounded riled as fuck.

"You did, when you didn't kill me or let me charge you," Ross told him, watching that flush actually rise to engulf his ears. "If you'd stood still like you were going to take a beating even though it was just practice, I would have known to not fuck around. But you're competitive as hell. If you'd put your toe on it and leaned back, I would have known you expected some bullshit on the bag."

Tenner let out a snort, and Ross knew he'd called it. "You are a running bag of bullshit, Ross McTierney, don't you deceive yourself. If my father had seen that crap when I was in school, he would have burst a blood vessel in his head."

"That's no fun," Ross said, a little sorry and a lot appalled. "My dad never even taught us baseball—he taught us pickle. I was in grade school before I realized baseball had a diamond and an outfield."

"Mm, that actually sounds fun."

"You don't think it's fun?" Oh *no*!

"Well, I do now!" Tenner said with a little laugh. "Nothing like not getting to play it for eight years, you know? But when I was in school, baseball was for scholarships, and fucking around was a sin."

"We're grown-ups now," Ross said easily, storing the ache in his heart for a rainy day. "Baseball's for fun and fucking around is a pleasure."

Ah! There it was. Tenner's reluctant grin.

"That's the plan," he said primly. "Have you eaten?"

"I'm starving for tube steak."

And that made him chortle. "I've got actual food in the fridge!" he protested when he could breathe. "Like, we can take turns in the shower and eat and relax and…." He blushed. "And see what happens."

"Sure," Ross lied. "We'll see what happens."

Yeah, Ross could eat. He planned to eat. But first, he planned to make Tenner come, hard, and *then* there could be showers. Ross was going to wring climaxes out of Tenner Gibson like a washcloth, making him limp with sex and sweat and pleasure.

And after Tenner got up in the morning and stumbled into work, wondering what had hit him, Ross was going to do the same thing when they got home. With one night's worth of exception, this man hadn't had sex that satisfied him in more than eight years. Ross was going to make it his personal mission to redress that heinous wrong.

Yup. *That* was the plan.

Ross gave Tenner his space as he opened the door and made his way into the house, thinking about a surprise kiss and then some slamming sex against the door.

But first they had to not let Joe the cat out, and then, when they were all situated inside, Tenner hit the lights, and Ross got a look into the kitchen and saw that the table had been set for two, and there were flowers on it.

His plan for ravishing Tenner fizzled to a puzzled halt.

The guy had brought flowers. And whatever he had in the fridge, it probably wasn't mac and cheese and hot dogs.

Ross abruptly changed strategies. Reaching out, he snagged Tenner's hips and pulled him in so Ross could nibble on the back of his neck. It was tangy with sweat, and Ross actually shuddered as he reminded himself that he'd switched from ravishment to seduction.

"I'll go shower in the guest room," he murmured. "You go upstairs. We'll meet down here."

Tenner didn't quite melt—probably for the same reasons Ross was holding back. He'd gone to some lengths to make this special. Ross had to let him.

"Fine. There's, uh, wine or beer or soda or milk or—"

The sweetness would kill him. He closed his eyes and nuzzled Tenner's ear. "Go before I ruin all your plans."

He let go and turned resolutely to the guest room, duffel in hand. God, he'd been right. He was in so over his head.

That didn't stop him from making an effort. No, he didn't have silk pajamas, but he figured sleep pants and a T-shirt with a little bit of aftershave would do. He still beat Tenner to the kitchen, and as he pulled the bottle of wine out of the refrigerator—chilled white, his favorite— and poked through the offerings for dinner, he hoped he wouldn't be too disappointed.

In addition to the regular groceries, and Ten kept a well-stocked fridge, probably mostly for Piper's sake, there was a plastic container of steaks marinating and a salad-in-a-bag.

Bingo.

Easy dinner for two guys making a late start. It was like Ross could read his mind.

He preheated the oven and pulled the broiling pan out from under the stove, then poured himself a glass of wine before he got comfortable in Tenner's kitchen.

He'd gotten the steaks in when it occurred to him Tenner was taking a long damned time.

"Tenner?" he called, coming around the corner. "Uhm, you having second thoughts? It's only dinner."

"Coming!" Tenner called back, so quickly Ross had to wonder if he hadn't been staring in the mirror, asking himself what in the hell he was doing.

Well, that was understandable too.

Because it wasn't just dinner.

This here had taken preparation and care. Steaks, wine, flowers— the evening had all the hallmarks of a man who hadn't dated in a while and who wanted to do things right.

"What?" Tenner asked irritably as he trotted down the stairs. "You were expecting a peignoir?"

"I didn't expect us to be twins," Ross said, hiding his laugh behind his hand. Plaid sleep pants—the same plaid—and white T-shirt. "I take it Target had a sale?"

"Is there any other place to shop?" Tenner asked sourly. "I mean, I seem to remember spending a lot of disposable income at PacSun and places like that, but then there was Piper and interview suits and—"

"Slacks and a button-down," Ross finished sympathetically. "Yeah. I do jeans and a button-down, but that's because I'm a consultant and I can flaunt the bullshit like a rock star."

Tenner rolled his eyes. "You'd wear jeans if you knew the dress code stated specifically that anyone wearing jeans would be skinned like a fish."

Ross had to shrug. "Yeah, that's fair. I mean, when you're tramping through deforested wastelands and trying to save the world, you don't really think about the clothes on your back."

Tenner's narrowed eyes told him he'd caught the self-important swagger added in there for spice. "You gonna tip your hat, pardnuh? I mean, you can't be John Wayne of the wasteland if you don't got a hat to tip."

Ross smirked and barely refrained from just pouncing on him right there, in the living room, bent over the couch like he'd planned all along. "Busted."

Tenner sniffed the air. "Did you put the steaks in to broil?"

"Yeah." Ross turned and grabbed his hand, pulling him into the kitchen and the set table and the flowers. "I figured those had our name on them, right?"

"You're very astute," Tenner mumbled.

"Well, you're very sweet. I haven't been wined and dined in quite some time."

"I'd ask about that other thing, but it's none of my business."

Ross laughed quietly. "Sure it is. Here, sit. Let me pour you some wine. It's tasty stuff, by the way. California has some of the best."

Tenner made himself comfortable at the table, swinging the chair around so he could watch Ross work. "I like it. White, not red, though. Sorry. Red gives me a headache."

"Yeah, it does that for lots of people. White's fine." Ross poured Tenner a glass and topped off his own before putting the bottle back in the fridge. "Here. You had carrot sticks so I figured we'd amuse-bouche."

"Is that really a verb?" Tenner challenged, and Ross had to laugh again.

"God, you're a handful. Now sit and let me regale you with my many sexcapades, so you might judge me for the manwhore I am."

Tenner laughed outright at that. "*This* is a sales pitch? Buddy, I might want my steak back."

"Too late, steak's mine. I licked it before I put it in to broil."

More laughter, and Tenner hadn't even had a sip of chardonnay. "You did not!"

"You'll never know," Ross returned primly. "Now, let's see... how many ways are there to get laid in the Amazon jungle?"

"Not that many, I'd wager," Tenner said, sobering.

Ross waggled his eyebrows. "You'd be surprised." But Tenner was just regarding him with that intent expression, so he figured he needed to stop dancing around the point. "Okay, fine. I've been doing fieldwork since I've gotten out of college. I go somewhere for a few months, then I come home to the most lucrative consultant job, I get my grant written, and I go back out. Most of the time, I avoid entanglements. We work damned hard out there, and male or female, everybody needs sleep."

"But when you're here in the States?" Tenner prodded.

"Well, it's like vacation. I'm in, I'm out—everybody knows the score. This time's different, though," he acknowledged. "This time I'm coming back to the same place."

"Are you waving that in front of me like a carrot?" There was bitterness in his voice, and Ross had to take a breath.

"I'm... I'm telling you not to judge a relationship before it starts. I mean...." He bit his lip, finding himself in deep water. "What I do, it's an act of faith and hope, Tenner. We have not been kind to our environment, and I have to scrape and money-grub and kiss a lot of ass to convince corporations to help me go out and fix things. And it could take a price out of my soul if I let it. But it's worth it, because what's the alternative? Give up? It's the same thing with a relationship. What's the alternative? Give up? Assume there is no happy ending... ever?"

Tenner took a thoughtful sip of wine. "No," he said.

"It's like fixing the planet. Reduce carbon emissions. Stop fracking. Stop dumping toxic chemicals into our food supply. So many small steps we can take. So, you know. A glass of wine, step one. A steak, step two."

"I hear you," Tenner said. "What made you decide to do what you do? I mean, it's amazing. Just knowing that you go out into the world and tramp the jungle and look for ways to reforest and clean water supplies and revitalize growth, I think that's really awesome. But how did you get started?"

Ross checked the timer on the steak and took his own thoughtful sip of wine to try to track the memory.

"Did you grow up in California?" he asked.

"No. The Midwest." Tenner breathed in thoughtfully. "Nebraska. Nina used to call it Nebransas, and she wasn't far wrong."

"Lots of flat land there," Ross agreed.

"It was like a prison of farmland," Tenner said with a shudder. "God, that scholarship to Sacramento—of all places, right? There's still a lot of rural in Sacramento. But there's also the ocean and the mountains. It really is still like an escape."

Ross smiled a little. "Yeah. So farmland—were your parents farmers?"

"No. Dad's in law enforcement. Mom worked at the school. Why?"

"Because… you tend to be attached to the seasons here in California. I mean, we just got out of one of our longest droughts in history, and when there's no drought, areas are flooding. Well, when I was a kid, there was a drought. And it was… scary. Really scary. I remember washing my hands—my mom was going on and on about how filthy they were because I'd been looking at bugs—and the water came out of the faucet, and I'd heard adults talking about the drought for a year, and here I was, wasting precious water on hands that didn't seem all *that* dirty." He winked, and Tenner laughed like he was supposed to. "And it hit me. We could run out of water. The world could run out of water. And I asked my dad, and he… he told me the truth. That it could happen—places could run out of water to drink. And… and I cried myself to sleep that night. And the night after that. My parents finally asked me what was wrong, and… I had a hard time putting it into words. It was like… like the sun going out. Like the stars extinguishing. The threat was that real to me. So…."

He drained his glass of wine, realizing that this was sort of a buzzkill. "Are the steaks done yet?"

"No, you've got five minutes. Finish." Tenner leaned forward, eyes fastened hungrily on Ross's face, and suddenly Ross felt naked, more naked than he'd been in front of another human being since his first time—Gabby Raines in the eleventh grade, and Paul Wright in college, if you were counting. But in the midst of all that nakedness, he felt safe.

Tenner wouldn't laugh or judge. Tenner just wanted to know him better. It wasn't a crime.

"Well, you know my sister, and you've probably guessed my parents are big barrels of awesome."

"I met them," Tenner acknowledged. "At Pat and Desi's twentieth. You were out of town, but there was a big to-do. They're…." He smiled wistfully. "It's like if you could fill out a special-order form for parents, you guys got the best set. Too bad they're limited edition, you know?"

Ross grinned, filing the quiet sadness away again, wondering when he and Ten would get to unpack *that*. "Yeah, well, we didn't know that when we were kids, but I sure haven't taken them for granted as an adult. Anyway, I wasn't looking too hot, and my mom asked me what was wrong one morning on the way to school, and I unloaded. I was so scared. This was our world and we weren't *doing* anything. So she kept me home, and we spent the day looking up things I could do. And you know, I was in, like, the sixth grade, and school had been easy, and I hadn't really cared that much about it. But once I found out what sort of grades you had to have to become an environmentalist, to go out and do what I'm doing now—I'll tell you what. My grades were top-notch. I got into UC Davis on a full ride. It's like... like she gave me the power to do what I had to fix the world, you know?"

"That's amazing." Tenner breathed softly, and Ross felt all that wonder deep in his soul.

Had anybody ever looked at him like that? He wanted to taste that appreciation, and he leaned forward, brushing Tenner's mouth with his own, just as the timer went off.

"Fuck," Ross muttered, put out. He stood up and got the steak out, then left it to rest on the stovetop while he turned off the oven and started on the salad.

"Here," Tenner said practically, "let me help."

"No, no." Ross shook the bag of salad into the bowl they'd used the week before. "I... I've never seen this sort of organization in my honor before. I want to give it the appreciation it deserves."

Tenner sighed and sat down. "Does it bother you?" he asked. "That I tried to... I don't know."

"Make things special?" Ross turned and smiled at him. "Not at all. I'm not usually that guy in people's lives, you know? That special guy? It... it means a lot to me. I want to do my part."

He heard Tenner swallow from across the kitchen and went back to fixing dinner.

DINNER CONVERSATION flowed pretty freely after that, but they both seemed conscious of not having too much wine.

Just enough.

Just enough to bring out the flavor of the meat (and Tenner's marinade was sort of wonderful as it was) and to give a late dinner in their pajamas a hint of occasion. When they were done and the leftovers stowed and the dishwasher set on cycle, Ross grabbed Tenner's hand again, tugging him out of the kitchen.

"There's gelato in the freezer," Tenner said, and for a moment, Ross thought he was going to get away.

"Later," he said throatily. God, that look in Tenner's eyes—dark earth brown with a hint of sepia, with the wonder and the appreciation and oh my God, the dry sense of humor—made him yearn for sweetness you didn't ordinarily find in the bottom of a gelato carton.

"We just ate," Tenner said, allowing himself to be herded up the stairs. "I may have gas."

"I don't care," Ross said. "I've done this before. I know the dangers."

"But—"

Ross shoved him up the last step and caught up, pulling his shoulder so they were face-to-face.

"I got tested Monday," he said, leaning his forehead against Tenner's. "All clear. Have you changed your mind?" he asked seriously.

Tenner's mouth, usually lean and tight-lipped, parted, and he wet it with a pink tongue. "All clear?" God, he probably still tasted like wine.

"No condoms, if you don't want. You'll feel me come inside you." Tenner's little gasp made him swell. "Have you changed your mind?"

"No," Tenner whispered. "No, just—"

Ross had been a good boy. There had been dinner and conversation, carnations, daisies, and wine.

And this man, looking at him like he was important and fascinating, and baiting him and debating him and giving Ross a safe place to be himself in the midst of what nobody knew better than Ross was a big scary world.

Ross had earned this, earned Tenner's little whimper of surrender, earned his no-bullshit kiss back, the way he cupped Ross's cheeks and took over his mouth without hesitation.

Tenner whirled Ross around and backed him against the wall, taking over with such ease, Ross wondered what fantasies *Tenner* had been entertaining.

"Just what?" Ross asked, tilting his head back so Tenner could nip at his neck, his collarbone under his T-shirt, his jaw.

"Just nothing," Tenner said. He shoved his hands under Ross's shirt, and Ross sighed in appreciation. Slightly rough, callused with work and play, Tenner swept his palms up and down Ross's chest, kneading, scraping lightly with his nails, pinching—"Ah! Oh, man!" His nipples were ultra-sensitive.

Ross stripped his shirt off right there in the hallway and gave Tenner full access, and Tenner, oh yes, went straight for his nipples again.

"Mmm... okay, do that as long as you want," Ross purred, massaging Tenner's scalp under his hair. Tenner spent a long time pleasuring one side, until Ross couldn't stop himself from rocking his hips back and forth in need. With a sudden switch, Tenner was on the other nipple, and Ross felt helpless, exposed, while he gave Tenner permission to ravish him.

"Gah! Ten, you're killing me here!"

"Your skin tastes magical," Tenner muttered, and before Ross could laugh or widen his eyes and remark that was the weirdest thing anyone had said to him while making out, Tenner sank to his knees and stripped Ross's sleep pants down to his ankles, and his boxer briefs with them.

"Here?" he asked, surprised.

"Oh my God." Tenner was staring at Ross's cock, fully erect and sticking straight out, with hunger in his eyes. His breath fanned the sensitive head, and Ross dropped his hand to stroke his own length, but Tenner stopped him.

"Please?" Tenner begged.

"Yeah, sure, why not." Ross leaned against the wall, eyes closed, Tenner's firm grip along his shaft a tender form of torture.

"I didn't even get to see it," Tenner told him, his tongue flicking out to tease the head between words.

"That's a shame." Oh God, his grip was so tight, so sure. Ross was going to expire, on the rug in the hallway, naked.

"Do you know how long I've dreamed about sucking your cock?" Tenner's voice rose, and his stroking kept up firmly.

"Two minutes longer than necessary!" Ross whined. "God, Tenner, you're killing me!"

To his horror, that stroke on his shaft stopped, and he lowered his gaze to Tenner's wickedly flashing brown eyes.

"What?" Ross asked while his heart thundered in his ears and time ceased to move.

"Beg me," Tenner whispered, flicking his tongue out again.

Ross had to stop himself from coming. "Oh, you evil, evil little man."

The lick across his head was a little longer this time, long enough to make Ross shudder and moan, but short enough to leave him practically in pain.

"Beg me," Tenner said again, his other hand cupping Ross's balls. Oh wow. Tenner might be the one to fuck *Ross* tonight. Anything was possible. This gorgeous sexual mastery was so much better than Ross had expected.

"You think so-*o!*" Tenner squeezed—not enough to hurt, just enough to make him…. *Oh no. Not that easily. No, no, no, no….*

"Beg me," Tenner repeated, his voice throbbing with the knowledge that Ross was only stretching this out for his own pleasure.

"God, yes. Suck me. Suck my cock. Jesus, Tenner, *suck my fucking cock!*"

Hot and hard, Tenner gripped and stroked with a fast, strong rhythm. The world shrank to a pinpoint, to Tenner's mouth on Ross's cock, and there was no showing Tenner who was boss, and there was no making this night the be-all and end-all of Tenner's sexual experience. There was only mouth and cock and—

"Fuck, Ten, I'm gonna—"

Tenner shoved his mouth all the way down to Ross's root, his throat working urgently, and Ross saw stars and came.

Spurt after spurt, the heavens dancing before his eyes, and Tenner swallowed so happily, like this was the best thing anybody could have done for him. Ross stroked his hair, his cheek, thinking brokenly that he wanted to do so much more for Tenner Gibson.

As soon as he could see past the stars.

Tenner finally pulled away and rested his head against Ross's thigh, his breath coming in pants. He gave a little shimmy as he crouched, a sound of need, and Ross felt steady enough to tighten his fingers in Tenner's hair and tilt his head back.

"Think you're something?" he panted.

Tenner gave a sultry smile and licked a trickle of come from the side of his mouth. "Show me different."

Ross pulled him slowly up, taking his mouth when they were even, exulting in the taste of his own come, wanting Tenner's in his mouth as well.

"I'm going to show you the world," he promised in Tenner's ear, and kiss by kiss, they slow-walked to the bedroom so Ross could make good on that promise.

By the time they got to the bed—a surprisingly solid four-poster masterpiece, decked in sage green—Tenner was naked, his remarkably wiry, muscular flesh hot and smooth against Ross's.

There was a dusting of dark hair on his chest, and he had bronze nipples that Ross had to taste. Tenner's hands flailed, finally finding purchase in Ross's hair, and his tugging goaded Ross on even more.

He practically tackled Tenner, shoving him backward onto the bed and falling on top of him. Tenner laughed up into his eyes, apparently delighted. "You think you're topping this time?" Tenner taunted.

In reply, Ross kept kissing him, plundering with his mouth and ravaging with his hands, until Tenner bucked mindlessly beneath him. Shoving his knees between Tenner's thighs so he could anchor him on the bed, Ross pulled back and grinned at Tenner, who was very much sloppy and swollen and mussed.

"First I'm gonna rim ya. Then I'm gonna finger ya. *Then* I'm gonna fuck ya!"

Tenner's mouth fell open in surprise, and Ross pushed at his thighs until Tenner's knees bent over Ross's shoulders.

God, his body was gorgeous. That silky dark hair dusting everything, the fair skin flushing brightly. Tenner's backside was taut and muscular—not soft and welcoming at all—but then, where would the challenge be?

He spread Tenner's cheeks and lowered his head, grinning up at those big brown eyes over the length of that compact body. "Don't touch your cock," he ordered and then lowered his head and licked up that preciously pink crease.

"Gah! Fuck you!"

"Not happening just now," Ross told him and then licked again.

"Holy fuck!" Tenner's hips practically came off the bed, and Ross gave him a playful smack on the ass.

"Stop that," he said, using his best schoolteacher/Dom voice.

Tenner moaned slightly, his stomach muscles quivered, and his cock splatted on his stomach. Ross remembered Tenner's eyes, challenging him, *Beg me!* and he got an idea.

"Stay right there," he said with deliberate sternness. "And put your hands over your head. Boy."

Tenner moaned again, his thighs falling apart lewdly, and he put his hands up where they were supposed to be.

"Nice. Sock drawer?"

"Top right," Tenner said, nodding to a standard long and low chest of drawers against his wall. Ross left him on the bed, missing his heat, his smell, even as he started rooting through the drawers—yes. Dress socks. Stretchy. While he was there he saw… ooh, lubricant, which he grabbed since he'd left his own downstairs. And wow. Oh wow. Two items, a little on the conservative side, sizewise, but one of them was very lifelike, and the other one vibrated.

Nice. He snagged everything and went back to Tenner, putting the vibrating plug on one side of Tenner's head and the dildo on the other, so whichever way Tenner looked, he would see them and imagine. Think of the possibilities. Maybe he'd start giving orders. Maybe they'd make him burn.

Tenner's eyes went from object to object, a flush of embarrassment washing his naked body. Ross stood, stroking his face for a moment while those eyes, limpid and blown with passion, searched his.

"Those things," Ross said, his eyes wicked, "are too small."

Tenner's breathless laugh went straight to his groin. "If I hadn't seen it myself, I'd say you were bragging."

Ross rubbed Tenner's lips with his thumb, and Tenner sucked it into his mouth.

"You didn't just see it," Ross told him, smoothing his hair back with his other hand. "You sucked it. You pleasured it. And now I'm going to pleasure you."

In response, Tenner sucked harder.

"Trust me?" Ross murmured, pulling his thumb out and using it to tease Tenner's nipples.

Tenner bit his lip for a moment as he lay splayed out in front of Ross, thighs spread, hole still shiny with Ross's spit. "Yes," he said, and it sounded like he was surprised himself.

"I'm gonna tie your hands. And then I'm going to use you hard. But your safe words are *stop*, *no*, *ouch*, and *I don't like that*, okay?"

Tenner's lips quirked. "Okay."

"This isn't a scene. This is me, keeping you still, so I can make you come so hard you'll scream."

A soft breathy sound issued from Tenner's throat, and his white teeth worried his lower lip. Ross's cock swelled with blood to the point of aching. "Yeah."

He bound Tenner's wrists, making sure there was plenty of play so Tenner could slip free if he needed to. A tiny corner of his mind engaged with padded cuffs and a little paddle and all of the delicious implements of very, very naughty sex, but when he was done, his naked body stretched over Tenner's, all of the "later" disappeared and there was only "now."

Now, he kissed his way back down Tenner's fine body, pausing at his nipples again, sucking, nipping, until Tenner started to squirm.

"No," he said, and he felt Tenner shoving his hips down against the bed. "Good boy." He stroked Tenner's outer thigh and then the inner, listening to the changes in Tenner's breathing. Slowly, touching just enough for Tenner to know he was there, he ran his tongue from the tip of Tenner's weeping cock to the base, chuckling and blowing on it when Tenner spurted precome.

Then he positioned himself back where he had been, between Tenner's spread thighs, looking up his torso.

This time, Tenner pulled at the socks binding his hands and thrust his hips down into the bed. "Good boy," Ross said again, running his tongue along the pale skin of his inner thigh. Down, down, down, right to the crease, and Tenner's heavy balls.

He tongued one, sucking lightly at the skin, and Tenner murmured, his hips flexing again. God, he was so sensitive. Then he snagged a pillow and shoved it under Tenner's hips, and parted him again, licking without mercy.

"Oh wow," Tenner gibbered. "Oh, damn. You… you weren't kidding. That's amazing. Oh God, Ross? Something more? Something harder? Please? Please? I'm begging. When I begged you—ah…."

Ross slid a finger inside him, stretching some more, playing, but not pumping. He took the opportunity to run his tongue from the base of Tenner's cock, which in the light was impressive and girthy, to the tip, tormenting the bell a little, lapping the precome like nectar.

He'd tease and feel Tenner quiver, tease some more, and savor his shudder, and the way his breath shook from his throat. Ross himself was hard enough to ache, and he was careful not to grind too much against the bed because he could, very realistically, lose control and come.

He snicked the lube bottle to dump some slick, and then added another finger inside Tenner's tight passage. He could feel Tenner's moan against the palm of his hand. Tenner's back arched and Ross flicked his bottom barely hard enough to sting.

"Bastard," Tenner muttered, shoving his hips down again.

"Want me to stop?" Ross asked, tasting the head of his cock again. His precome was so sweet, it was all Ross could do to keep from gobbling it down.

"N... n... no...." Tenner let out a moan.

So Ross stopped. "Is that no, don't stop, or no, don't keep going?" He was pretty sure he knew the answer, but God, having Tenner at his mercy made him hot.

"Don't stop. Please don't stop. Fuck me. God, fuck me."

"Fingers or cock?" Ross tantalized some more, adding a third finger to his ass. Tenner arched his back again, and this time, Ross took the thrust of his cock straight to the back of his throat.

"Cock!" Tenner begged. "Please, cock!"

"Are you sure?" Ross taunted. He dumped some more lube on his fingers and stretched, playing with the fourth at Tenner's entrance.

"*Please*!" Tenner snarled, and Ross pulled his fingers out and leaned his head against Tenner's thigh, closing his eyes and counting to five to keep from coming.

"Ross?"

"You destroy me," Ross said gruffly, shoving up the bed and knocking the toys aside. He reached up and grabbed Tenner's hands, wrestling briefly with the sock. Tenner flexed his fingers and then met Ross's eyes.

"Ross?"

"Destroy," Ross whispered, taking his mouth. He pulled back and positioned himself at Tenner's entrance. "Annihilate." He closed his eyes and thrust in, glad for the time he'd spent stretching, because Tenner gripped him tight and slick and sure. "Ah, gods. Obliterate." He pulled back and thrust forward. "Unmake." Kiss, long and slow and sweet while he lost himself in heaven. "Unravel. Undo."

Tenner moaned into his mouth, and Ross kept thrusting, losing his words.

Please. Please! The difference between a plea and a command had blurred, the edge of passion honed sharp on the distinction.

Tenner wouldn't bow. Tenner wouldn't give. He was who he was, and Ross didn't have the strength to change him. Ross needed what he had to give, and Ross had to be the one to bend.

He thrust hard into Tenner now, his hips pistoning, his rhythm merciless. Tenner had gone beyond moaning and was crying out, keening in arousal, gibbering in need.

He needed, and Ross had to give him and give him and give him....

Everything.

Ross rocked back onto his knees and pulled Tenner up with him, penetrating again and attacking from a new angle. Tenner's eyes were closed, his head tilted back in abandon, and his cock flopped hard against his abdomen, full and leaking.

Ross slowed down enough to grab it, to milk it in time with his thrusts, and as he rubbed his thumb across the head, squeezing under the bell, Tenner arched up in a loud, unapologetic howl.

His spend jerked slowly from his cockhead and leaked onto Ross's fist until Tenner fell back against the bed.

Ross raised a hand covered in ejaculate to his mouth and tasted, and it was the tang of come that sent him over, pumping into Tenner's body, as unmade as he'd known he would be.

He fell forward, shaking, his hips still in rut, and buried his face against Tenner's chest. When Tenner stroked his hair back, stroked his cheek, his shoulders and back, Ross knew he was done for.

He'd tried. He'd tried so hard for hard-core, no-holds-barred sex. He'd even gone for kink because it seemed to turn Ten's key.

But there was a rawness to Tenner—an honesty and realness—that didn't play games and couldn't be denied.

At least, Ross couldn't deny him.

He pushed over to the side and kept gulping air, turning his head so he could rub Tenner's chest for his own amusement.

"So...," he said, pulling together a cocky smile like he hadn't just been shattered.

"Bet you think you're something after that," Tenner said, giving a sly smile of his own.

"Not so's you'd notice." Ross's grin cranked up a notch. God, Tenner was stunning.

"I've got your come leaking out of my ass," Tenner murmured in wonder. "That's... damn." He gave a sexy little shiver, and if Ross hadn't come twice in less than an hour, he might have thought about getting hard again.

"You want me to clean it up for you?" Ross mumbled, and he would have done it—God, anything to hear Tenner beg again.

"No," Tenner said dreamily. "Leave it. It's proof you were inside me."

Ross leaned in close to take his mouth again, and as he did so, with his hand he knocked one of the articles he'd pulled out of the drawer. It was the smaller, nonvibrating one. He smiled at it, some of his kink and play returning through the haze of spent desire.

"Here," he murmured, "prop up your other leg."

Tenner did without question, making himself more accessible, and Ross used the lubricant and come still at Tenner's entrance to pop the plug smoothly in.

Tenner's eyes opened a little more, and his mouth made a round moue in surprise.

"Keep my come inside you," Ross whispered in his ear. "Keep yourself open for me. That's mine now, you hear? And this is far from over."

Tenner dropped his leg and rolled to face him. "Yeah?" he asked, a fine tremble passing over him from being stimulated all over again.

"Yeah," Ross whispered, liking Tenner's eyes like this, the pupils so blown from passion, Ross couldn't tell if they were black or brown.

"Good," Tenner said, lashes fluttering closed. Another fine tremor passed through him, but he fell asleep like that, his arousal not quite spent, his body dilated and ready for Ross's possession again in the night.

Ross got up, turned out the lights, and set the lubricant and the other sex toy on the end table for possible use. Then he set his phone to wake him up in an hour—it wasn't quite time to go to bed for him anyway—and settled himself back down, this time with Tenner in his arms and the covers over both of them.

"All good?" Tenner surprised him by saying softly. "Your territory all marked? Did you pee in the corners?"

Ross chuckled, burying his face against the back of Tenner's neck and undulating his hips until his groin hit the plug, and Tenner caught his breath.

"I marked what I needed to," he said mildly. "Be ready, okay?"

"I'll be asleep," Tenner slurred. "You be ready."

"This time."

But Tenner didn't respond, and Ross figured he'd fallen asleep on that, which was fine. Because he didn't want to admit the truth.

"Be ready" was empty posturing. Ross hadn't been ready—not even close. He'd come here tonight for a romp, for some solid sex, for a challenge.

And Tenner had vanquished him, literally with both hands tied over his head, just by being honest and himself.

This man in his arms was solid and real, and he wasn't going to quit his job or leave the child he'd already sacrificed for behind. And Ross wasn't going to quit seeing him, quit trying to make nights like this happen, not while they were in the same town and had time.

Something was going to have to give, and it wasn't flesh and it wasn't sex, and it wasn't a sock.

Ross lay awake until his alarm went off, thinking about what the future could look like. So many amorphous shapes, and they all depended on a man who couldn't even tell the people in his life who Ross was.

He killed his phone and began to move practiced hands over Tenner's body, picking up on the way Tenner undulated his hips, made little gasps under his breath, whimpered when Ross brushed his erogenous zones.

That was the best. Ross rolled him to his back again and was surprised when he saw Tenner's eyes, glinting in the light from the window.

"Are you going to take me again?" he asked, arching his hips, thrusting.

"Do you want me to?" Ross licked his jaw, because everything was open to taste.

"Sure," Tenner slurred. "All floaty... and a little sore."

"Mm...." Ross kissed him. "Don't worry, then. I'll do you right."

He kissed his way down Tenner's body again, thinking he knew the path by now, but it was all so new, so delicious, he loved doing it again. When he got to Tenner's cock, it was full, again, thrusting without urgency into the air.

Ross took it into his mouth and nursed it tenderly. There was no play here, no kink, no "beg me." There was just Ross, giving Tenner everything he needed. Tenner moaned and thrust, no inhibitions holding him back from seeking pleasure, and Ross took his rocking motions and used them, bringing Tenner closer and closer to his peak.

As Tenner started fucking his mouth in earnest, Ross tugged gently on the plug, until the widest part was stretching him, and Tenner cried out, hands beating weakly on the coverlet. One more thrust, one more lick, one more tap on the plug, and when Tenner's next cry turned into a hoarse shout, Ross pulled it out and Tenner came and came and came.

Ross got up to clean off the toy and returned to bed with a cloth. "How you doing, cowboy?" he asked when Tenner waved him off.

"Don't leave," Tenner mumbled.

"No." Ross squeezed his eyes shut in the dark. "I can't. You're my ride."

Tenner made a fuzzy sound and rolled into Ross's chest. Ross gave up any more thoughts of cleanup.

Tenner was marked, like they'd joked about, but for real.

Oh God. This might have started as a quick fuck in a dark park, but Ross knew—and maybe Tenner knew now too—that this had never been playing around.

DOUBLE HITTER

TENNER STARED at the screen in front of him and saw absolutely nothing.

"Ten?" Pat said from his doorway. "Tenner? You there?"

Tenner shook himself and tried to concentrate on his work. It was hard when his body was so damned mellow. "Sorry, Pat," he said, faking a little yawn. "Long day yesterday."

"Turn off the alarm on your screen before we all kill you," Pat said sternly, and Tenner *really* made an effort to snap himself into the present this time.

"Sorry, Pat," he said sheepishly, hitting the alarm that said the test was run.

"Wow," Pat said, shaking his head. "I mean... wow. I sort of knew Ross was, like, a sex shaman and everything, but I had no idea he had a magic penis. Did he tell you how much he paid for it? Was it in gold florins or cold hard cash?"

Tenner flailed and held his hands to his mouth and then his finger to his lips as he tried to remember how to shut a grown man up about stuff he should *not* be discussing at work!

"Do you want people to hear?" he growled.

Pat narrowed his eyes. "Don't we already know you're gay?"

Tenner frowned. "Only you?" He tried to think about the rest of his department, but he couldn't remember. When he and Nina had split, there had been so much misery. He'd told Pat, and since Pat was his boss *and* his best friend, that had seemed like enough.

But according to Pat's frown, it really wasn't.

"You are despoiling my brother-in-law and you are not even out?" he hissed, outraged. "Tenner! That's not fair to *him*!"

"Well, what am I supposed to do?" Tenner hissed back. "Stand up at the water cooler and scream 'I'm gay'?"

I'm gay came out a lot louder than he'd intended, and as he and Pat stared at each other in horror, the rest of the office noise died down completely, and the world's most awkward silence descended.

A tentative voice floated over the cubicle walls then. "Uh, Tenner? We know. We've known since the divorce. You and Patrick aren't exactly quiet. It's a cubicle. Can we all go back to work now?"

"Sure," Tenner said, his voice strangled. He rested his forehead on his fist. "Do you have any ibuprofen?" he asked Pat miserably.

"Let me check my cubicle," Pat said.

"Could you check it for cyanide? It might be more effective." God, Tenner was just going to die of embarrassment on the spot.

"Suck it up, Tenner," Pat said with the same tone of voice he must have used on all his children to get them to attack their first soccer ball. "You can tell me about Ross's magic penis at lunch."

Oh God. "Sure, but can we not do Indian food? It gives me gas."

LUNCH PROVED to be decidedly less awkward. Pat had, predictably, wanted to check to make sure Tenner was okay, and Ross was okay, and everybody was all happy fine.

"So," he asked, over a veggie burger and fries, much to Tenner's relief, "are you okay with him leaving?"

Tenner's own veggie burger went down a little harder than he'd anticipated. "Yeah. Sure. I guess I have to be."

"Hey," Pat said gently. "He's coming back this time."

"Not necessarily to me." Tenner thought about Ross's brashness, the way he filled a room. "Would he really be happy being my weekday guy?"

Pat sighed. "Have you talked to Nina?"

"Yeah. She… well, she didn't yell or cry or get nasty. Maybe… I don't know."

"Maybe she's ready?" Pat asked delicately.

"I can't push her just because *I* am," Tenner said on a sigh. "But… but right now, I get to take a really amazing guy home tonight and play softball tomorrow. I mean, how much better could life be?"

"We could be eating real beef," Pat said without equivocation.

"Well, yeah. But, you know. Compromise."

Then Pat met his eyes. "You shouldn't compromise on a guy you like to make your ex-wife happy."

Tenner took another bite and wished for beef. "Jesus, Patrick. Way to get real."

"I have children about to date. You and Ross need to be settled so I only have one focus."

Tenner snorted. "Mm… are Ross and I really dating?"

Pat rolled his eyes. "Did you set a date to interact, regardless of how that interaction would occur?"

Tenner poked at that with his brain and could find no holes. "Yes."

"*Did* interaction occur?" Pat waggled his eyebrows, and Tenner's face heated.

"Yes."

"Was it *good* interaction?" Pat prodded.

"Why is that important?" Tenner's face was on *fire*, and he didn't even have the cover of Indian food to explain it away.

"No reason. I'm just curious."

Jesus. "You suck."

"No, no, I don't. But Ross does, and excuse me, I'm curious if he does it well."

Tenner's mouth went dry as memories of that second round drifted behind his eyes—his pliancy, the utter sensual saturation of every moment he spent in Ross McTierney's arms.

"Zero complaints," he managed to say, and he could swear his ears were sweating. "None. None at all."

"That is good to know," Pat said as if they were discussing the weather. "His sister will be so proud."

"You are not telling his sister!" Tenner snapped. "No sister needs to know that about their family!"

"I beg to differ," Pat said, then scooped a fry in ketchup and ate it with bliss. "See, if she knows, then she can give him sound life advice. Like, you know… 'Yes, Ross, you should come back to Folsom when you're done saving the world this time because Tenner will wither away and die without your magic penis!'"

Tenner set his veggie burger down and gave up. "You two are terrible, terrible people. My only consolation is that you have children, and they will be just like you."

Patrick dropped his next fry. "You take that back."

"Oh no," Tenner told him smugly. "No. You'd better spoil those kids rotten, or when it's time for an old age home, forget about it. You'll be in some sort of basement with nonstop SpongeBob on the television and cheap butter noodles for breakfast, lunch, and dinner."

"After we sent those little so-and-sos to Stanford," Pat said, indignant.

"Allison isn't even in high school yet," Tenner argued.

"No, but I've set her up nicely in the college department. She *could* go to Stanford if she ever stops fucking around and does her homework."

"She'll go to art school, and you'll love it. All I'm saying is, you go ahead and meddle however you want—they're waiting. You put your cheaters in the freezer one too many times and you're going to end up in Silver Corners, rocking your retirement away and forgoing all those cruises Desi's been planning."

Pat narrowed his eyes. "You've got a real mean streak, Ten-Spot. I'm thinking I should have a long talk with Ross about why you might be the worst idea since Astroturf."

"You do that." Tenner regarded his veggie burger with hope. It really wasn't bad. "I'm sure Ross will tell me all about it, and I can assure him there are no bodies in the basement."

"What about between the walls or behind the washer."

Tenner winked, feeling Ross's optimism, his chutzpah, infusing him from the inside out. "Well, we won't tell him about those."

"Of course not."

Veggie burgers. Good for him and tasty. Change wasn't always the worst thing that could happen, right?

TENNER PICKED Ross up as they'd planned—or as Ross had ordered—and took him home to cook dinner.

"Think I'll be able to run this off?" Ross asked, looking at the pasta primavera Tenner was working on in the kitchen.

"We can try in the morning, if you want. I usually go running before work."

Ross laughed softly. "I'm going to hazard a guess that we'll be too tired tomorrow."

Tenner shrugged and remembered Patrick's boundless optimism. "I mean… we don't have to do it all… you know, tonight. There's, uh, next week, right?"

Ross moved behind him, doing that thing he did, with his hands on Tenner's hips and his breath in Tenner's ear. It turned Tenner on, that's what it did.

"Yeah," he murmured. "You set the rules here, Ten. You've got the kid and the involvement and the complications."

"You've got the plane ticket," Tenner replied. "I… I'm not sure how involved you want to get."

"I loved having dinner here last Sunday," Ross said, surprising him. "No sex—I get it. Kid in the house, you didn't want her to get attached. I don't even know if you're out yet to her. That is entirely your call. But spending time with you makes me happy. I'll let you know if it gets too hard."

Tenner smiled briefly. "So, the safe words are *please stop*, *too much*, and *let me go*. I get it."

"Good," Ross murmured. "Can I come to your Sunday practice and come home with your kid again?"

Tenner closed his eyes. Family time, and the sweet little fantasy that Ross was part of his. Even if Ross slept in the guest room again, it would be worth it to have a friend there with Piper, someone to make him feel like he wasn't in the parenthood thing alone.

"I'd love that," he said. And then, because that conversation with Pat had been light and fun but it had held a kernel of truth, he revealed one of his bodies. One that Ross had guessed at. "And I don't know what Nina has told Piper, but together, our story was that we still loved her but that living together didn't make us happy anymore."

He sighed, a vision of Ross doing this, holding him, being tender to him after work while Piper did her homework at the table, taunted him.

"I… until recently, it had not occurred to me how much I wish I could tell her and make it normal."

"Recently?" Ross goaded.

"Don't make me say it. I'll want things I can't have."

"It's good to want things," Ross told him. "You just have to do something about it."

Tenner wasn't stupid. "Like telling my daughter who I am?"

"Mm… however you want to do it." Ross kissed the side of his neck. "We're not going to sort it now."

Tenner tilted his head for better access. "No. But we're not going to have sex now either."

"Dinner ready?"

Tenner had to—he turned in Ross's arms and caught his mouth. "Yes," he said, after a brief taste. "Apparently we're dating now, so feeding you is important."

Ross grinned. "Dating? Is that what the kids are calling it these days?"

"That's what Patrick's calling it these days. He's my boss and my friend, and I've learned not to question him. Set the table. We have work to do before the sex."

"Is there at least dessert?" Ross asked, all indignant.

"Does gelato count?"

"Salted caramel?"

"Or dark chocolate raspberry," Tenner confirmed. "Not just dessert—dessert for people with champagne taste."

"Fine. I may *tolerate* the presex ritual of dating. If I have to."

Tenner kissed the corner of his mouth. "You're very patient. Now set the table."

CONTRARY TO their play-whining, Ross was a charming dinner companion once again. Tenner could spar with him for hours. Even when silences fell, they were contemplative rather than awkward. It was funny how the two of them could wander off independently on a subject, come to a conclusion, and then restart the conversation as if they'd never left it.

By the time they'd wrapped up the dishes and dessert, Tenner was relaxed and happy to the point that he'd almost forgotten what his endgame was.

He went to sit in front of the television, thinking they could watch a movie or something, and Ross said, "Really?"

Tenner blinked up at him. "We... I mean, it doesn't have to be about sex all the time, does it?"

"No," Ross said, frowning. "But you liked the sex, right?"

"It was *amazing*." There was no question. "I just...." Tenner sighed and stood up. "Sorry, wrong fantasy, I guess."

"Wait, you mean, your fantasy had us watching television on the couch?"

Tenner shrugged, embarrassed. "You know... like a couple. People dating. Never mind. I guess you've got an agenda and—"

"Sit," Ross said. "And give me the remote. I'm driving."

"My house, my remote," Tenner returned, so happy it was like his stomach was flying.

"No, if I'm passing up sex—"

"Nobody said we were passing it up. We don't need bells and whistles and clowns and a trapeze," Tenner returned smartly.

"I didn't even get to the whistles, and the clowns aren't until next week."

"No clowns."

"But me and the clowns got a schtick!"

Tenner shuddered. "If I give you the remote, can there be no talk about clowns again?"

"Fine. I'll call out the strippers!"

"No! Just you! It's fine! Jesus, the hoops a guy has to jump through to watch TV with a good-looking guy in his own house."

Ross gave a long-suffering sigh and sat down, then crooked his finger for Tenner to come lean on him. "Fine, but only if we watch something dumb with explosions."

"Thoughtful with serial killers," Tenner countered.

"Dumb with serial killing explosions."

"Done!" Tenner had been saving the series on Netflix for weeks. He grinned at Ross like the man had saved his day. "One episode, and then we can go ring some bells and blow some whistles."

Ross lowered his head and captured his mouth in a surprisingly sweet kiss.

"As long as you want. And if I fall asleep, wake me." He yawned then, in a way that was no bullshit, and Tenner realized they might really be making a choice here. But God, Ross's chest was solid and warm, and his thighs around Tenner's were so reassuring.

"Me too," he said, snuggling back. He started the episode and thought if they could squeeze sex in on top of gelato and grown-up television with another grown-up, it could be the best date in the history of ever.

QUIET SURPRISES

THEY MADE it through one episode before they both had to admit they were nodding off, and Ross helped him lock up and feed the cat before they went upstairs together. This time they both undressed to their briefs, and while Tenner used the hamper, Ross used his duffel. They crawled into bed, and Tenner reached to turn off the light before rolling over in Ross's arms and surprising him with a kiss.

Passionate.

A passionate kiss.

Not a "sweet boring couple who are too complacent to have sex" kiss, but a passionate kiss. Ross responded, a tiny corner of his universe setting itself right again.

He'd been sort of afraid he'd done something wrong.

Tenner had been his usual irascible self during dinner, but in a happy way—the two of them had maintained playful banter for most of the meal, and then, when Ross was thinking, "Showtime!" Tenner had dragged him to the couch.

Ross had been wondering what was wrong with him that after one night—okay, two—Tenner wanted to chill in front of the TV for an hour, but now, tasting him as Tenner aggressively pinned him to the bed with kisses, he realized that wasn't the thing at all.

She stopped touching me. Stopped smiling. Stopped being my companion.

Ross allowed himself to be pinned, opening his mouth in surrender. Tenner hadn't just been looking for two days of balls-out sex. He'd been looking for companionship, and he apparently enjoyed Ross for his company as well as for his prowess.

The thought was humbling.

Ross had sold this idea of a relationship based on the sexual connection alone. Tenner had done him one better. He'd been rooting for a *human* connection, and by God, he'd made one, one that Ross wouldn't risk by breaking out the clown cars or the trapeze.

Or ending this kiss, the sweet, passionate, sensual kiss that involved tongues and hands, undulating bodies and bare skin.

Tenner swept palms and fingertips down Ross's chest, along his stomach, along his hip, and suddenly those places—which had never ranked very high on Ross's erogenous zone list—became sensitized in ways not even he had imagined.

When Tenner broke the kiss to move his lips down Ross's chest, Ross actually whimpered in protest, pulling Tenner's head back up and claiming his mouth again.

They'd cuddled during that movie, Tenner leaning into his chest, their body heat making up for the mild chill of the spring night and the overhead fans. Ross got it now, that need for connection, the way their mouths were more intimate together than on each other's bodies. And Tenner wasn't reluctant. He slid to the side and pulled at Ross's shoulder until they were facing each other. Ross felt his hand, shoving at the waistband of Ross's boxers, and suddenly wanted that. Wanted this kiss to continue, and the urgency it was building up to be relieved in the throes of the kiss.

He tugged at Tenner's shorts and found his erection thick and long, as he'd tasted the night before. He moaned as Tenner's hand closed around him, their bodies so close, his nerve endings firing so powerfully, differentiating his touch on Tenner's cock from Tenner's touch on his became a blurry sort of thing.

They were one.

They didn't have to penetrate or fuck to be one—they were one, mouth to mouth, hand to cock, and he squeezed Tenner's length exactly as hard as he liked his squeezed, shuddering when Tenner's moan shook them both.

And then Tenner's thumb skated across Ross's cockhead, not gently, the slightly callused pad sending his arousal into the stratosphere.

"Keep that up," he managed to gasp. "I'm going to come."

"Wanna taste," Tenner insisted.

"Me too."

They had to break the kiss off, but God, they were both so desperate. Their shorts practically disappeared, and Tenner moved so his head was at Ross's erection, and his erection was tantalizingly near Ross's mouth.

Ross could feel the breath they both took shuddering through them. His mouth on Tenner's cockhead happened exactly when Tenner's mouth took his in, and after that....

There was no rational thought.

There was only the thing in his mouth—the hard, salty, explicitly male thing in his mouth—and the exquisite touch of Tenner's hands, his mouth, his tongue, on his own.

Concentrating on what he was doing grew harder and harder and harder, and stars washed behind his eyes as he fought orgasm because he wanted Tenner's spend flooding his senses first.

Tenner's finger, spit-slick, tapping at his entrance tipped the scales, and Ross was not nearly as delicate with his two fingers shoving in the same place.

Their muffled moans filled the bedroom, and Tenner bucked hard, filling Ross's mouth with come just as Ross lost all of his senses when climax unleashed his hold on his mind.

God! So good! Ross swallowed, the taste bitter and salty and earthy and good. Tenner did the same, both of them cleaning up until the other one let out a sound of protest. Tenner rested his head against Ross's thighs, and Ross did the same.

"Ten, honey, you have to move your head up here. That's no way to sleep."

With a heave and a less-than-graceful set of scooting movements, Tenner eventually righted himself and the covers and the pillows, and they were face-to-face again.

Tenner had closed the drapes this time, but there was a nightlight in the bathroom, and Ross had enough glow to see that Tenner looked utterly debauched, his hair in spikes, and trails of come running from the corner of his mouth down his cheeks.

So beautiful.

Ross kissed him, licked him like a cat, cleaned him off, and then pulled back from the kiss and smiled drowsily.

"That was… spectacular."

"No clown car necessary," Tenner mumbled smugly.

"We'll bring it out next week."

"'Kay. I'll be ready to get it up again by then."

Ross's laugh was sleepy and filthy. "Oh, baby. You need to up your stamina."

"Mm… you coming to practice Sunday?"

"To see your adorable and preternaturally well-behaved child again and have hot dogs? Wouldn't miss it."

"Don't forget Mario Kart."

"Do I have to let her win?" And wow—last Sunday's quiet domesticity next to the last two night's sensuality—such a toss-up. Suddenly Ross wanted it all.

"Naw. Maybe Piper can have a tantrum, just to make you feel more at home." Tenner had a smile on his face, and his eyes closed, like he would reply to Ross's foolishness in his sleep.

"I like your home. Maybe I'll get used to it. Start freeloading off your beer and Wi-Fi."

Tenner chuckled. "You could always pay for dinner."

"I would love to take you out to dinner."

The sudden thought of Tenner, dressed nicely, sitting across from him at a restaurant, at a concert or a baseball game, passed behind Ross's eyes, and he almost gasped, he wanted it so badly.

"Not in Folsom," Tenner mumbled. "Not now. But I'm trying."

Ross blinked. "What do you mean you're trying?"

"Asked Nina to think about it. Asked her why we shouldn't both be happy. Asked her how she thought I should date. She didn't get mad. It's a first."

Ross's eyes burned. "God, Tenner—"

"Gotta keep you coming back without the clown car," Tenner said, and suddenly his eyes glinted in the glow from the bathroom again. "I don't care if it *is* only eight weeks. I want it to be the best eight weeks."

"Me too."

Tenner kissed him softly and then rolled over, probably to his most comfortable side, since he'd put the end table there, and backed into Ross's embrace, letting him be the big spoon.

Ross tightened his arm around Tenner's waist and kissed his shoulder, eyes still burning.

The best eight weeks. Sounded like a plan.

Except it was after midnight, so now it was only seven weeks and two days.

And that didn't sound like enough.

ROSS WAS careful to clean up the next morning, making sure his dirty clothes were in the duffel with his toothbrush and shaving kit, and his clean clothes were on his back, and his softball uniform was on top. They were both changing clothes at work so the games could start on time.

He had to be careful, he thought. A T-shirt left there, a spare pair of briefs—those could lead to….

What? That he'd think of you? That he'd want you there over the week? That he might have a reason to push some more, get the thing he wants most of all?

That you might be that thing?

Because no kid noticed their dad's T-shirts—Pat's kids would probably not notice if their father wore his underwear on the outside of his pants. But Tenner would know.

And that would be enough.

Ross waited until Ten was downstairs on his way to make coffee before he took the sleep shirt he'd worn that first night and put it in Tenner's hamper. He was wider in the chest than Tenner, and a couple of inches taller, so he wore a size larger. Tenner would notice.

The thought of Tenner wearing his shirt sometime in the next week would have to sustain him.

They both seemed preoccupied, in morning news mode, as they drank their coffee and had a breakfast of cottage cheese and fruit. Ross looked up from the newsfeed on his phone to see Tenner looking at him, teeth worrying his lower lip. He looked away when Ross caught his eye, and Ross went back to his phone, feeling a little empty.

Maybe that's why, as they were both heading for the door, Ross stopped at the threshold.

"Did you forg—"

Ross kissed him, hard. Hard enough to make Tenner's mouth swollen and shiny, hard enough to muss his perfectly pressed shirt and break some of the gel on the back of his hair. Hard enough to make him scrabble at Ross's button-down, knead his back, and grind against Ross's thigh.

Hard enough to make a groan of frustrated arousal and pull back, as he probably should have, because now was not the time.

"What are you doing to me?" Tenner asked, leaning against the door and closing his eyes.

"Don't forget about me after the game, okay?"

"It's just until Sunday," Tenner mumbled, but it sounded like he was trying to convince himself.

"Yeah, but then it's just until Wednesday again. Don't put me in a box, Tenner. Remember that kiss. Wear it on your skin."

Tenner let out a humorless laugh. "You dumb jock. Do you think I have a choice?"

Tenner took his mouth this time, a little softer, but still intense intense, and Ross was the one who pulled back. "Sunday. Text me if you can't make it. I'll stop by, okay?"

"Yeah," Tenner murmured. "Piper'll look forward to it."

"Good. If I can charm her, the rest of the relationship is a piece of cake."

Tenner snorted, and maybe it was that little bit of humor that got them both out the door.

"HEY, BATTER batter, sha-*wing*, batter!"

Ross tried to keep up the energy during the game, but he had to admit he was a little tired. He was tired, and Tenner's team was playing someone else, and it wasn't as much fun to bait anyone other than Tenner when they were trying to hit the ball.

The ball came flying out to right field, and Ross fielded it easily. Three up, three out. He trotted toward the dugout.

"Seriously," Tenner said on the other side of the fence. "Is that all you got? That's weak shit right there. You'd better be hitting a ton if you're not even going to put your heart into the shit talk."

Ross grinned, some spark coming into the game. "Don't you have a team to captain? A kid to pick up? Something else to do?"

"God, no. I have a team to lead into last place! *That* I can do! And I'm on the way to pick up the kid. I just wanted to see you strike out first."

Some of Ross's swagger came back. "Gimme a kiss for luck and I won't strike out."

Tenner's eyes narrowed, and Ross could see him weighing the odds as to whether a simple kiss for baseball would get back to his ex-wife.

"How about I don't give you a kiss for luck, but I sit back here and admire your ass. And you hit the damned ball anyway because you're good at it?"

"If I get a home run, will you give me a kiss?"

"Get a home run and I'll think about it."

"God, you're demanding."

"Ross, get up here. You're first at bat!" Patrick called, and Tenner winked.

"You ain't seen demanding yet. Get your ass up there and hit!"

Ross trotted to the plate with some go in his step. The team they were playing was good but not great. If Tenner had been batting, with his ferocious concentration, the game would be over by now. They were in the bottom of the last inning and that home run Ross was boasting about would tie the game.

He'd known this before he'd gone into the chain-link dugout, but here, crouching over the plate, the eyes of the guy he'd woken up with that morning on him, he felt a sort of thrill he hadn't felt since high school.

And then he heard Tenner's voice, taunting, ridiculously arrogant, and completely adorable.

"Hey, batter batter, sha-*wing*, batter!"

He took a deep breath, ignored the pitcher, and kept his eye on the ball. Up, up, up, down, down, *swing!*

And it sailed up over the center fielder's head, clanging off the fence in challenge.

Ross was running before it even passed over second base. He rounded first as the center fielder ran out to snag it, and hit second as the guy turned to throw. Could he get there? Third? His team screaming from the dugout, Tenner's voice loudest among them, spurred him on. *Go! Go! Go! Go!* It was going to be close. He saw the ball launched into the air when he only had a few more steps to get to third, and slid in under the baseman's glove.

His team was applauding on the sidelines, Tenner leading the cheer, and as he stood and dusted himself off, he gave a wink before turning to face home plate.

The next batter hit him in, and as he jogged over to the dugout afterward, his team rewarded him with back pats and lots of "Jesus, McTierney, showboat much?"

"As much as I have to!" he told them.

He went to his gear bag and turned toward Tenner, who was shouldering his own bag and making to leave. "Wait!" he said through the fence. "What about that kiss?"

"That wasn't a home run," Tenner told him. "You'll have to wait until next week."

As Ross's jaw dropped, Tenner gave him a saucy wink and sauntered off, like he knew Ross would never fight free of his team in time to get to him.

But Tenner was waiting for him in the parking lot, leaning back against his vehicle, grinning with such self-satisfaction, Ross couldn't even be mad.

"You think I still want that kiss?" Ross taunted. Of course he did.

"Just waiting to see if you'd come and collect when you didn't deliver." Tenner's eyes danced, but he licked his lips.

Ross wanted him all over again, but he sobered. "You need to go," he said softly.

"I do. I, you know… didn't want to leave you."

Ross closed the distance between them and cupped his cheek, lowering his mouth for a hard, powerful kiss. Tenner opened for him, giving as good as he got, and for a heartbeat, the two of them were lost.

Pat's wolf-whistle broke them out of it, and Ross leaned his forehead against Tenner's. "Sunday."

"See you then."

And then Tenner got in his car and drove away.

Ross turned back around to Pat. "Is the bag of bases still on the field?" he asked gruffly. "I can go get it."

Pat regarded him steadily for a moment. "Yeah. I'll drive around and get you after I load the back."

Ross strode toward the dugout, wondering when Pat was going to co-opt the kids' wagon to do this shit instead of relying on forced labor.

He grabbed the bag and had swung around when the lights clicked off, the sound hitting him just a moment before the darkness.

He stood still, letting his eyes adjust, and was forced to deal with the fact that his chest ached.

It was a date.

It was a date to follow up another date.

It was sex, which happened on a date.

He'd done this before. He'd done it several times. Dating was pleasant. Sex was a helluva lot of fun. There was no reason, no reason at all, to feel put out because his date had to leave and go be a family man.

Tenner had never lied to him, not about his priorities, not about how out he was, not about any of it.

Pat's headlights cut through the darkness, and Ross made his way to the minivan, pausing to throw the last bag into the back with his duffel, which he mentally made a note to take to the laundry the next morning.

"So," Pat said as Ross got in.

"What?"

"It's what I'm asking you. How was it? Your sleepover. Or date. Or whatever?"

"Uneventful," Ross lied. "Ate dinner, watched television, got to be grown-ups together. No serial killers. No drama." No clowns or a trapeze.

"Yeah, Ross?"

"What?"

"You want to convince me it was no big deal, you gotta not look like someone kicked your puppy when he leaves."

"I've known the guy a week. Eight days. It's fine."

"Sure it is. When you hooking up again?"

"Well, I'm helping his team practice again on Sunday. He'll have Piper with him. There might be dinner and video games afterwards."

"Totally platonic," Pat said, to clarify.

"Well, it's his daughter, Pat. He's not out to her. I don't get to expect more. Jesus, not after a week."

"I know that. But think about it. He's letting you talk to his daughter as a friend."

Ross swallowed. "Yeah."

"If you think this means any less to Ten-Spot than it does to you, you're really not paying attention."

The tightness in Ross's chest eased. "I always pay attention," he said softly.

"Good." Pat started whistling on the way home, batting Ross's hand away when he tried to turn on the radio.

"You're going to make me listen to that all the way home?"

"It's happiness, my boy. Don't shit on my mood."

He was whistling "I Dreamed a Dream," and Ross just let him go.

"YO, MCTIERNEY!" Ross looked up from the plans he was assessing to see Jimmy Dowd, his boss, bearing down on him at full speed.

"Yo, Jimmy!" Jimmy was a big guy, flushed face, shiny dome, heart of gold. He'd been the one to recruit Ross for Green's Hill in an attempt to align the company *and* the city planning commission with solid goals for water and energy conservation throughout the area. Green's Hill was a conservancy agency based out of Foresthill and they did everything from raising political awareness of environmental exploitation to helping companies change their protocols in order to help conserve the environment.

Ross liked Jimmy very much, and he sort of loved the little, eclectic bunch of people that made up Green's Hill conservancy.

"You done with those plans yet?"

Ross grimaced. "No," he said shortly. "Jimmy, there is no way this project isn't going to impact the local wildlife. See this?" He pointed to a wavy line. "That's the goddamned fish hatchery right there. That thing was implemented for no other reason than to help keep the salmon population steady, and this proposes blasting a quarter of a mile away. What's that going to do to the salmon, when half the canyon falls on their heads and they can't swim or breathe?"

Jimmy grimaced. "Well, shit and fuck me."

"I've done the first already today, and no, thank you, Jimmy, you're not my type."

"What is your type?" Jimmy asked, not flirting, really, but in a broad-stroked attempt to get to know him.

"Well, right now, it's a single father who likes to play softball." Ross let out a soft sigh. "He might be my type for a while." But there was the inevitable.

"Well, you want to come back, don't you?" Jimmy asked. "Because seriously, man, Mr. Green wants you here bad. The development in this area over the last twenty-five years has been hard and fast. We're going to have flooding problems during the next big rain, and people keep wanting to go solar when they live on top of a hill and wind might do them more good."

Ross took a deep breath and nodded. He thought of Tenner in his arms that first week—of Patrick's little dig with "I Dreamed a Dream." This wasn't so much for a certain irritating computer engineer/baseball player (sure it wasn't) as it was for the knowledge that staying with his sister this time around had made him part of a community. (Tenner was part of that community, right?)

"I need to see how things are going in the Amazon," he said soberly. "I got a couple of texts from the outfit I'm working for down there, and it's looking like they might need me more sooner than later."

Jimmy hissed through his teeth. "We can hold a position for you," he promised as if this had been something he'd already discussed with Mr. Green. "We can even give you two months leave a year to go out and do field work. Just let us know, okay? We'll need an answer sometime before you leave, preferably in the next couple of weeks."

Ross nodded thoughtfully.

"Yeah," he said. "I'll… I'll do that." He looked at the plans again and then looked outside at the bright spring day. "Hey, Jimmy, you want to go walk this area? I think we need to get a real idea of what they want to do here. I have the feeling this 'recreational area' is going to be as environmentally friendly as those theme parks that put roller coasters next to wildlife."

Jimmy grunted. "You mean actually walking? In the sun?" He rubbed his bald pate. "Seriously?"

Ross grinned. "It'll be worth it. I've got a sun hat in the Tahoe."

Jimmy gave a heavy sigh and started to unbutton his suitcoat in anticipation of the heat outside.

"Yeah, whatever. If you're going for two months, I'm going to have to know what the hell you were talking about when you were here. Let's motor."

It was a solid answer—he was game and ready to try.

Ross thought about Tenner again, and thought that maybe he could be no less game.

WHEN THE CLOWNS COME HOME

"I'M SORRY about this, Ten," Nina said, looking sincerely apologetic.

"Next weekend?" Tenner grimaced. "Are you sure you want me here? I mean, I can bring Piper back early, no problem. You know that. They're her grandparents."

"Yeah, but they're your parents, and they asked that you be here this time."

Tenner grunted. "Did they say what this was about?"

Nina shook her head, and both of them looked down the hall to where Piper had run to pack her pajamas and books. "They... they still think we're getting back together," she murmured. "I keep trying to explain that it's never going to happen, and your mom's like, 'Oh, sweetie, the Lord works in mysterious ways.'"

"Obviously," Tenner muttered, because how else would you explain a boy who never had a sexual thought about girls in his life being born to Mr. and Mrs. Conservative Christian Law Enforcement.

Nina snorted a little, and she risked a look down the hallway. "And the thing is, I was thinking about what you said at dance class. I... I was mad, so mad, when I had my lawyer draw up that agreement, and...."

"You had a right to be," Tenner said softly. He got it. He'd promised her happily ever after, and had, to her eyes, wimped out.

"I really don't want a bunch of strange men running in and out of your house—"

He opened his mouth to protest, but she held up a hand.

"But it occurred to me that you probably feel the same way, and never once did you accuse me of whoring around. Because you trusted me with our daughter. And... I'm thinking about it, okay? I want you to know that I trust you with Piper too. I know whatever you do, you'll want what's best for her."

Tenner nodded. "Thank you. I do. And about that—" He was just about to mention Ross coming to dinner Sunday when Piper came running down the hall.

"Daddy! Daddy! Look what Mommy got me!" She held out a small, perfectly tied baseball mitt and a softball much smaller than the ones Tenner's league played with. "She said I could practice with you and Ross!"

He gave Nina a full-blown smile of gratitude. "That's really kind of Mom," he said. "Thanks, Nina."

"She's been talking about him," Nina said. "Pat's brother-in-law? I guess he plays on your team."

Tenner had to *make* himself not respond with a double entendre.

"Actually, he plays on Pat's team, but my team needed some practice, so he stopped by to help."

"Well, Piper loved his company, and you know, Pat and Desi are good people."

"The best," Tenner confirmed, and Nina's wistfulness pulled at his heart a little. He'd gotten Pat and Desi in the divorce, hands down. Unfortunately, Nina's family hadn't been the warmest people either. Tenner had gotten the only functioning set of parents between the two of them, and he'd never wanted her to feel alone. "Uh, would you like me to invite you to their next get-together?"

She shook her head. "No… it would be awkward, you know? I'll just keep my friends, and you keep yours." Most of her friends were out of town—she saw them on business trips, but very seldom on her weekends home.

"But Nina, they'd be fine with it—"

"No, Ten." Her look turned almost fond. "But it's sweet of you to ask. You're a good guy."

And Tenner *really* cursed Piper's timing there, because he would have told her about Ross, at least that Ross was the guy he wanted to date, except Piper was *right there*.

"When I can be," he said gallantly, and she gave him a bittersweet wink.

"Of course. C'mere, Piper. Give Mom a hug. You ran off without one last time."

Piper gave her a cursory hug and grabbed Tenner's hand. "So, we can play baseball on Sunday? And gymnastics tomorrow? And what else? Can we see a movie?"

Tenner looked over his shoulder and saw Nina's forlorn expression. One of their biggest arguments had been about how Tenner was the worst Disneyland Dad in the history of the species right after the divorce. He hadn't known what to do about it then, but now, when he had hope that she might accept him for who he was, he thought he might have an inkling.

"You want to see a movie with us?" he asked Nina, and she shook her head.

"Naw. I've got work to do. But thanks, Ten. Again, it was sweet of you to ask."

And like the invitation had been all she needed to let go, she went back into the house, and Tenner took Piper to her weekend home.

"SO WHAT'S this movie about?" Piper asked, settling down with her extra-large popcorn the next day.

"I think there's cats and dogs in it," he said. Truth was, it had looked pretty terrible. He usually went for animated features from Disney or Pixar or Sony—he loved a good animated feature as much as the next repressed twelve-year-old boy. But this one had realistic talking animals, and while Piper adored them, Tenner was not a fan.

"Yay! Want some popcorn, Daddy?"

It would probably make him sick *and* fat. "No, thank you, sweetheart. I'll stick with my giant soda, thank you."

Piper kept her eyes glued to the preshow show on the screen—the one they put on before the lights went down, and Tenner felt his pocket buzz. He pulled out his phone and saw Ross's name scroll across the top.

What's doing?

Watching a terrible movie in five. You?

Helping my nephew build a kite. His old one disintegrated.

By accident? Tenner was pretty sure that could not possibly be true.

It wasn't my fault, I swear!

At that moment the movie lights went down, and Tenner had barely enough time to type *I don't believe you!* before he signed off.

"Movie's starting, Daddy."

He put the phone in his pocket and as the absolutely horrible talking animal vehicle began to roll, it started to buzz in his pocket practically nonstop, Ross's name flashing across his watch with every text.

Tenner covered his wrist and double-checked to make sure it was just foolishness and not something important, and for the rest of the movie, at least every ten minutes, his pocket would buzz and his watch would flash.

He didn't return any of the texts, of course, but in a weird sort of way, it was like Ross had been there.

"YOU *ASSHOLE*!" he hissed at Ross when he showed up for practice the next day.

"What?" Ross held his hands to his chest and had the gall to look offended. "What could I have possibly done?"

"Does yesterday's movie ring a bell?" he asked, wanting to throw a mitt at that smug leonine head.

"Mm…." Ross pretended to think. "No, no, it doesn't. Does it ring a bell for you?"

"No!" Tenner threw up his hands. "No, it doesn't! And do you know why?"

"Because you fell asleep and snored in Piper's ear?" Ross asked sweetly.

"Because some lunatic was texting me every thirty seconds and I couldn't concentrate on the movie!"

"It was literally called *Cats Drool, Dogs Rule*, Tenner. How much was there to concentrate on, really?"

Tenner just shook his head. "No, seriously, there was no way for that to get any worse."

"So you should be thanking me, then?"

Tenner rolled his eyes. "I'm not going that far."

"You're welcome."

"I said I'm not going that—"

He saw it then. Saw Ross's abortive movement to reach out and touch his hip, probably to pull him close enough to kiss. Ross's hand froze, and they both took a quick look around, but it didn't appear anybody else noticed. Piper was busy throwing her little ball back and forth with Hanford, and the other players were warming up the same way.

"Shit," Ross murmured.

"I'm sorry," Tenner said reflexively. Then, because he'd been planning to tell Ross this after Piper went to bed anyway, he continued, "Nina is… well, she's softening. My parents are coming to dinner next week, so no practice next Sunday, but let's see how that goes. If it doesn't suck too badly, maybe she'll... I don't know... be okay when I tell her we're dating."

Ross's smile was lopsided, but it was still a smile. "When?" he said.

"Yeah," Tenner murmured. "When." He looked at Ross's hand as it sat by his side, flexing. "That would have been a good kiss."

"Always," Ross said, and without another word, they both grabbed their mitts and went out to the field.

It was time for serious game.

Their date that week was awesome. Amazing. Life changing.

And normal.

Nothing to see here, folks, two guys getting home from work, fixing dinner—Ross went shopping this time—and then watching some TV before going to bed.

Just two guys, skin to skin, breaths harsh in the darkness, touches tender, playful, arousing.

Two guys coming, in hands, mouths, asses—Ross coming in Tenner's ass, because Tenner hadn't yet had a brain in his head to top when the time came, and Ross was damned good at it—and coming and coming because to stop coming would mean the touch was at an end.

Two guys who were in it for a fling, for Ross's version of a summer romance, for Tenner's first relationship since a bad divorce.

Two guys who would die for one more kiss.

Two guys... who were irrevocably falling in love.

TENNER SHOWED up at Nina's with Piper in tow. He'd asked Nina for a dress for after practice, and Nina's eyes had grown bright and shiny. Piper loved her tomboy clothes, Nina knew that, but they both knew his parents wanted to see her in something lacy and girlie, and Piper didn't mind those either.

That Tenner had remembered was important.

As they got out of the car, Tenner grabbing Piper's bag because she was excited to see Grandma and Grandpa again and forgot, his pocket buzzed.

He pulled out his phone as he walked, and saw a picture of the practice he'd left early. Ross had, apparently, ordered pizza, and all his guys were digging in.

Should I bring you some later?

Tenner grimaced at his parents' rental car as it sat in the driveway. *Yeah. I'll text you when this is over.*

Good deal.

And then he put the phone away and summoned his best plastic smile.

"Grandma!" Piper squealed, running in for a hug. Tenner's mother—a severe woman with gray hair scraped back into a ponytail— hadn't been particularly warm when Tenner had been a child. Something about having a grandchild, though, had made her soften. Her smile and hug had all the hallmarks of the things Tenner had missed when he'd been a kid, and he was glad that, if nothing else, his daughter didn't have to know about chilly voids and disapproving scowls in the same way he had.

Tenner walked up quietly behind his daughter and waited to be let into the house.

His mother sobered when she saw him, her face drawing into lines of lemon-eating disapproval. "Tenner."

"Edith," Tenner said dryly. He hadn't been able to call her Mom since he'd told them about the divorce and was told, in no uncertain terms, that he wasn't their son anymore.

"Be respectful," his father said behind her.

"I am being respectful, Timothy," Tenner replied, meeting his father's eyes. "You said I wasn't your son, so I'm addressing you as fellow adults."

"Tim." Tenner's mother put her hand on his father's shoulder and looked at him pleadingly, and then looked at Piper.

Timothy Gibson swallowed whatever he was going to say and glared at Tenner, but he stepped back into Nina's house and gestured for Tenner to come in.

"Grandma!" Piper said a little desperately. "Did you see what Mommy got me? It's a baseball glove! I practice baseball with Daddy and his team!"

Timothy Gibson gave Piper a fond look. "You don't really play with the team, sweetpea. They're just having fun with you, is all."

Nina entered from the kitchen at that moment, her face flushed and her eyes way too bright, and her glare at Tenner's father was fierce.

"She practices with the team," Tenner said before his daughter's lower lip could start quivering. "They all take turns with her, helping her throw, helping her hit. Hanford brings his sister's kids—"

"Who's Hanford?" his mother asked sharply.

"Co-captain," Tenner responded, a little startled. "Ross brought his nephew today."

"Who's Ross?" she asked with the same tone.

And Tenner got it. "Piper honey, why don't you go put your backpack and toys away and go help your mom with dinner, okay?"

"Okay, Daddy." She beamed at him and then went in for a surprise hug. "I don't care how I get to play, you know," she said, her voice a little wobbly. "Tell them not to be mean to you."

He bent down and kissed the crown of her neat double plait. "I definitely will. Now shoo." They'd left softball a half an hour early so he could get her hair done specifically that way, because she wanted to make Grandma and Grandpa happy.

She trotted off, Nina at her heels. Nina threw him a beleaguered look of compassion over her shoulder, and he understood immediately. She'd love to help, but she needed to get Piper out of the room before the fireworks began.

"You two," he said pleasantly, "need to just stop. I'm gay. I'm not banging my entire men's softball team. Most of them have wives, a few of them have boyfriends, and all the single ones are probably not interested." He conveniently left Ross out of it because Ross was not the point here. "Piper loves you right now. You show up with toys and hugs and desert, and that's great. But Nina and I take care of her from day to day, and if you keep crapping on me, or start in on Nina, you are going to make that little girl hate you. And that would be a shame."

They both recoiled from him like he was a snake, but he didn't care.

Nine years ago, when he'd been a dumb, confused kid, he'd given up who he was for what they wanted him to be. Piper had been the result—and he'd do it again, for her—but he and Nina had been collateral damage, and that wasn't fucking fair.

"You have no right to talk to us in—"

"In Nina's house? I think I do. What have you been saying to her, M—Edith? She looked like she was ready to cry."

"Your mother was trying to make a point," Timothy growled. "The way you two are raising that little girl isn't right. Splitting her between two houses, you off doing God knows what in front of your little girl while that woman works herself to death as a single mother."

"Fifty-fifty, Tim. We split custody fifty-fifty, and we both have jobs. Do you think I hire a maid to do her hair?"

"Everybody knows you people have no problem doing hair," Edith said, trying to be conciliatory.

Tenner's eyes widened, and he ignored her because... God. Because.

"Piper's doing great. Her teachers have said so, she has friends over—Nina and I live less than two miles away from each other for exactly that reason."

"Oh, you've got an answer for everything, don't you!" Tim barked.

"As far as our daughter is concerned, we both do!" Tenner snapped back. "What is this about?"

"We just think," Edith murmured, "you know. Neither of you are looking to get married again, and if you're not going to get back together, we just think it's best that Piper be in a stable household."

For a moment, Tenner's brain blanked. Completely fuzzed out. All he saw was white static and all he heard was a roaring in his ears. His temper hair-triggered, and he was about to open his mouth and roar when he remembered he was in his ex-wife's house.

He took a deep breath and held up a finger. "Excuse me."

And with that he walked back to Piper's room, where Piper was emptying her backpack and explaining what they'd done that weekend. "Honey, I need to talk to your mother for a minute. Nina?"

Nina turned red-rimmed eyes toward him and bit her lip. "I'm so sorry," she whispered. "They ambushed me with it, Ten. I swear, I would have managed to be out of town if I'd known."

"Not your fault," he murmured. Piper was still unloading her things, and he leaned in for Nina's ears only. "How about you tell Piper that you, me, and her are going out for dinner. Then get her out to the car, okay?"

"I've got stuff in the oven," she protested.

"Mind if I turn it off?"

"Not at all." She smiled tightly. "Tenner, I feel like crap. The things they've been saying about you—"

He twisted his mouth. "You knew they were like that."

"Yeah." She let out a big breath. "But for the first time it hit me, why you might want to try to be… be what they wanted. Instead of who you are."

His own eyes burned. "I keep telling you—"

"It wasn't to hurt me." She let out a short laugh. "You know me when I'm mad, Ten. I don't listen to reason."

"And when you're hurt, it lasts a really long time," he murmured, remembering the one time he'd tried to break up with her when they'd been dating.

She nodded. "Yeah. Yeah. Me and Piper'll take off. Meet at the usual?"

"The usual" was a chain restaurant they'd eaten at every Friday night for Piper's first four years. It had been a break from cooking, for both of them, and a chance to go out as a family. It wasn't fancy, wasn't perfect, but it held good memories for the three of them. They'd gone there for Piper's birthday since the divorce, and maybe it would make the disappointment of what Tenner was about to do easier for Piper to bear.

"See you there," he said. "I'll lock up."

He turned back toward the living room and stalked right past his parents and into the kitchen. "In here," he muttered, making sure they both followed him. Aw, damn. Nina had made her chicken bake recipe in an attempt to make nice with his parents, and he sort of liked that one. He made a big production out of checking it to make sure it was done, and it was, which was good because she and Piper could have leftovers for the next week. Then he took it out of the oven and clicked the dial to Off before turning around and looking his parents in the eyes.

"No," he said pleasantly. "Timothy, Edith, no. You're not getting custody of our daughter. There's no judge in California who would allow it. It's ridiculous."

"But *you*—" his father began.

Tenner held up his hands. "It's not illegal to be gay. It's not illegal to be divorced. And it's not illegal to be gay, divorced, and a parent. The world is all sorts of complicated these days—you should turn on a TV sometime. And you know what? Even if I *was* the scum of the earth you want me to be—"

"We never said that!" his mother protested, but Tenner wasn't going that way either.

"Even if I was, Nina is a good mom. Our custody agreement is between the both of us. Whatever we do to it, that's us. It has nothing to do with your disapproval of me, or your prejudice, or whatever is driving you. You *disowned* me, remember? Nina asks you here literally out of the goodness of her fucking heart, and you bring this bullshit into her house?"

"You don't even like women!" His father looked legitimately baffled. "How can you defend her? She'd rather go off and be Ms. Bigshot than take care of her own kid—"

"I don't like them to sleep with!" Tenner crossed his eyes, because laughter was all he had at this point. "That doesn't mean I hate women as a rule."

"Don't be crude, son."

"I'm not your son, Tim. Not anymore. Nina's a good mother, and she's good at her job. If we were still married, it would be my job to support her. She's the mother of a child we both love, so it's still my job. And she supports me. I get my softball team, she gets her business trips, we both communicate when we get the chance. And yeah, Piper has a nanny sometimes when Nina's gone, but I also get to come get her if my schedule allows. She's not neglected—"

"You don't even take that girl to church," Edith sniffed.

"Because one way or another, you'd make her hate God, herself, and other people," Tenner muttered, and then held up his hand. "At least the way you guys do it. I've been there, remember? I want something better for her. You guys—you need to leave."

They both started at the abrupt change of subject.

"I'm sorry?" Timothy said.

Tenner double-checked the oven and reached into the drawer for some foil to put on top of the casserole. "Piper's not here anymore. She and Nina left before we really started to go at it. I heard the door slam. We're done here. You lost out on the chance to see your grandchild, and this is not your house."

They gaped at him.

"I'm done," he said. "You and I are already estranged, and we'll keep it that way. But now you and Piper are officially estranged as well. You won't be able to see her unless you sign something that says you'll never try this crap again." He had no idea if Nina's lawyer could do that or not, but then, maybe like with him, just the threat alone would do it. He was surprised at how many people wet themselves and forgot what facts and the truth were when people said the word *lawyer*.

"But... but, son...." Timothy James Gibson looked legitimately shaken. "I don't see how—"

"I will seriously call the cops," Tenner said, and he realized that the ball of ice in his chest, the one that Ross had worked so hard at defrosting over the last few weeks, was frozen in his core again. He shuddered and wished hard for Ross.

"Fine," his mother said, tugging at his father's shirtsleeves again. "But we'll be back."

"Then we'll get a restraining order."

And that shocked them both.

"Tenner—"

He squeezed his eyes shut, that ice core taking the vitality from his bones. "You could have had Piper's love," he said, wondering where that lost note came from. "You could have had a good dinner tonight. But... but you had to ruin it. Like you ruin everything. You ruined falling in love for me—the first time. I was in love. I came out to you and said I had a boyfriend, and... and you froze me out. And now you're trying to ruin Piper. But I won't let you. Nina and I have our differences, but Piper is our strength. Just go."

And a miracle happened. They did exactly that.

"Fine," his father mumbled. "But we won't be held accountable for what happens to that child—"

"That's fine, Tim. Nina and I are doing a pretty good job at accountability. Now shoo. You guys leave first. I'm locking up."

He followed them outside, making sure the doors were locked and Nina's alarm set. He had keys to her house, as she did to his, because it only made sense.

They were, for better or worse, going to be in each other's lives until death did they disentwine.

But Nina wasn't who Tenner was thinking about as he got into his CR-V and waited for his parents' rental to take off. He pulled out his phone to see Ross had texted him sometime while he'd been inside.

You surviving?

And, like his parents hadn't been able to do, the simple concern made his eyes burn.

No. Kicked parents out of Nina's house. Am meeting Nina and Piper for dinner. God, what a clusterfuck.

The phone rang in his hands. "Oh, baby—when you said it would be awkward, I had no idea."

"They… I don't know. Apparently decided Nina and I were going to fuck things up. They wanted custody, out of the blue. It's…." He flailed. "God. No. I'd die before I let them raise my kid."

"Oh, Tenner!"

Tenner realized that might have come out sounding a tad overwrought, and he tried to reel it in. "Anyway, Nina was barely holding it together. I told her I'd handle my parents, then meet her and Piper for dinner. Piper was so proud of her dress, you know?"

"Yeah. She told the whole team about it, Ten. Couldn't have missed that."

Tenner swallowed. "I… never mind. I'm just glad you called. I gotta go."

"Text me when you're done with dinner. I want to know, okay?"

"Deal. Later."

They signed off, and Tenner tried to forget what he'd been going to say to Ross but he'd chickened out on first.

I needed you here so bad.

It wasn't Ross's fault he hadn't been there. Tenner needed to make that right.

NINA HAD ordered for him, which was fine. He was starving, and sirloin and broccoli sounded as good as anything else.

"I'm gonna miss the chicken bake," he told Nina, with a smile, though. "I put some foil on it so it should keep."

"Thanks," she said briefly, and they both watched Piper playing the restaurant's electronic game with complete absorption. She seemed to have taken the change in plans relatively well, but then, she'd caught on that Tenner hadn't been happy pretty quickly too.

"Ten?" Nina said hesitantly, for his ears only.

"Yeah?"

"So, when you talk about dating… do you have someone in mind?"

His heart started to pound. "Yeah."

"I… I don't want anyone spending the night at the house while she's there. Not in your bed."

"Deal," he said. "Why the change of heart?"

"Because there's nothing like seeing the ultimate in judgment to realize you don't have a place to throw stones," she told him, sober and hurt.

"I'm sorry, honey—"

She shook her head. "Let's just say I had a chance to think about it before you got here, and… God. You were right. We both deserve to be happy. Being like *them* isn't going to make me happy."

Wow. Oh wow. "I won't argue. When does the same-bed thing change?"

She visibly swallowed. "Until I meet them?"

Okay. So, serious. He got that. "Same," he said. "But…." He'd already done this, but it made him look generous, right? "Guest room is fine."

She gave him a brief smile. "Deal."

"But we need a way to tell—"

And at that moment, the waitress arrived with their food, and Piper was suddenly paying attention to Mom and Dad again.

So, not out to Piper yet. But there was progress. Improvement.

And he and Ross, maybe this week, maybe the next, could go out on the town in their nice clothes. They could see a River Cats game together. They could hold hands in public.

The freedom he felt under his breastbone melted some of the ice that had formed there when he'd been alone with his parents.

Seeing Ross, waiting in his car as Tenner pulled up to his house, melted the rest.

Broken Rules

ROSS HAD come to expect a certain amount of stoicism from Tenner. He could be a smartass, but his humor was best classified as "dry," and he had the habit of understatement that made Ross want to grind his teeth sometimes.

The look of naked relief, of longing, on his face as he parked his SUV in the driveway and met Ross on the walkway came up against the barrier Ross usually kept between him and his "fling" lovers and pounded it to dust.

"Hey," he started, keeping his voice gentle. "I hope it's okay that I stopped—"

Tenner swept him up into a kiss—blatant, carnal, and needy as fuck.

Ross was needed.

Wow. He wasn't used to being needed; he was the youngest of four. People liked him and enjoyed his company, his banter, his sex, but they didn't *need him*. He returned the kiss with a hunger he could have sworn he didn't have.

He'd been prepared to be sensitive, to be kind, to listen. He had not come prepared to be ravished. And with any thought of a barrier barely a memory, he was vulnerable as he never had been before.

Tenner's hands in his back pockets, kneading his ass, woke him to the fact that they were dry-humping each other on Tenner's front lawn.

"Inside," he gasped.

Tenner practically ran to the door, and they fell through the threshold, then slammed the door against the jam and dodging before it bounced shut. Their mouths meshed, hands shoved at clothes, breaths mingled—

"Shit!" Tenner pulled back. "Did we let the cat out?"

Ross's heart stuttered. *Oh God, no.* Not before what could be the best sex in his entire life!

Behind them, Joe let out a plaintive meow, and Tenner sagged against the couch while scratching Joe behind the ear. "Sorry, buddy. Could you, I don't know, park it a minute? We've got something going no—"

That was sweet, the way he talked to the cat. Ross was captivated, charmed, and he needed Tenner now. He took over the kiss, took over the undressing, until they were both naked in the living room, kissing.

Ross took command first. "You stay down here. I'll get the lube up—"

Tenner turned and bolted for the stairs, Ross at his heels.

"First one to the lube tops!" Tenner called, and Ross had to pause at the staircase to shudder.

Tenner got to the bedroom first, and by the time Ross recovered, he was putting on a show. Tenner stood at the bed, covers turned down, oiling his cock with a fierce hunger in his eyes.

Ross took the bottle from him, standing close enough to smell the heat from his skin. "Give me that," he murmured before turning toward the bed and putting one knee up on the mattress, spreading his backside, exposing his opening. Then he squeezed a little slick onto his two fingers and reached behind himself, turning his head so Tenner could see his expression as he shoved his fingers in.

"Ah…." A plaintive, needy note crept into his voice as he breached his entrance, stretched, made himself wide and ready. He loved to bottom—had toys for it when he didn't have a partner—but he was always so aggressive, it didn't happen often.

Tenner, fierce, demanding, wanting inside Ross's body as if his cock was the key to Ross's soul—Ross wasn't going to pass that up.

He was going to do anything he could to goad Tenner on.

Tenner, throwing off heat, buzzing with electricity, lined up behind him. "You want me to take you like this? Bent over the bed? Or face-to-face?"

And Ross had to hide his face. God, he couldn't let Tenner see how—

Tenner shoved at his shoulder, rolling him to his back. "No hiding," he muttered. "Forget it. Took too long. My choice."

Ross had enough time to spread his legs, bracing his feet on the edge of the bed, before Tenner positioned himself and thrust in.

"Ah!" Ross threw his head back, eyes squeezed shut, because he'd prepped just enough, and they were both slick. Possession was sweet and wonderful and it burned.

Tenner rocked forward, taking him over, and the sound he made was no less surprised, no less wounded, for all he was the one penetrating.

"God!" he groaned. "So good."

"Tell me about it." Ross started to tremble as Tenner pulled out shakily, thrust back in with exquisite care. "Not made of glass, here—fuck me!"

"*God*!" And it was like Tenner had been waiting for permission. Harder, harder, faster. The sound of their flesh slapping off each other probably scared the cat. But Ross was in heaven, possessed, owned, taken, his cock swollen and aching and his ass being plowed in the best of ways.

Ross managed to pull up a taunting smile, although his head was swimming and orgasm felt like it lurked under the surface, a leviathan waiting to break into the world.

"That all you got?"

Tenner stopped, and Ross almost screamed.

"You *bast—augh*!"

Tenner's fist around his cock, still slick, squeezing hard, from base to tip, while Tenner was still solidly lodged in his ass—it was like a new form of torture, a delicious, masterful way to have sex.

"Gonna move?" he almost begged, and Tenner managed a little rocking motion that was designed to drive him out of his mind.

"Want me to?"

Ross whimpered, and Tenner squeezed his cockhead gently, skating his thumb through the precome at the end. "Not so's you'd not—*ice*!"

Tenner pulled out until his bell stretched Ross's entrance. "I notice," he rasped. "I notice that you're gorgeous"—he thrust his hips hard—"and kind"—and he thrust again—"and all I ever wanted and you're just fucking out of reach!"

He stopped again, stroking some more, while Ross slid seamlessly into subspace, simultaneously needing to come before he exploded and able to wait until Tenner said it was okay.

"I'm here," he almost wept. "I'm here. Whatever you need, Tenner. However you need me, I'm here."

Tenner made a surprised sound, an indeterminate sound, and then thrust forward again, the final flurry of fucking, the moment designed to drive Ross mad.

"I need you to come!"

Searing climax roared through him, and he closed his eyes and gave himself over to it, convulsing around Tenner's cock and spewing come across his own abdomen, chest, even shoulders. He kept shaking as Tenner cried out and fell forward, hips still pumping, coming inside Ross's body, filling him up and overfilling him, possessing his ass, his heart, his soul.

"God," Ross mumbled into the silence, still in the floaty place where words were hard. "What was that?"

Tenner buried his face against Ross's neck, some of the dominating fierceness easing from his body, and then some more, and finally melting into Ross's arms with all the sweetness he'd shown the damned cat.

"I really needed you tonight," he confessed, his voice throbbing. "So bad. I just kept thinking, if you were there, I'd know I was doing the right thing. If you were there, I'd be stronger. If you were there, it wouldn't...." His voice hitched, and he shook gently, like he was trying to get himself back under control.

"Hurt so bad?" Ross whispered.

"Yeah."

And then Ross was holding him, comforting him, relieved, finally, because this need he felt for Tenner in his body, by his side, in his heart— this need for the two of them, joined somehow, always touching—it wasn't his alone.

Finally, Tenner slid away and went to wash up. Ross followed him, because he didn't want Tenner alone in his almost pristine bathroom with the brown tile and the matching brown towels, looking in the mirror and wondering who he was.

Ross knew that's what *he'd* be tempted to do, if he went to the washroom alone.

Tenner soaked a washcloth and met Ross's eyes in the mirror, and tried to smile. Ross kissed his sweaty shoulder and shook his head.

"Here," he murmured. "Let me."

He could hear Tenner swallow.

"Okay."

Ross washed Tenner and then rinsed out the washcloth and hung it up.

"Not you?" Tenner asked.

"You think you're the only one who wants to feel marked?"

Tenner closed his eyes. "Thank you. For... for wearing me in your skin, I guess."

Ross trailed fingers along his spine, down the small of his back. "Thank you for trusting me with…." *Your need. Your want. Your gracious little family. Your time.* "You."

Tenner caught his mouth again, the kiss a simple blessing. "I'm gonna jump in the shower—wanna join me?"

Ross smiled slowly. "Yeah."

No acrobatic sex—just simple touches, made more sensual by the pounding cool water, the soap. They emerged and Tenner wrapped a towel around his waist and ran down the stairs, then came back with their clothes—and a mostly full quart of gelato and two spoons. He gave a small smile as he handed a still-naked Ross the gelato and pulled his phone out of the pants he'd brought up to put on the end table.

"Since I get you on a Sunday night as a treat anyway."

"So I'm already dessert?" Ross set the gelato on the dresser long enough to put on his briefs and climbed into bed, watching as Tenner grabbed a clean pair and did the same.

"And the main course and the appetizer," Tenner assured him with a quiet smile. He climbed in next to Ross and scooted until the lines of their bodies were touching.

"Talk to me," Ross said quietly.

Tenner took his spoon and a healthy bite of gelato, tilting his head back and sighing as if the sugar and cream was a hit of the good stuff.

"I fell in love in college," he murmured. "Like you do."

"So dramatic," Ross agreed. "All six times."

Tenner shot him a grin. "Wow—six?"

"Three boys, two girls, one enby. I was positive I was going to marry each and every one of them."

Tenner nodded. "And then…?"

"Life. Summer vacation. A fight like a summer storm."

"Yeah. I was going to marry a boy. He was out and happy, and his family was… so kind. And I flew home over Christmas vacation to the ice and the snow and the house in the middle of the vast nothingness, you know?"

"Nebraska is really that bad?"

"Geographically and emotionally—at least for me. Anyway, I flew in for Christmas and texted Blaine the entire time. And I told my parents, and… and my mom said, as long as I continued to believe in the devil's path, she and my father would have nothing to say to me. This was Christmas, mind you, and suddenly I... I was a ghost. I didn't have a plate set at dinner. They didn't listen to me when I spoke. It was...." He shuddered.

"That is the most chilling goddamned thing I've ever heard," Ross said, horrified.

"It wasn't fun. And I thought, 'Okay, I can do this.' And I was fine with it. They didn't open the presents I brought them. They didn't put any for me under the tree. Christmas was just a big day of me being... a shadow in their house. I left five days later, pissed and absolutely sure I would never see them again."

"What happened?" Because obviously he had.

Tenner pulled up one shoulder. "On the way to the airport, I watched as the house got smaller and smaller and realized I'd never felt so alone in the world." He closed his eyes and leaned back against the pillows. "I... I went back and ghosted Blaine. Broke his heart, I think." He let out a sigh. "Not my best moment."

"Mm." Ross teased his lips with a bite of gelato, pleased when Tenner opened up and sucked it off the spoon. "Well, obviously you're going to have to suffer for all eternity for being a mixed-up college kid."

Tenner rolled his eyes. "I think the memory is sort of a torture as it is, don't you think?"

Ross nodded thoughtfully. "That if we want to be good people, the bad stuff we did—even if it's unintentional—really does come back to haunt us? Yeah. I think we punish ourselves a lot."

"Well, wherever Blaine ended up, I hope he found someone he deserves. He was a truly awesome guy. I... I mean, I was in the middle of breaking up with him, and he didn't call me a coward or blame me or any of the things he should have done. He just kept saying, 'Don't let them do this to us. Don't let them do this to *you*.'" He opened his eyes and searched Ross's face. "But I did."

"Was that when you met Nina?"

Tenner's smile turned bitter. "She was a baseball groupie. Stalked the team. So when she got a crush on me, I... let it happen. Told my parents I was dating a girl. They sent me a Christmas present the next week."

Ross sucked air in through his teeth. "What'd you get?"

"A mint set of baseball cards. I sold them for baby furniture after I got Nina pregnant." He grimaced. "She, uh, she lied about birth control. I haven't told many people that. It makes her sound awful, but she was just… like me. Young and stupid. She confessed before we got married, and I promised I'd never hold it against her." He let out a sigh. "It's easier not to do that now. But yeah. I had to drop out of baseball when we got married."

"You hadn't graduated yet?" Ross didn't know this part.

"No. Piper was born about six months before I got my degree and my job at CompuCo with Pat. By the time Pat met me, Nina and I were a nice young couple, starting out."

Ross finished off the gelato and set the container on the end table. Then he settled in with his head on Tenner's chest, soothed when Tenner started to stroke his temple.

"None of this means you should die old and alone, Ten."

"You know? I'm starting to figure that out."

Ross swallowed. "I'm… I'm sorry tonight sucked."

"Well, it had some good points."

Ross had to smile before kissing Tenner's nipple, which was really too close to resist. "The sex was rocking."

"Besides that," Tenner said seriously, and Ross pushed up on the bed so he could see Tenner's face.

"What?"

"Nina and I talked at dinner. You and I, sir, are officially dating out of most of the closet."

Ross's heart started thumping in his throat. "Most?"

Tenner looked away. "I still haven't figured out how to tell my daughter. I'm sorry. I'll figure it out. And until you and Nina are ready to meet, you're in the guest room when Piper's here. But that's—"

"That's fair," Ross said, voice rough. "You negotiated that tonight?"

"Nina… she had sort of an epiphany, you know? Not… not completely, I think. But enough. Enough to say what you said, that neither of us deserves to be alone. She hadn't realized that's what she'd essentially done to me. She wanted to make it better."

Complicated. Wasn't that what Ross had said to Patrick? The whole thing was complicated. But Tenner had been working to untangle it.

"There's so much I want to do," Ross said, surprising himself. "I want to take you out to dinner this week. I want to take you and Piper to a Giants game one weekend. Or the River Cats. I'm not picky. Does Piper like amusement parks? I could do roller coasters. Did you know the Republic plays all summer? That's soccer, you know, in case the other kind of ball confuses you—"

"Bite me!" Tenner laughed, and Ross was so happy, he did. A sensuous little love bite, right at the join of Tenner's shoulder, another down his throat, another on his left pec, and one on the soft skin of his abdomen.

Tenner's noises went from tickled to tantalized, and Ross's body was ramping up for round two. He took a small mouthful of skin right above Tenner's cockhead and sucked, teasing with his tongue.

"Have I bitten enough?" he asked huskily. "Because you just practically promised me a Disneyland summer."

Tenner's eyes went from passionate to sober. "Remember, not out to—"

"Piper." Ross sobered too. "Baby, I can come play at your house anytime I want. You and your daughter will find your way—that is completely your decision. But you and me are a you and me, and I'm going to celebrate by sucking your cock. Do you mind?"

Tenner laughed and knotted one of his hands in Ross's hair.

Which was the sweetest request Ross had ever heard. Ah! So much goodness—Tenner's hand in his hair, his happy sex noises, his taste. When he let out a gasp and flooded Ross's senses with come, it was like he was flying.

He had all the hope in the world.

ABOUT AN hour after they'd fallen asleep, Tenner's phone rang.

"Mo—Edith?" Tenner mumbled. "What in the hell?"

Ross squinted at him. "Edith?" he mouthed.

"My mother," Tenner mouthed back. "What do you need?" He sat up. "No. No. I told you no. I don't care if you bring an *exorcist*, you can't see her. Nina and I agreed. And no, you can't call Nina." He set the phone down and started to text. "She's blocking you, Edith. I'll file a restraining order against you guys tomorrow. I'm not kidding around. God*dam*—hey!"

Ross held his hand out for the phone, and Tenner gave it to him, eyebrows raised skeptically.

"Hi, Edith? Tenner's mom?"

"Yes," said a sharp female voice. "Who's this?"

"Yeah. I'm Tenner's boyfriend. Yes, I'm in bed with him right now. We're naked. Do you want pictures?"

He had to hold the phone from his ear when she squawked. "How dare you—"

"Look, what you're doing right now? It's considered harassment. When he says restraining order, he's not kidding. But more importantly, why are you doing this?"

And that seemed to shake her. "What?"

"Why? This thing you're doing—trying to take a little girl away from people who obviously adore her—it makes no sense. I need you to explain why to me." God, if nothing else, he was curious.

"You don't have any right to—"

"You're hurting someone I care about. Isn't that what this is about? Doing right by the people you care about? You obviously care about Piper—you want what's best for her, right?"

"Yes. Yes, we do." And for the first time, he heard a softening, some humanity, in that sharp female voice.

"Okay, well, that's good. But I need you to tell me what you think she's missing out on."

"They don't take that girl to church." Ooh, she sounded sort of smug on that one.

"Well, I hate to break it to you, but I don't go to church a lot either. My parents go, but I'm out of the country a lot. That doesn't mean I don't worship in other ways, you know. Have you ever seen the sunset in the Amazon? That'll make you believe in the Divine. I mean, the forest has been really depleted—that's why I'm there, you know."

"I, uh, no. I didn't know. Why are you in the Amazon?"

Okay, this was better. No defensiveness. No anger. That was one of the problems with talking to your own family sometimes. The things that made you love them also made you want to throttle them.

"I'm an environmentalist. Our atmosphere has been impacted by the fires in the Amazon. I'm sure you've felt it."

"My husband's asthma is really bad," she said, a little tearfully. "We worry, you know. All the smog out here, and that little girl's lungs."

"Yeah, that's a shame." He meant it. Stories like this one made him want to do his job. "I'm sorry to hear that. But Piper's happy here. She knows she's loved. Why would you want to pull her away from that?"

"Tim…. Tim's afraid," she said, her voice softening. "He's not sure he's going to be here for long, you know? And when I get older…. Tenner was supposed to be our comfort in our old age, you know?"

"Well, he still could be," Ross said, keeping his voice gentle. "Threatening to take away his daughter isn't going to help that happen."

"But what am I supposed to do?" she asked. "How do I—how do I make him my son again?"

"You have to love him for himself. Don't you see?" Ross fought to keep impatience from threatening. "He's… he's such a good man. He's such a good father. How could you not love him like he is?"

"But what he's doing is wrong!" And Ross had her. Because she was desperate, and because this was the part when people usually recognized they were parroting something they didn't understand.

"What's he doing that's wrong?" Ross asked, waving away Tenner's outraged look. "Be specific."

"He's sleeping with a man!" He loved the way she said that, like Ross wasn't the man in bed with him.

"Except we're not really sleeping right now, ma'am. We're having this delightful conversation. And so far, you seem to think I'm okay."

She started to sputter, and he thought that was a start—and more than enough for the evening.

"I'm going to hang up now, okay? You must be exhausted, and I know I need my sleep. Now let's not hear any more talk about kidnapping children and calling police, okay? Can I get your promise on that? You're hurting Tenner's feelings in a thousand ways. Do you want to do that to your son? Hurt him like that? Because we seemed to be getting along so well."

"I don't want to hurt him," she said softly.

"Well, good. How about you send him a letter when you and the mister get home. I'm sure this whole thing will be much easier to resolve using good old-fashioned pen and paper. What do you think?"

"But the girl—"

"Is very happy. And no lawyer in the world is going to take your money to take her from her parents. And if you try it, you'll be criminals. Do you understand, ma'am?"

"Yessir."

"That's a girl. So I'm going to say good night, okay?"

"Good night."

"Good night, sweetheart. Let Tenner know when you get home safely, okay?"

"Okay?"

"Good."

Ross hit End Call and sagged against the pillows before Tenner took the phone from his hands.

"That was…. That was amazing," Tenner said, setting the phone in the charger. "Oh my God. Ross. You're like… like magical. You're a lion with wings or something. How did you do that?"

Ross yawned and went back to burying his face against Tenner's neck, which had become his favorite way to sleep.

"Nobody agrees on what my job should be," he said on another yawn. "Nobody. And people pull God into it, and big oil and stupidly bad ideas about economic theory. And I don't want to be a politician. I really fucking don't. But I gotta explain to people that they're stone-cold wrong without pissing them off. It's a job skill."

Tenner reached to switch off the lamp again, and Ross pulled him back as soon as darkness fell.

"It's a you skill, sweetheart," he said throatily. "You. Nobody else in the world could do that. Only you."

"Keep saying sweet stuff like that," Ross mumbled. "You never know when it's gonna get you laid."

Tenner chuckled, and Ross sank halfway to sleep.

"Night, Ten."

"Night, Ross. I love you."

"Love you too."

He didn't even realize what they'd said until he woke up in the morning. And by then, the words had settled into their skin, like they'd always been.

How to Always Be

REAL LIFE had to intervene sometime. Ross had needed to leave early the next morning for work, and had called Tenner at the office to… well, to see if he was okay, mostly.

"You get enough sleep?" he said over the phone, and Tenner pictured him as he'd been that morning, rumpled and shy and vulnerable.

Those words—hopeful, damning words—hovered over both of them like shady rain clouds after a scorching desert summer. The blessed life-giving rain threatened, but they needed to raise their arms and their faces to welcome it.

"Not so much," Tenner admitted, yawning. He set his computer to rest mode and stood up, stretching. Pat was very pro on a short stretching break every forty-five minutes or so, and doing it while on the phone was the ultimate in multitasking. And for some reason today his body felt extra, extra achy. "You?"

"Slept like a baby, just not for long enough," Ross said, yawning back. "Do you want me over tonight—"

"Yes," Tenner said before he could think. "I mean, shit. I have to work late, and if you need to sleep…."

"I should see Pat's kids," Ross admitted. "There were certain promises made about my time here this go-round. You go ahead and work late. I'll see you Wednesday."

"Uhm…." *I want you. I want to sleep next to you. I want to talk to you over dinner even if it's about traffic or work or the weather.* "I… uh…." The silence on the other end of the line was deafening. "I meant it. Last night. Don't stay away because you're afraid I'll take it back." *Good. I said it. Sort of.*

Ross's laugh was soft and only a little bitter. "I love you too, Ten. I said it too, remember?"

"Yeah. But your heart is so big, and I don't know how you can believe a thing I say if I haven't told my daughter and—" Oh God. His voice was wobbling.

"I'm going to have some faith in us, okay?" Ross yawned again. "And seriously. Sleep. You still have dance lessons tomorrow?"

"Yeah."

"Good. Take a picture of her in her get-up, okay? I bet she's hella cute."

Tenner's heart beat a little faster. "You... you are really good dad material," he said, like it had just dawned on him. Then... "Oh, shit—I didn't mean.... You probably aren't ready to.... Sonovabitch, you're leaving in... when. I keep forgetting when. I keep trying to pretend it's not happening, and I make all these plans in my head and—"

"Four weeks today," Ross said, and he didn't sound happy about it either. "And every time I think, 'Ten and Piper at a Giants game' or 'Disneyland,' I remember she has gymnastics and grown-ups have to plan for these things. And I'm nobody to her."

"That's not...." True? Right? Who was he to Piper? Uncle Ross? Was he even Uncle Ross? Was he Dad's friend who came by after practice on Sunday? Tenner hadn't even invited him the first time. "Forever," Tenner said, coughing a little. Besides the fatigue that felt like it was draining his lifeblood, there was also a raw throat that often came with lack of sleep. "That's not forever. I'll talk to Nina at dance tomorrow. There's got to be something about this in the manual."

Ross's laugh warmed him. "Of course, Ten. Parenting manuals have whole chapters for this kind of thing."

"I like that you call me Ten," he said miserably. "It's a stupid name, and you make it sound fun."

"Get to work so you can get home and nap. I'll text you later." Pause. "I really do love you."

"I really do love you too."

Tenner sat down abruptly, and the call ended. He logged back on to his computer and gazed at it sightlessly, trying to pull his concentration from the pile of cotton wool that his head seemed to have become.

About an hour after Ross called, Pat came by his desk with a hot mug of tea. "You look like shit," he said amicably. "Here."

Tenner picked up the tea, and before he could even drink, Pat closed in on him, schwacking something to his forehead and putting a hand on the back of his neck at the same time.

"Help, I'm being harassed?" Tenner managed.

"Drink your tea, son, and shut up."

Tenner did what he was told, and Pat unschwacked the thing on his head. It said, "100.1."

Tenner blinked eyes that had gotten increasingly heavy and tried not to wrap himself around the mug in his hands and die. "That explains the body aches," he murmured. "I thought it was lack of sleep."

"Yeah, well, if it's what the kids brought home, it's about to get ten times worse. There will be throwing up and high fever and crap that you can't get out of your lungs with a snowplow."

Tenner squinted at Pat in horror. "Why do you look so fucking chipper?"

"Because Desi and I called the doctor when Polly *and* Ally both puked, and we've been on Tamiflu ever since. Abner didn't get it in time. All three kids, walking, talking scenes from *The Exorcist*. It's terrifying. I was surprised Ross hasn't given it to you yet, but apparently it was in stealth mode, like a plague cat."

Tenner thought about their subdued morning, the sort of tiredness neither one of them could shake, the way they'd both crashed incredibly hard after Ross had gotten off the phone with his mother.

"Fuck," he muttered. He picked up his phone and texted, *Buddy, we both have the plague. Go get some Tamiflu, stat!*

Even as he sipped his tea, his stomach gave an unhappy little gurgle.

Patrick took the mug from him. "I'm sorry, Ten. You've got about fifteen minutes to get home before the world goes tits up and purple. I'll see you in a week."

"A *week*?" His stomach gurgled again, and this time it meant business. "I can't take a week off! I've got a project due for you, and softball and Piper and *Ross*!" Oh, he hadn't meant to say that last one, but they only had four weeks!

"Ten-Spot, go home," Pat said in his best "I love you, but you're being an asshole, son," voice. It worked, maybe because Tenner knew Pat would never ghost him as long as he kept showing up for potlucks.

Oh God.

Potlucks.

His stomach gurgled again, and he gave Pat a despairing look, grabbed his keys and his phone, and bolted.

HE BARELY made it home.

An hour after he arrived, he emerged from the downstairs shower cleansed, both inside and out, and not sure he had the muscle tone left to get him up the stairs. He kept all his old robes in the downstairs closet, and had just put one on when the doorbell rang.

He staggered to the door and opened it in time for Ross to bolt inside and toward the guest bathroom. Tenner was still staring after him, appalled, when there was a honk from Pat's Odyssey by the curb.

"We'll bring you chicken soup tomorrow!" he called through the passenger window. "You should be able to keep it down by then!"

He drove away, leaving Tenner to stumble to the couch and park himself, dozing a little in misery for a good hour before Ross emerged in the same state, wearing another one of Tenner's old robes.

Ross threw himself onto the other end of the couch and gave a shaky breath. "Oh my God, that sucked."

Tenner whimpered. "Pat says we've got days of this." The thought would have horrified him, if he could move.

"Yeah, but the nausea's over in the first day." Ross groaned. "Pat gave me a big thermos of tea and a box of the stuff to brew on our own. If I ever move again, I'll get us some."

"If I have to get up, I'll raid your duffel." Tenner listened to his stomach for a moment. *Not yet. But soon.*

"So," Ross said, and Tenner could hear that familiar indomitable humor teasing his voice. "You got the remote?"

Tenner actually thought about smiling. He found it on his arm of the couch and tossed it over. "What do you have in mind?"

"Sitcoms. Something with at least five years to shotgun. You game?"

"Can we watch sports movies and explosions as palate cleansers?" Honestly, he didn't really care, but challenging Ross let him know they were both still breathing.

"No," Ross said, telling him the same thing.

"I'll whine," Tenner threatened.

"You don't know how to whine."

Tenner laughed hoarsely, his throat going like broken glass. "Watch me." And his stomach gurgled. "In about half an hour. For now, I need to go die alone."

Ross grunted. "I may need your upstairs bathroom, then."

They looked at each other miserably.

"One, two, three, break?" Tenner punctuated the "break" by pushing himself weakly off the couch, and Ross followed. They split at the stairs, and the next two hours were spent in painful puking solitude.

THIS TIME, Tenner managed to fall—clean and shivering and wearing only briefs—into the guest bed. Ross was there too, making him drink some of Patrick's tea. Tenner gulped it down because apparently Pat and Desi knew their home remedies, and the tea really did help him feel better. But when Ross would have made him drink more, Tenner paused.

"Have you had any?"

Ross grunted, and Tenner made him drink the last of it.

"Okay," Tenner mumbled. "Get me another robe."

Ross was already in bed next to him. "Where are you going?"

"To brew more tea. I want gallons of it. It shall be the only thing we drink. We shall both be brilliantly translucent vessels filled with whatever wonderful chamomile and ginger magic is infusing me right now."

Ross whimpered, shivering in the bed. "Can you bring me some ibuprofen, Oh Translucent One?"

Tenner gave his own shudder. "Sure. I'll take some of that myself."

LATER, TENNER would claim not to remember much of that week—but he lied. He remembered every moment of it. He remembered the fever, the shakes, the torn-up throat, the ripped-up chest, and coughing until he was afraid he'd crack a rib.

He also remembered the hours of stupid sitcoms that made him and Ross giggle like children because God, anything was better than the misery of being sick.

He remembered calling Nina and bailing on dance and then calling Hanford and bailing on the game and then calling Nina and bailing on the weekend.

"Honey, are you okay?" Nina asked the second time he called. "That's a long time to be sick!"

"Ross is here," Tenner told her, too sick to care about propriety. "We got sick at the same time, so Pat kicked him over here so he and Des could take care of the kids."

"Oh no. Poor guy. Stuck at some stranger's house for a week. What were Pat and Desi thinking?"

Tenner opened his mouth to say, "They were thinking since we were sharing germs anyway, we might as well just share the joys of being gross," but then Piper's voice came on the phone. "Let me have it—Daddy! You're sick? You can't be sick! Are you all alone?"

"No, sweetpea. Ross is with me."

"Oh, good. Ross won't let anything bad happen to you." And then, in an aside to Nina, she said, "Ross is really strong, Mommy. And he's even taller than Daddy. He can take care of Daddy."

"I take care of Ross too!" Tenner said, feeling defensive. "We take turns."

"Good, Daddy. You tell Ross that's fine. You can take care of him too. I said it was okay."

Tenner's head ached fiercely, and as he spoke, he started rooting for the ibuprofen in the kitchen cupboard. He'd made this phone call after Ross had drifted off to sleep in front of the television, and Tenner was feeling like they both needed to be in bed soon.

"I'll tell him that, baby. Me and Ross will take care of each other and you said it was okay."

"Good. I love you, Daddy. Mom says we can come by and visit tomorrow to make sure you're not dead."

Oh God, he must have missed that part of the conversation. He leaned his head weakly against the cabinets. "No, honey. Nina, no. Don't come. You'll both get the crud. No, no, no. You can't touch us or breathe our air or touch anything we've touched. I'm going to have to burn the furniture. Nina, don't. Save yourselves."

"Have the two of you even eaten in the last week?" she asked, taking the phone again in exasperation.

"Patrick keeps leaving big pots of soup at the door, ringing the doorbell, and running away." Like the coward he was, Tenner thought bitterly, even though that wasn't fair. "We've started washing the pot and leaving it on the step when we're through with it so Desi doesn't run out of cookware."

"Honey, I'm taking my Tamiflu, and I've got Piper on something for kids. We won't lick your face or anything, but she really needs to see you're okay."

"Just not for long. I'm serious about you guys not wanting a piece of this, okay?"

"I understand. I need to make sure you and this virtual stranger aren't dead."

"He's a friend," Tenner mumbled, needing to sit in the worst way. "One of the best. More than a friend. A—" *boyfriend.*

"Sure, he is, honey. You're brothers in germs. I get it. Now go to bed. I still have your key. I'll just swing by tomorrow after work, okay? No germ swapping, I promise."

"Sure. Whatever. Going to bed now."

What could possibly go wrong with that?

Because he knew. He knew that one look at the two of them together, the way they touched, the way they bickered, and Nina would get what Tenner had been trying to tell her, and all of this good feeling between them would be gone.

But then, he thought fuzzily, he'd be left in the house with Ross, in sickness and in health. And God knew, they were dealing with the sickness at the moment, and they didn't seem to hate each other. In fact, Tenner wanted nothing more than to climb back in bed and cough out his lungs next to the man he loved.

So, not a total loss.

"Bye, Ten. Feel better."

"Bye, Nina. I'll try."

By the time Tenner got back to the couch, he felt like he'd been on safari for months.

"Whowuzat?" Ross mumbled, shoving his back into the corner of the couch and opening his arms. The day before, Tenner would have told him to fuck off, because they'd been sweating like lathered moose. Today, they were down to a midgrade fever—uncomfortable, exhausting, but a much better cuddle temperature. Tenner burrowed in and turned bleary eyes toward the TV.

"Nina. She's gonna bring Piper by tomorrow. We should probably get dressed." They'd managed two loads of laundry—sheets, underwear, and pajama bottoms—and were ready for a third.

"I'll break out the sharp threads and dancing shoes," Ross told him. "Tomorrow."

"It's a date."

"Speaking of… seriously. What day is it?"

"Saturday."

Ross grunted. "Fuck. Fuckity bugger me fuck."

Tenner let out an amused breath. "Not anytime in this last week, no. Why do you ask?"

"That's why I'm mad. I'm down to three weeks."

Tenner grunted. "Fuck is inadequate," he said, his heart aching. "I want my week back." Ross would be gone two months—if he came back. Tenner hadn't wanted to ask. How could he? He hadn't even come out to Piper. God, how could he expect—

"I'll come back," Ross whispered.

"I should have my shit together by now," Tenner muttered, broken. "I was going to be all functional, and my family was going to be happy and accepting, and my daughter was going to be so well adjusted, and—"

"Aw, baby. You *are* functional, and your daughter is perfect. Like scary perfect. No, seriously, I've been living with Pat's kids for five weeks, and they're pretty awesome, but they're horrible to each other. I swear, Abner borrows his sisters' yoga pants for dance so he can fart in them. They're rotting out at the crotch. It's terrifying."

Tenner managed a weak chuckle, wondering how Ross could make him laugh even when they were both dying of the plague. "But I haven't told her yet," he bemoaned, and Ross gave one of those sounds that told Tenner he might have some bad news.

"Ten?"

"Yeah?"

"Look, I have no concrete way of knowing this, and we need to act like I'm wrong, but… uh…."

Tenner pushed himself up on Ross's chest with a concerned look. "What?"

"Look, everything I know about kids tells me that she might have an inkling. That's all. So, you know, don't be surprised if she knows."

Aw. "So sweet," Tenner murmured, patting his cheek. "So naïve. Kids really don't give two shits what grown-ups do. You know that, right?"

Ross met his eyes with bleary amusement. "Sure, baby. Let's pretend that's true."

Tenner collapsed back on his chest. "You make me tired just talking to you. Press Play."

"What're we watching?"

"Anything you want. You win today. Maybe tomorrow I win."

Ross yawned. "Good luck with that. Do we know when she's coming?"

"Sometime after ten."

"*How* do we know that?"

"Because that is the absolute earliest the two of us can be up and showered and in clean clothes."

"That is totally fair." He didn't question any further, but he should have.

But then, Tenner should have too.

THE NEXT morning they felt marginally better—their fevers were still low-grade and exhausting, but they both managed showers, and after two loads of laundry, Ross could wear his own pajama pants and underwear as well.

Pat had awakened them that morning with a half-gallon of orange juice and a big tub of sliced mangos, kiwis, and strawberries. He actually brought it to the door this time and didn't just drop the supplies and run.

"How you guys doing?" he asked seriously, scowling at them both. "Ross, you've lost ten pounds. Tenner, you've lost fifteen, and you're shorter." He yawned. "I'll order you guys some groceries. You can eat and sleep for the next two days and maybe make it to work on Tuesday—"

"Wednesday," Ross said without batting an eyelash.

"But Ross, I can make it back by Tue—"

"Wednesday," Ross said, looking at Pat meaningfully.

Pat nodded. "Wednesday it is! But Ross, you've got to spend Wednesday night at the homestead so the kids know I haven't killed you and buried the body."

Ross snorted. "They're the assholes who gave me the plague. Burying my body would have been a kindness."

Pat nodded and yawned again. "Yeah. I'm not arguing. They're going back to school tomorrow, but I think Desi and I are staying home and sleeping. This week, man. It's like it dropped off the fucking map."

Pat took off after that, and Tenner and Ross had orange juice and all the vitamin C fruit they could handle—which wasn't much at this point—and then sat down on the couch, exhausted.

"Why Wednesday?" Tenner asked as Ross found the remote in what felt to be a routine they'd been practicing for years.

"So we can have sex all day Tuesday."

Tenner stared at him. "Are you shitting me?"

"I don't know why that freaks you out. Dammit, the world owes me. I fall in love over an eight-week break, and one of those weeks is stolen by the plague? I want some sex!" He let out a little yawn. "Just as soon as we can both get it up, there will be sex."

"I have never in my life taken a sick day for sex."

"Heh, heh, heh. Well, technically, it's a personal day for sex. If you were sick, you wouldn't be having sex."

Well, couldn't fault that logic. "Witness the last week." Tenner yawned too and checked his phone. Nothing from Nina yet. He slumped against Ross, who in turn slumped against the pillows. Joe jumped up on his backside, determined to get every bit of snuggling out of his two human heating pads, and they both gave a prenap cough, then settled in to watch TV.

Or really, settled in to sleep.

Which was where they were when Nina let herself in.

RECKONING AND WRECKONING

"TENNER?" THE voice was unfamiliar, but the tone was everything.

Ross opened his eyes and looked into the face of the enemy.

"Shh!" he said, maybe unnecessarily, because Tenner was limp on his chest and didn't seem to be waking up for anything. "God, he's asleep. Do you have any idea how much we would have given for real sleep this last week?"

She gaped at him. A pretty woman—delicate, with dark hair pulled into a ponytail, pale gold skin, and wide brown eyes. She had the cutest little cupid's bow mouth he'd ever seen. Obviously Piper's mother, and those wide brown eyes were filling with hurt and anger.

"Sorry," Ross murmured. "Here, let me…." He wiggled out from under Tenner, who slid to the side and mumbled incoherently before hugging the throw pillow that had been bolstering Ross's back.

He stood creakily to his feet and grinned at Piper, who threw herself at him without reservation.

"Ross! You and Daddy were napping together—it was adorable!"

Ross wanted to shake Tenner awake so he'd hear that and know Ross was right. Naïve! Ha! But he contented himself with giving Piper a quick hug and then setting her at arm's length.

"All right, little Piper Cub, you need the rules. Me and your daddy have been very sick for a long time. No more hugs." Her face fell, and he felt like an ass. "Here, let's do elbow hugs. Stick out your elbow like this." She did, shy delight taking over the disappointment, and he matched her stance and rubbed elbows with her. "That's the only kind of hug we give when we're sick, deal?"

"Yeah, Ross. Can I go wake Daddy up and elbow hug him?"

"No, Piper—" Nina said, but Ross shook his head, and to his relief, she quieted down.

"Sure, sugar. Just only touch his elbow, okay?"

"Okay! See, Mom? I told you he would take care of Daddy!"

The closed expression on Nina's face made Ross swear softly under his breath.

"Yeah," Nina said bitterly. "Ross can definitely take care of Daddy."

"Don't be mean," he said softly. "You being mean in front of Piper is his biggest fear. C'mon, Nina. You're raising such a happy kid. Don't wreck that."

Nina's expression turned stricken, and she stalked into the kitchen, hauling several bags of groceries. Ross followed, hard on her heels.

"He should have told me," she muttered, setting the bags down so she could pace. "He should have...." She stopped and swallowed. "He tried," she said as if to herself. "It's like I can hear all the things he was trying to say and I just ran right over him. He tried to tell me, taking it slowly. 'Cause God knows I don't take surprises well. I suck at it. They make me fucking stabby. But...." She trailed off and looked at Ross in misery. "This was a surprise. It shouldn't have been, but it was. And now I'm pissed off. And I probably have no right to be, but I am. I'm trying to make myself be a nicer person or a better person, but it isn't working. And you guys are sick, and I'm pissed, and—"

"Shh...." He smiled reassuringly. "You're doing fine. Don't beat yourself up too much. We...." He grimaced and gestured to the kitchen with the clean sink and swept floor. "We sort of cleaned up for you, and I'm afraid it tuckered us out. Ten even managed to spray-bleach the furniture and throw a sheet over it. He really didn't want you guys to get sick."

Nina watched him as he spoke, her big brown eyes luminous and wide. "It is so hard," she said, her voice gruff, "to reconcile the Tenner who works so hard to keep us healthy, to make us happy, to accommodate everything I need, with the guy who was asleep in your arms five minutes ago."

Ross blinked several times, not sure how to help with this one. "I.... See, I'm too close to this," he said apologetically, thinking about how easy it was to soothe Tenner's mother compared to the nightmare of understanding and resentment that was building in his chest toward Nina. "I can't see anybody else. He's the same guy. Piper is his priority—yes, even over me. I'm fine with that. My parents raised us all to worship the baby god. Give the child absolutely everything they wanted or needed, no questions asked. And you'd think that would make us all spoiled rotten. I mean, I'm the youngest, right? I should be a nightmare of self-interest. But that's not what happened at all."

"What happened?" Nina asked blankly as if surprised to find herself in this conversation.

"We grew up to worship the next baby god. The young person in the family comes first, and that love rolls downhill."

Nina swallowed again and reached for the bags, but Ross beat her to it.

"Here, let me put these away." He yawned into his shoulder. "You brought us food and that was so nice—"

And that, of all things, seemed to help. "Sit," she said shortly. "You've both been sick, and I'm here trying to do something nice, and I can't make that happen if I'm having a bitch conniption." She started pulling essentials out of the bags—fresh bread, preshredded chicken, salad fixings. When she opened the refrigerator, she made approving sounds. "Desi's been making you soup," she said happily.

"Yeah. My sister's the best."

She glanced at him, chewing that adorable little mouth. *Oh, Tenner, if you were going to try for a girl, this would be the one.* Ross could see how she'd appeal to him, to his chivalry, to his pixilated sense of humor. She wasn't Ross's type emotionally—high maintenance, even when she was working hard to be a lower-key person—but he had to give her points for trying.

"You're really Patrick's brother-in-law," she said, almost musingly. "I... I heard Pat and Desi talk about you a million times, you know. You're sort of the family hero. I...." She shook her head. "Okay, I didn't realize you were gay, and that shouldn't mean anything. I mean, with Desi and Pat, it didn't. You were just her little brother and she's proud of you. Why would she mention that you're gay? Like, she's not going to tell me your sex life. It shouldn't matter to me. So why am I surprised?"

He smiled briefly, liking her repeated attempts to talk herself down. He could see why Tenner worked so hard to keep her happy—worked so hard to introduce things like his new relationship a little bit at a time. She wasn't evil. She wasn't even really bitchy. She was complicated. And obviously a good mother. Ross was going to have to work hard too.

"I'm bi," he said, like it was an introduction. "And you're right—it shouldn't matter. But it does, because now I'm involved in your life in an unexpected way."

She nodded, shoving food in the refrigerator. "That's it. I'm...
I'm so bad at the unexpected," she said, like she expected him to
contradict her.

"Some people are," he said neutrally. "I'm actually sort of good at it."

She gave him a dry look, and he returned it with his most winning
smile.

At that moment they heard Tenner from the living room. "Ross?
And your mother? In the kitchen together?"

Tenner's bare feet on the hardwood came next, and Ross got up just
in time to catch him as he bounced off the doorframe with his shoulder.

"Take it easy," he said, steadying Tenner's shoulders. "She hasn't
killed me. She probably doesn't feel like cooking, and we're too sick to
be the main course."

"Ou—"

"Tenner, are you okay?" Nina called from the other side of the
counter.

"—uch...," he finished, rubbing his shoulder and looking down at
his toe.

"Here, baby. Come sit." Ross guided Tenner to the kitchen table
and sat him down. "I'm going to grab us some ibuprofen and maybe
some crackers, okay?"

"I'll nuke some soup," Nina said helpfully, and Ross saw her eyes
darting from Tenner, who was still a little dazed, to Ross and back.

Well, awkwierd *and* helpful.

Complicated in spades.

"Daddy, are you okay?" Piper came running in from the living
room, and unlike her father, she wasn't disoriented from fever and
congestion, so there was no running into the doorframe.

"Fine, pumpkin," Tenner said, eyes on Nina.

"Daddy's fine," Nina said, and her eyes did that little dart from
Ross to Tenner and back again. "You were right—Ross is taking care
of him."

"Can I go get my color books and pet Joe?" Piper asked happily.
"He was asleep on Daddy's bottom when we got in, wasn't he? Wasn't
it funny when Ross got out from underneath him and the cat stayed on
Daddy's bottom?"

"Laugh riot," Tenner muttered, and Ross chuckled.

"Go ahead," Nina said. "Joe probably missed you this weekend." She wrinkled her nose. "Although I think Daddy missed his cat box this week."

"Shit," Tenner said abruptly.

"I think that was her point," Ross said, smirking. "Here, I'll get it—"

"No," Tenner said, fighting to rise. "I can do it."

"Both of you sit down," Nina said sharply. "God. I'm not that much of a bitch. Let me get you guys some lunch, then I'll take care of it. Believe it or not, I know how to change the cat box."

"Sorry, Nina," Tenner said wretchedly, and Ross ignored the ex-wife and rubbed soft circles on Tenner's lower back.

"No, I'm the one who's sorry," she said, putting a two-person serving tub of soup in the microwave and pressing buttons. "It's not your fault I'm a freak who can't deal with change."

"Harsh," Ross muttered.

"Just shut up, both of you, and let me pretend this is all normal and fine, and eventually it will be normal and fine, okay?"

Ross got it. In fact, he was pretty sure this was how prejudice in all its forms would eventually be conquered. By people working really hard to forget all the things they'd been programmed to believe. It didn't come easy. Children had to learn to hate—adults had to learn to let go of it.

"That's fine," Ross said, feeling the tiredness that had taken him and Tenner out when they'd been on the couch resurface. "Honestly, I don't know if either one of us is in any shape to fight you."

She gave a grim smile. "And maybe that's a blessing. I've got to tell you, it's really hard to get pissed at Tenner for something that isn't his fault when he looks like a stiff wind is going to knock him over."

"I am not that pathetic," Tenner mumbled, setting his chin down on his fists.

Ross blew on him, laughing at his outrage. And as he was laughing, he heard an amazing sound.

Nina was laughing too.

Piper came in and joined them for lunch, everybody being very careful not to breathe on each other. Nina shooed them back into the living room to sit while she cleaned up, and Piper marched in, giving them directions.

"So Ross is going to sit in that corner, and Daddy's going to lean up against Ross, and I'm going to put a pillow here and lean up against Daddy, and that way I won't get sick."

Ross quirked his mouth. "I like this plan."

"Good, because we've been making this plan A all week," Tenner responded. He yawned into his shoulder and swore. "Darn it. I don't want to sleep anymore."

Ross made himself comfy and raised his arm, gratified when Tenner leaned up against him. Well, whether Piper knew what it meant or not, Tenner couldn't deny that the cow had left that particular barn.

"Okay, Daddy. You and Ross are all cozy. I'll go get you a blanket." She disappeared into the guest bedroom and came back with the quilted fleece blanket that usually sat at the foot of Tenner's bed upstairs. She gave Ross one corner and Tenner the other, and together they huddled under the blanket in absolute perfection.

"Good," she said. "That's how you should be."

She got her coloring books again and sat on Tenner's other side, singing to herself. Tenner took the remote control and found a station with cartoons on it. Then the two of them slid underwater again, but this time, it was a wee bit warmer.

THE NEXT day they were fever-free and exhausted. Ross told Tenner he hadn't slept so much since he'd spent sixty hours traveling from Finland to Colombia, then back to the States.

"How did you even know which country you were in?" Tenner asked fuzzily from his accustomed spot on Ross's chest.

"I had no idea. An airport's a fucking airport. Unless you're in Detroit or Dulles, and then it's a portal to hell, and I don't want to talk about it."

"Poor, poor, baby, who gets to travel a lot. Your life must be very hard."

Ross grimaced slightly at the bitterness. "I keep telling you, I'll return here." He had, in fact, already told Jimmy Dowd this. "I mean, you're giving me something to come back to, aren't you?"

"Yes," Tenner said unequivocally. And then, because he was Tenner and nothing could be easy or simple with the guy, he added, "But I'm not out to Piper yet, and—"

Ross snorted. "Says you!"

"Fine. I haven't had the talk with her."

"The talk. Is that in italics or all caps or in quotation marks or what?"

"Shut up," Tenner muttered.

"I think we need to make a rule that you can't use 'shut up.'"

"Can I use 'bite me'? Is 'bite me' a thing we can use?"

Ross pretended to think. "Only if actual biting will be involved. For example," he said experimentally, "if I bit you gently on the neck *right now*, what do you think your reaction would be?"

Tenner also pretended to think about it. "I'd call you a freak and tell you only two-year-olds bite people."

"And what if I bit you tomorrow?"

More thought. "I would probably bite you back in a potentially sexually pleasing way."

"Then no—you may not use 'bite me' because you do not *mean* 'bite me.' And honestly, you do not, at the moment, want to be bitten. You are going to have to find better words."

Tenner growled. "I want you to come back," he said, sounding tired and out of sorts and dear. "I want that more than I think you know. I want that more than I think you even guess. But you are doing something really fucking important. I mean, let's see, send Ross into the world so my kid can have oxygen when she's grown, or keep him here with us because I am...." His voice faltered. "I am lonely and sad and grumpy without him and would rather have him here by my side than off in some distant place doing the world good. Which one of these is great for me but bad for the rest of the world? You tell me."

Ross lowered his head to Tenner's neck and bit gently, pleased when Tenner didn't smack him or tell him he was a freak. Instead, he let out a low, pleasured moan, and Ross's body gave a sleepy response that made taking Tuesday off to have sex seem like the best idea ever.

"Ross!" Tenner argued, squirming against Ross's body, "this is serious!"

"Yeah, I know." Ross pulled back and sighed. "Look, I'm not taking the job here because it's easier than the ones overseas. I'm taking it because getting funding to the places we need in our country is one of my biggest concerns. Cleaning up toxic waste or e-waste takes a lot of money—private citizens can't do it all. We need to make corporations accountable. And seriously, I had to explain to people how *not* to kill fish last week. You'd think it would be easy, but somehow, they thought blasting away at the riverbed was going to be all okay fine for the fucking fish. And when I'm done saving the damned fish, I may end up doing a lot of work lobbying for more government money, but I'll be working for the environmental cleanup company here in Folsom. It's not a cop-out, Ten. It's a way to help and to see my family more. And...."

Oh. Oh, this felt unexpectedly bare and vulnerable.

"And that includes you. And Piper. And I know I'm not even 'Uncle Ross' to her yet, but she thinks I keep her daddy safe, and I want to be that guy. I... I was thinking about coming back already—I told you that. I just need to give my boss the final okay. This whole week, he hasn't badgered me about work I haven't done, or about how I'm a consultant who almost died while on sick leave. No, he's been asking me to give him the go-ahead to hire me back when this next gig in the Amazon is up. What should I tell him?"

Tenner swallowed. "Tell him...." He buried his face against Ross's neck. "Tell him your chickenshit boyfriend is terrified that he's not a good enough reason for you to come back. That every time I think about you leaving, this big black hole opens up in my chest as if you're going to be gone forever and I'm going to be wondering what I've done wrong. And you're not that guy. I know you're not that guy. But I yanked 'happily ever after' from Nina when she was not expecting it, and I don't fucking deserve you."

Oh.

That hadn't been the answer Ross had been hoping for—or expecting—and for a moment, his throat closed up with hurt.

He took a few deep breaths then, wondering if his heart was going to be able to bounce back from this when he was pretty sure it had shattered on the road outside Tenner's little suburban mansion, and then some of what Tenner said sank in.

"You do," he said gently. "You deserve me. Come on, you haven't backed down from a fight yet, Tenner, even if we're just arguing over the remote control. Can't you trust me to come home when you give me such a good home to come to?"

Tenner nodded against him. "If you come back to me, you gotta know, I'll twine around your heart like ivy. I'm not ever letting you go."

Well, good. Ross might need a little ivy to hold him together after that kersplat his heart did on the pavement. "Okay," he whispered. "It's a deal. But if I come back, you and me are holding hands in public, and when Piper's over, I'm staying in your bedroom still. We're together, like a couple, in front of everybody. I want to be a part of your family, Ten. Can you deal with that?"

Tenner nodded again, raising red-rimmed eyes to meet Ross's. "Can you deal with the extra work to make Nina be okay with it? With trying to make her part of our little family? I know some guys would be jealous, but you've got to know it's not like that—"

Ross smoothed his hands back from Tenner's face and kissed his forehead. "You don't want her to be alone. It took me a while to figure it out, you know? Most other guys would be losing their shit with her, torching her reputation to her friends, bitching about their evil ex. But you care about her, and you want her to be happy so Piper is happy, but also, so she's okay herself."

"Yeah," Tenner said, biting his lip. "She... all she wanted with me is what I want with you. A life, a good life, of having someone she can laugh with and someone who loved her and someone who wanted to touch her in a way that made her happy. I couldn't be that guy, but that doesn't mean I don't want to be her friend. I...." He looked embarrassed. "We were truly good friends there, for the first couple of years."

"Do you really want that with me?" Ross asked, getting it.

"So much. I'm so afraid to hope—you know that. But God, I want you to get off the plane and come fall into my bed and never leave."

"Then that's what I'll do," Ross said softly. "If you can hang on for those two months, that's what I'll do when I get home. I promise."

Tenner still looked a little terrified, but he swallowed and said, "Then tell your boss you want to come back. You've got family waiting for you here."

Ross smiled softly. "I will—on one condition."

Tenner waited, eyes sober. "What?"

"Sometime, and I'm not saying this week or the next, but before I get on that plane, I want you to hold my hand in front of Piper. Deliberately. So she can tell her classmates that her daddy's boyfriend is far away, but he'll be coming home to you. She thinks I'm going to take care of you.

She needs to see you have faith in that, or she'll never believe I'm part of her family forever."

Tenner swallowed. "I can manage that," he said gruffly. He gave a grimace. "I think you're right—I'm pretty sure it won't surprise her much."

"I'm pretty sure it won't either," Ross murmured. He kissed Tenner's temple. "Sleep, okay? And dream of tomorrow, when I'll keep biting you until something *really* interesting happens."

Tenner went limp against him. "I can do that," he said.

Ross's heart fluttered in his chest like a struggling moth. Tenner had said it, said it out loud. All Ross had to do was believe in that promise and tell his boss that he meant it too.

"As long as there's no clown cars," Tenner added.

Ross narrowed his eyes. "What do you mean, no clown cars?"

"You keep talking clown cars and a trapeze, and seriously, just you is fine."

"Fine?" Oh, that wasn't going to slide.

"Great!" Tenner amended. "You're great! We don't need a clown car! Or a trapeze!"

"Don't you trust me to catch you on the trapeze?"

"Of course I do! But that doesn't mean I need a clown car up my ass while we're swinging from the ceiling."

"Heh, heh, heh, heh...."

Tenner pulled back. "What?"

"Nothing." Oh God, he really really wanted to do that thing in his head.

"No, seriously, what?"

Ross's sadness, the threatened heartbreak, eased up. God, even if Tenner couldn't trust in fate, hadn't that always been Ross's best thing? And even if Tenner couldn't—even if he broke Ross's heart by telling him to fly and be free or some other horseshit that was basically a stand-in for the fact that the guy was afraid to get his own heart hammered—Ross still wanted to spend as much time inside that marvelous body as possible, still wanted to fly with Tenner inside him.

"I think it's going to be a surprise," he said with some satisfaction.

Tenner narrowed his eyes. "Clown cars up your ass are never a good surprise."

"They're only bad when you fart and run over the cat," Ross said, spoiling the joke by snorking on his own laughter in the middle.

But it didn't matter because Tenner was laughing openly on his chest, and for all Tenner's doubt, Ross had an abundance of faith.

AND BETTER OR WORSE

MAKING LOVE to Ross was always such a whirlwind. A roller coaster. A hurricane cluster in a tsunami.

All Tenner could do was hold tight and hope Ross could navigate the maelstrom.

After their afternoon nap the day before, Ross had borrowed Tenner's car keys and returned an hour later, giggling to himself like an unhinged asylum inmate. Tenner had an idea of where he'd gone, but not what he'd gotten, and he glared.

"No clown cars," he threatened direly.

"You will be *begging* for clown cars," Ross assured him, that easy smile on his face. He was a little pale and a little thin, but God, he was still the irrepressible man who had barged into Tenner's life and not taken no for an answer.

"Why can't I just beg for your—" Tenner swallowed, realizing what he almost said out loud, in the middle of his kitchen, as he was preparing their first nonsoup meal in a week. "Uh. You."

"Heh, heh, heh, heh…."

"Shut—"

"Nope, that's a rule."

Tenner narrowed his eyes. "I would prefer it if we kept all discussion of a sexual nature confined to the bedroom," he said primly, setting the chicken in the oven to broil.

The expression on Ross's face was not promising. "Oh, really?"

Oh, no. "We are *not* having sex in the kitchen!" he said, somewhat panicked.

"Sure, we're not," Ross said, and then he dropped his cargo shorts— since he'd been out—and his underwear right there on the kitchen floor. Just dropped them, and stepped out of his shoes.

Tenner wouldn't have been more surprised if he'd turned into a rabbit.

"What in the actual hell?"

Ross grabbed one of the cushions from the wooden kitchen chairs and threw it on the ground on top of his clothes, then deliberately looked from the cushion to Tenner.

Tenner had the image, suddenly, himself on his knees, in front of Ross, his mouth on Ross's cock, his hands clenched against Ross's asscheeks, his throat full of Ross's come.

He took a shaky breath and tried to stand his ground.

"Uhm, no?"

TEN AMAZING, thunderous, fantastic, filthy minutes later, Tenner was kneeling on a pillow in the middle of his kitchen, but now he had come all over his face, and Ross was still running around without pants.

"Stay right there," Ross mumbled, running to wash his hands in the sink, using plenty of soap from the pump while he was there. He hit the alarm for the chicken when he was done, dried his hands on a paper towel, and then grabbed the hot pads and pulled the chicken out and put the steaming veggies on a cool burner.

Tenner stayed where he was, lapping dazedly at his own come on his hand. "You are cooking naked," he said in disbelief.

Ross looked up from where he was running some paper towels under water, and grinned unrepentantly. "And you just came all over yourself and the kitchen floor. Will wonders never cease?"

Tenner shook his head. "You know, you really are a magic human. I have no idea how you even get that to happen."

"It's easy," Ross said, a spasm of what looked like sadness crossing over his self-satisfied features. "You trust me."

Tenner moved to stand, but Ross held out his palm.

"No, no. Stay there."

Ross came back with a damp paper towel and started cleaning Tenner's hands and his mouth off and then his face. "Close your eyes."

Tenner did, Ross's studious, careful expression branded on the back of his eyelids. "Why were you sad?" he asked after a moment. "Just now. Why were you so sad?"

Ross let out a sigh, and Tenner, sensing he was done, opened his eyes. "Because you trust me so beautifully when it's about sex," he said with a shrug. "From the very beginning—you'd challenge me about baseball, about the time of day, about pretty much anything under the sun, but by God, you trusted me about sex. Why can't you trust me with your heart?"

And Tenner heard the unspoken part of that. *With your family.*

"I do," he said, surprised to find he didn't need to leap at all to find this faith. "I do. I will. Can you trust me? To do this right for them and not let you down?"

Some of Ross's sadness lifted. "That depends," he said, darting his face close so he could lick Tenner's nose.

"What are you doing? What does it depend on?" Tenner took the paper towel from his hands and wiped his nose himself.

"Licking the come off your nose." Ross stuck out his clean tongue, indicating he'd swallowed, and Tenner felt his face heat at the same time he rolled his eyes. "And it depends on…." Ross stood easily, and then offered Tenner a hand up. Tenner hauled his sleep pants and briefs up his backside and to his waist before he took it.

"What?" Tenner asked, taking the opportunity to stroke Ross's chest, since he was still naked in the middle of the kitchen. "What does it depend on?"

Ross gave one of those lazy smiles, the kind that had infuriated Tenner from the first—and had hooked him, reeled him in, and never let him go.

"Depends on whether you trust me with clown cars and the trapeze tomorrow," he said cockily.

Tenner shook his head and stalked around the counter so he could wash his hands with soap this time and finish their dinner.

"Is that a no?" Ross asked, eyes widened ingenuously. And oh my God, he was *still naked.*

"Get dressed!" Tenner managed to say. "Get dressed, set the table—"

"But is that a no?" Ross goaded, bending to get his cargo shorts and briefs from the floor first.

"Sure," Tenner said shortly, his body still tingling from unexpected bondage sex on the kitchen floor. "Sure. You can bring the whole circus. Elephants. Nipple rings. Electric shock. Whatever. I'll obviously go with it. Just keep the clown cars in the bedroom, will ya? I'm trying to cook dinner here!"

"Heh, heh, heh. There's gonna be clown cars," Ross all but sang.

"Man, if you got me a butt plug that squeaks when I clamp down, I will never forgive you!"

Ross's eyes went anime-character luminous. "Do you think they make those?"

"No," Tenner said in horror. "Absolutely not. I think they're a myth. Set the table. The vegetables are overdone. The chicken's dry. Dinner is ruined. Let's eat."

And Ross gave him a fond smile. "Says you. I think it's the best dinner we've had in a week!"

Tenner suddenly remembered how sick they'd been, how much better they felt now—and how far they'd come since their first angry, sexy, frenetic coupling behind the restroom in the park.

"Sure," he said, smiling fondly back. "Now get a move on!"

"I'm on it, Ten." Ross winked. "You can trust me."

Of course Tenner could. He couldn't remember why he'd ever harbored a doubt.

THE NEXT morning Tenner popped up bright and early, his internal clock finally well enough to think it was time to run before work and not sleep.

He was rolling out of bed when Ross snaked out an arm and hauled him back next to his warm body and whispered in his ear, "Where do you think you're going?"

"Running?"

Ross's filthy chuckle in his ear made his body tingle—and warned him that, like so much with Ross, things were not going to go exactly as planned.

"Go use the bathroom and shower," Ross instructed, and he had a timbre to his voice, a particular note, when he was talking about sex, that melted all the bones in Tenner's spine and left only jelly. "When you're clean, inside and out, come back in here and wait for me. I'll be downstairs doing the same thing."

Tenner swallowed. "Uhm... running?"

"Trust me, Ten. This'll be better. If you've got the energy to go running after this, I'll wave to you cheerfully as you rabbit out the door."

Tenner smacked his arm. "You'll come running with me and like it," he muttered. "You won't be nearly as excited to bang me when I'm as big as a house!"

"I will too," Ross said, affronted. "I wouldn't complain about some meat on that ass, you know. It's like banging a set of bleachers right now."

Tenner glared at him. "If this is your seduction technique, it really sucks. Which is more than I'm going to do."

"Heh, heh, heh, heh…."

Tenner's throat heated, his cheeks heated, his ears heated. "Fine. We both know that's a big lie. I'm just saying—"

Ross stopped him by kissing him hard, until Tenner was on his back, rucking Ross's shirt up, swinging one leg around Ross's hips in an effort to get closer. "You all done getting huffy?" Ross teased gently, his own color high enough to tell Tenner he wasn't unaffected.

"It is embarrassing how bad I want you, all the time."

"Heh, heh, heh, heh—"

"God you're insufferable," Tenner said, but without any real heat.

"You suffer me and love it." Ross kissed his neck and Tenner moaned. "C'mon, Ten, we can plan to be gods later. Let's get ready to fuck like gods now."

"Do I even get to ask?"

"Nope," Ross said smugly. "Just be aware—clown cars *will* be involved."

"And the trapeze," Tenner replied, his curiosity setting his skin tingling. "Understood."

That laugh, that filthy, insufferable laugh. In the end, it's what got Tenner out of bed, to see exactly what would make Ross laugh like that.

Twenty minutes later, Tenner was standing in his room with a towel around his waist, pulling out underwear and a clean change of clothes, mostly to kill time. He set everything on the dresser neatly and then started sorting his and Ross's clothes, relaxing into housecleaning that didn't wipe him out or destroy his plans for the rest of the day.

"What are you doing?" Ross asked, dropping his own towel on top of the neatly sorted piles.

Tenner looked up. "Uh, housework…." God, Ross was beautiful. That long, rangy body, the muscles as natural as that athlete's grace, it was there. Naked. Pale and lovely and—

Ross moved behind him and cupped his hand over Tenner's eyes. "Tenner? Baby? I love your practicality, don't get me wrong. I think when I get back from my trip, it's going to keep us together a lot, because you are firmly bred in the idea that man cannot live by sex alone."

For all his nagging, Ross's body was shower-warm up against Tenner's. The heat and the dampness and the smell of deodorant and aftershave were all doing their part to change the mood of the moment. Tenner smiled against the darkness. "But…?"

Ross leaned forward and whispered in his ear, "But we're not doing laundry now, are we?"

"No, sir," Tenner said smartly, and Ross let out a little gasp and grabbed his shoulder with his other hand, letting Tenner feel the silky length of his body from the back of his neck to the backs of his thighs.

"You do know how to turn my key," Ross murmured. "Do you want me to put a blindfold on you, or do you want to see?"

"Ah!" And it was Tenner's turn for his knees to go weak. This moment, in the dark, reliant on Ross for everything, trusting he would get it, was one of the sexiest moments in Tenner's life.

"I'll take that as blindfold time," Ross murmured. "Here, lie on the bed and close your eyes."

Tenner did, and he had to admit to himself that the only thing that made it possible to break away from Ross was the order that he do so. Wow. This trusting someone was pretty heady stuff. It was almost its own sex toy!

While he was there, with his eyes closed, he heard Ross rustling around in what sounded like his duffel bag and then the crinkle of plastic.

"Don't worry about the stuff in the bag," Ross said. "I washed everything while you were in the shower and brought it back up. That's what took me so long."

Tenner grunted. "I was actually not worrying about that," he said, eyes still closed. "Which means I'm not particularly bright."

Ross laughed shortly. "Or it means you really do trust me, which is probably closer to the truth. Now, the first thing I'm going to do is put on a blindfold, so you don't have to work so hard."

Tenner felt his head being lifted, and then the blindfold—whoop!— and the world beyond his eyes went dark. He didn't open his eyes, but he did relax them a little, and the darkness surrounded him, like a friend, touching his skin.

Intimately.

"So what's next?" Tenner asked, the slight quiver in his voice betraying maybe a little bit of nervousness and a whole lot of arousal. Somewhere on the bed, near his hips, Ross dropped a couple of items that had some heft to them. Tenner reached out and felt... oh, man.

"Is that a dildo?" he asked, his voice pitching. "It's sort of big. And the other thing isn't small, and is that lu—"

"Don't touch those," Ross said, laughing.

Tenner gave the dildo one last lingering stroke, marveling that it was almost as big as Ross's cock, but not quite. "Other than that?"

Ross's lips, running down his cheek to his ear, then pausing to linger at his jawline, coming back to tease at Tenner's mouth, was his answer.

"I touch you, as much and as long as I please. You talk to me and tell me what feels good. And I give you the occasional order that you can choose to follow," he said, dotting Tenner's face and shoulders with playful little pecks as he spoke.

"Can I touch you?" Tenner asked.

"God, yes. As much as you can manage. Be careful of the dangly bits, but do whatever comes naturally there too." And still those playful little kisses down Tenner's body. He paused at the nipples and began to tease unmercifully, and Tenner took him at his word and raised his hands to play with that curly hair.

Ross answered by sucking one of the nipples into his mouth and Tenner tilted his head back and gave a breathless moan.

"Ooh," Ross taunted. "If that's what I get for a little nipple nip, what'll I get for blowing your mind?"

"It feels good," Tenner defended, kneading Ross's scalp through his hair. "Ah! So good!"

"You are so easy," Ross marveled before sucking on the other nipple. Tenner whined and arched his back and Ross pulled off long enough to order, "Stop that. Wait until your mind is blown."

"Sadist," Tenner muttered, thrusting his hips down against the bed again.

"I just worry about you crushing my head between your thighs when I rim you," Ross said, and between his mouth, and his hands—oh my God, what were his palms doing to the inside of Tenner's thighs?— and at the thought of a rim job, Tenner had to admit he was right.

"No crushing," Tenner panted. "It's a deal. Ah!"

Ross bit softly on his stomach. "Good. Now I'm going to swing my hips up above you and straddle. In case you're interested, my cock should be right above your mouth, you know, if you want to play with that thing in any way, or suck it or... you get the picture."

"Yeah, su-*ure*!" Tenner's voice pitched at the end there, because Ross's mouth had found the swollen, aching bell of Tenner's cock, and was doing sinful, wicked things to it. Licking and sucking things—teasing things.

Tenner wasn't in a teasing mood.

Ross's cock buffered along the side of his face for a moment, and Tenner wasn't going to let it go this time without taking it down his throat, and without touching *everything* within his reach. After the night before, being on his knees, helpless to do all the things he'd wanted to, he needed Ross to know what he was missing when he told Tenner not to touch him.

Ooh, this wasn't just blindfolded sex with toys—this was *revenge* blindfolded sex with toys. That took things to an entirely other dimension.

Ross deep-throated him, swallowing slightly on Tenner's cockhead, and all thoughts of revenge fled.

He wanted Ross's cock in his mouth, filling him up, now.

He grasped it firmly, stroking once or twice before guiding it carefully to his mouth. Ah, yes! He used one hand to stroke the shaft and another to tease the balls, and the taste was exquisite. Ross let out a grunt, not unaffected, and obviously dedicated to his own task.

Their sixty-nine was passionate and merciless, and Tenner wasn't sure if Ross thought of it as a contest to get the other one to come first, but that's where *Tenner* was heading with this. The blindfold, Ross's touch, the competition—ah, all of it was glorious!

So glorious that Tenner barely noticed Ross fumbling on the bed beside him until Ross raised himself off of Tenner's cock and murmured, "Legs spread, baby."

Tenner did on automatic, lifting his hips and crunching his stomach to give Ross better access. He was prepared for the lubed finger, tapping, stretching, but it didn't deter him from his goal of deep-throating as much of Ross's erection as he possibly could.

The second finger, spreading, scissoring, gave him a little bit of pause. It had been over a week since they'd done this, and he wasn't sure—oh God! There went the third finger, and he had to fight to keep his concentration, full on both ends, needing—

All three fingers disappeared and he let out a frustrated groan, the sound muffled by Ross's cock.

Ross's laugh was strained to broken. "Impatient?" he goaded, fiddling with something on the bed.

Tenner whimpered, empty and wanting.

"You know, you could always give me a bit of the same treatment," Ross said. "Here, give me your hand."

Tenner dropped one hand down by his side and the sudden drizzling of lube on his fingers made him shiver.

Okay. Okay, fine. He was ready for some payback. It was awkward, but he knew the lines and curves of Ross's body. Keeping that cock lodged firmly in his mouth, he maneuvered his hand up between Ross's thighs and parted his cheeks, reveling grimly in Ross's gasp. Served him right, dammit. What was he doing down there?

A little rougher than Ross had been, but then Ross liked it that way, Tenner thrust two fingers slowly into Ross's backside—

At the same time, Ross thrust that giant sex toy that had been on the bed into Tenner's.

Tenner let Ross's cock flop out of his mouth to gibber, but he kept his fingers planted firmly where they were.

"Ross—oh, wow. Hey—"

"Tell me if it hurts or you want me stop," Ross said seriously.

"Yeah, no, I'm fi-*ine*—oh holy hell. Wow. That thing's… damn. Keep going. Oh, shit. Oh my. *Fuck!*"

Ross paused at what felt like the widest part, and Tenner flexed his fingers because he had to.

"Still good?" Ross asked, his voice decidedly shaky.

"You're just gonna stay there?" Tenner practically wailed. His whole body was trembling, sweating, and his cock splatted uselessly on his abdomen, rock hard.

Ross's laughter held a strained edge. "No, baby. I'm gonna shove it all the way in. You ready?"

"God, please," Tenner pleaded.

"A little louder," Ross taunted.

"Oh my God, Ross, please!"

"One more time for the cheap seats." Ross ducked his head to lap at Tenner's cock.

"Please, baby, fuck me with that thing!" Tenner practically yelled.

"Okay, but you can't come. I've got plans."

Tenner sucked in a breath and steeled himself. "I'll try," he said.

"That's all I can ask." And Ross rewarded him with a sure, smooth thrust to the hilt.

Tenner howled as it slid home, and fought back the climax that threatened to rush his spine. "Ross, I sort of, I sort of need, here. I don't know what—"

Ross gently moved his hand, hissing when Tenner's fingers slid out of his ass. Then, while Tenner was trying to orient himself in the darkness, the pressure in his hole, in his backside, the stretching, the things Ross was doing over him—

Wait, what was Ross doing over him?

Ross was... straddling him? Tenner ran his hands over Ross's thighs as Ross boosted himself up. Ross's firm grip on Tenner's cock was his first clue.

"Wait," Tenner gasped, stimulated from every end, adrift in the dark, his body a disparate collection of extreme sensation. "You're going to—ah!" Ross pressed Tenner's cockhead against his stretched entrance and lowered himself, fucking Tenner's cock with his tight, slick asshole while that toy pushed up inside Tenner's ass. Deliberately, he lowered himself until Tenner was completely sheathed.

Tenner's groan came from deep inside, where their pubic bones touched, and he clenched at Ross's thighs in desperation.

"So good," he managed to say. "God... oh, please... something... something's gotta—"

Ross kept Tenner inside him, and lowered his head, touching Tenner's lips with his own. The movement pulled Tenner about halfway out, and Tenner shuddered at the air on his base.

"Baby?" Ross asked, his own voice trembling.

"Yeah?"

"I'm going to take the blindfold off, and I want you to fuck me."

"Thank you, thank you, thank you—"

He kept his eyes closed as he started to thrust, and the light and the cool air on his face was secondary to the feeling of being invaded while he fucked. Ross let out a cry, as undone as Tenner, and Tenner opened his eyes, still pumping, and saw him, head tilted, back arched, unashamed, riding Tenner proudly, his hand on his own cock for his own pleasure.

The image seared itself into Tenner's brain, and the orgasm he'd been holding at bay hit critical mass.

"Ross, I've gotta come!"

"Good. Keep fucking me as long as you—ah! God! Yes! Yes! Jesus!"

Ross's pleasure did him in, his asshole clenching so hard around Tenner's cock, Tenner saw stars. Climax rushed him, his spine, his lower back, his ass where the dildo was lodged, his cock in that tight, warm grasp. All of it overwhelmed him, blew him apart, split him at the core, and he screamed hoarsely, shoulders coming off the bed as he came and came and came.

Above him, Ross gave a cry of his own, and Tenner felt the heat and spatter of Ross's come across his abdomen and chest before Ross fell forward, collapsing on top of him, kissing him hard and long, with so much need, it made Tenner proud of what he could give.

It took a long time to come down from that, but when he did, his first thought was less than romantic.

"Ross?"

"Yeah, baby?"

"I've sort of gotta… you know… bathroom?"

Ross laughed softly and slid to the side, where he closed his eyes and wiped the come off his chest, tasting it with a self-satisfied smile. "Go. Don't be embarrassed. That was the hottest moment of my life."

Tenner had to kiss him, had to take his mouth, had to take *him*, if only for a moment. "I love you," he said, fighting off that urge for the bathroom for just another minute. "I've never trusted another soul like I trust you."

Ross's lazy smile went serious, and he opened his eyes. "I won't ever let you down. I promise. Now go."

Tenner made as dignified a retreat as he could manage.

WALKING OUT the door Wednesday was a relief, and harder than Tenner had imagined. Ross had packed his duffel that morning with a little frown line between his eyes, and Tenner realized he was doing things like looking in the bathroom for his toothbrush, putting it in the duffel, then taking it out again and setting it in the spot it had inhabited for the last week.

The third time Tenner saw him do this, he grabbed a toothbrush from the closet and put it in Ross's spot.

"What are you doing?" Ross asked, zipping his duffel for the umpteenth time.

"It's there for Sunday," Tenner said. They both had work waiting for them, and the odds of them doing more than waving at each other from across two baseball fields on game night were slim.

"Isn't Piper here Sunday night?" Ross asked, sounding a little lost.

"Yeah," Tenner said, sitting down on the bed and pulling Ross down next to him. "She is. I figure you've met Nina—not the best meeting in the world, but you've met. She knows. I'll call her this week, okay?"

"And tell her what?" And again, he heard that lostness. It was reassuring in a way; Tenner was on uneven ground too.

"Tell her that you have to leave in two weeks and I don't want to waste any of that time with you in the guest room."

Ross raised his face to Tenner's and smiled a little. "We can't have loud sex with your daughter in the house," he said seriously as if Tenner didn't know this.

"Believe it or not, I don't want you only for the sex."

Ross smiled slightly. "It's the hair, right? I know I've got sort of fabulous hair."

Ass. Hole. "No, it's not the hair."

"The way I hit a softball? I may be the best player in the league."

Tenner laughed in his face. "The league, hah?"

"Not to brag, but there's this guy who might take my place on the team when I leave. He may be better."

"He just takes batting practice seriously," Tenner said softly. "Now kiss me, and let's go downstairs, grab some coffee, and get to work. I'll see you Sunday as we try to convince my team that they're not supposed to be afraid of the ball—they're *supposed* to catch it."

Ross chuckled. "You know, they're actually getting better."

Tenner wrinkled his nose. "*That* remains to be seen," he muttered. "We skipped a week, remember? Pat said they lost. Like, the other team never let them get to bat, lost. They timed out. First time it's happened in the league. My team is going to be the reason the league adopts a mercy rule."

"Oh, no!" Ross cracked up as he stood and offered his hand to help Tenner up. "Poor Hanford!"

Tenner grunted. "Patrick said he was in tears."

"Poor kid." Ross ruffled Tenner's gelled hair, just to watch him flail. "You know he's got a crush on you."

"Still?" Tenner said. "I mean, at the beginning, sure, but not now, right?"

Ross laughed some more, and Tenner glared at him, feeling the tiniest bit guilty.

"He still does, unfortunately. That's why his sister keeps bringing the kids. He wants you to think of him as good father material for Piper."

Tenner almost fell down the stairs. "That's horrifying," he said, not laughing with Ross. "You've been there from that first day!"

"Well, yeah," Ross said gently, "but we haven't been there as a couple, because Piper was there."

"Oh, no." This felt awful. Huge. Like he'd led that poor kid on and betrayed him in the worst way. "I didn't mean—"

"Ten, don't sweat it. Did you mean it when you said Piper would know this weekend?"

"Yeah," Tenner told him.

"Then we'll be a couple on Sunday. You might break his heart a little, but you haven't deliberately hurt him." Ross went after his hair again and Tenner fended him off. "It's going to be okay."

Tenner nodded. There was nothing he could do about it now. He grabbed his own backpack, his long-neglected laptop inside, and his car keys, and they both reached for their travel cup of coffee.

It was time to rejoin the rat race.

Unbroken Circles

"YOU DON'T look comfortable," Ross said, trying not to be hurt. He finally had Tenner, dressed up and on a date, but the circumstances weren't anywhere near what he'd had in mind.

Friday morning, Nina had called to say Piper wasn't feeling well—a mild fever, she'd said, a rumbly tummy. Tenner had stopped by after the game on Friday night to check on her, but she'd been sleeping.

He'd said Nina had been pale and tired too. He'd called that morning, but Nina waved him off and, Tenner had said, told him to go see his boyfriend and get out of her hair.

"She said that?" Ross asked when Tenner called him Saturday morning. "She told you to go see your boyfriend?"

"No, I made that part up. Yes, she said that, but I warn you, it didn't sound like she was happy about it."

And Ross could picture that too. "Well, forget *her* happiness. We are well, we are childfree and it's Saturday. I'll be over in an hour. We can catch a movie and go to a grown-up place to eat. Some place they serve beer. It'll be great."

"An hour!" The squeak in Tenner's voice was gratifying. "I have to shower! Shave! Find something to wear—"

"I'm not taking you to prom, Ten. I said beer, not champagne."

"I haven't been out on a real date with someone I wanted to bang since college," Tenner said firmly. "Just… just give me a minute."

"I'll give you an hour and you'll like it. Now go. I need to get dressed myself!"

The movie had been the best kind of blow-shit-up with attractive leads who kissed at the end, and Tenner hadn't even blinked when Ross had reached for his hand. And the restaurant was a sweet little hole-in-the-wall in downtown Folsom, the kind of place with only microbrews and local wineries. The appetizer had been oysters in the half shell—sautéed with butter and bread crumbs—and they were waiting for dinner.

Tenner, who had been attentive and happy for most of the date, was suddenly checking his phone, and Ross remembered—Tenner was a parent. Taking advantage of a free evening was fine, but it was going to come with an underlay of worry, especially since Tenner hadn't been able to see his daughter that morning.

"She... she should have texted me back," Tenner said apologetically. He glanced up from his phone, his forehead furrowed. "I'm sorry, this place is great, but—"

"But she's your kid and you're worried," Ross said, his own hurt fading. "I get it. Do you want to stop by after dinner?"

Tenner nodded, that furrow in his forehead not diminishing in the least. "Yeah. I just... this thing hit us like a ton of bricks. I know they were taking prophylactics, but those don't always work. What if they got the full-strength plague? Nina doesn't have a Patrick and Desi to keep them in soup and tea, you know?"

Ross nodded. "Yeah. But she's got us." He waved his hand at their waiter, who hurried over. "I'm sorry, his daughter is sick. Is there any way we can get our meal to go?"

TENNER WAITED a good three minutes after his first knock before letting himself in and gesturing Ross behind him. Most of the lights were off, with the exception of a lamp by the couch, but Ross still got an impression of a spacious, airy room. The floor was littered with dolls and clothes, a Barbie Dreamhouse taking a corner of the room, and Ross's opinion of Nina rose a little. This was where a little girl could play if she wasn't feeling good, and the thought of Piper, fretful and sick, going through her doll clothes to try to find the right one twisted his heart.

But the doll house wasn't the most important thing—the most important thing was the woman on the couch, covered in blankets, shaking.

"Tenner?"

"Oh, honey, what happened?"

Nina looked awful—face pale, hair a mess, and a large pot on the floor next to her head. Poor baby. Tenner stroked the hair out of her eyes.

"We were both sick today, and she had to throw up, and then I had to throw up, and I put her to bed after, and...." Two weak tears ran down her nose. "I was going to text you, but I left my phone in the kitchen. I just...." She let out a little hiccup. "It just got bad fast. I wanted to check on Piper. She's been so quiet...."

"Here. I'll go do that. Ross? Could you wait here?"

"Yeah, sure." Ross went to the head of the couch and crouched down, placing a tentative hand on Nina's back and rubbing.

"That's sweet," she mumbled. "God—why're you guys over here, anyway?"

"He was worried," Ross said softly. "He didn't hear from you. And he knows you'd text him if you were up to it."

She sniffled a little more. "This is so nice. I mean… you coming over. Making sure. It's really sweet."

"Well, you did the same for him."

She nodded, and more tears came, illness, lowered barriers, whatever. He kept rubbing, because he'd never seen anyone look so bedraggled in his life.

"But you're here too and…." She squinted in the lamp light. "You're both all dressed up. Tenner's wearing the shirt Piper got him for Christmas. Oh God. You were on a *date*, and I fucked that all up. I'm sorry. I'm so sorry—"

"Hey, hey…," Ross soothed her, rubbing gently, and her eyes had fluttered shut when Tenner came out of the bedroom, Piper bundled in his arms.

"Ten?" Ross stood up anxiously.

"Her temp is really high," Tenner said softly. "I got her to take a meltaway with some water, but I called the advice line, and they said bring her in. I…." He looked at Nina in mute supplication. "I don't want to leave her alone—"

And Ross got it. Complicated? Not so much. It was very simple. He leaned over and kissed Tenner's cheek, relieved when Tenner did nothing more than close his eyes in acceptance.

"I'll call Desi and have her bring supplies," he said. "And maybe get Nina to bed. She can't be comfortable here."

Tenner nodded, his eyes bright. "Thanks. God, thanks so much—"

"Daddy, is Ross gonna take care of Mommy?"

Tenner kissed his daughter's forehead as she lolled on his shoulder. "Yeah, honey. Ross takes care of all of us."

"Good. Thanks, Ross."

Ross leaned over and gave her his own kiss on the forehead. "Night, sweetpea. Get better, okay?"

"Yeah."

"I'll take Nina's car," Tenner said. "It's got the car seat, and that way you're not stuck here."

Ross shrugged. "I've got nowhere else to be. Now go. Take care of our kid, 'kay?"

Tenner nodded earnestly, grabbed a set of keys from a pegboard by the kitchen, and left through the garage door.

Ross looked down to where Nina had finally fallen asleep and sighed. He was definitely going to need some help here.

Without hesitation, he pulled out his phone and dialed. "Hey, Desi? You remember when we were sick and you brought me and Ten that amazing tea...."

BY THE time his sister arrived, he'd managed to get Nina off the couch and into the bathroom, and he was running her a bath.

"Oh, thank God," he muttered, opening the door. "She feels like shit, but God, she's been throwing up all day. I need a woman in there before I start undressing her, or I'll be the ultimate in creeper."

Desi grimaced. Her golden hair was pulled back into a ponytail, and she was wearing sweats and no makeup. Ross got the feeling he'd called her up from a lazy night watching television, and he felt some remorse—Desi and Patrick ran their asses off every day. A lazy night watching television had the same sort of luxury factor for Des and Patrick as going out to a nice restaurant in their best clothes had for Tenner and Ross.

She must have rung the doorbell with her elbow, because in her arms she had a giant vat of sun tea that looked like it had sat outside that very day.

"Take this, Ross, before I drop it."

Ross grabbed it, and Desi came all the way in, then turned and got the door. "You said Tenner's got Piper at the ER?"

Ross nodded. "They were waiting to be seen. He said he'd text me as soon as the doc came and told them what's up. But Nina's been sick all day. Thanks so much for coming over. Tenner didn't want to leave her alone, and I can totally see why."

Desi patted Ross's cheek. "You're a good egg, kiddo. Let's go take care of our newest stray."

Together, they managed to get Nina undressed and help her into the bath. Desi had her wash her hair for good measure, and by the time she was done, Nina was weak enough for Ross to just wrap her in a towel and carry her to bed. They got her dressed in sweats, and Desi brought in the hair drier and went to work on her hair while Nina sat on the bed, looking exhausted.

Ross brought her a mug of tea, and she sipped dispiritedly at first, and then she gulped the rest of it down and set the cup aside with a sigh as Desi turned off the drier.

"I'm going to come back with some crackers and some acetaminophen," Ross told her, and she nodded, snuggling under the covers. When he got back, she was crying softly into the pillow as Desi sang a song that she used when she put the kids to bed. Ross watched the two of them for a moment, his heart opening wider than he ever thought it could.

"Here, sweetheart," he said when Desi was done. "This'll help you sleep."

Nina ate obediently and washed the medicine down with more tea. "Have you heard from Tenner?" she asked. "How's Piper?"

Ross checked his phone. *They've got her on IV fluids and fever control. They'll probably let her go in the morning.*

Good—Nina was asking. How you holding up, champ?

She looks so small.

Ross touched the screen, his chest aching. *Yeah, but she's too tough to be down for long.*

How's Nina?

Pitiful and sad and worried. We'll take care of her.

We?

Called in the big guns, hoss. My sister taught me all the good stuff, remember?

Tell Desi thank you for me. We owe her and Patrick something huge for the last two weeks.

I have an idea, Ross typed, *but it will have to happen when I come back.*

There was a pause, and Ross realized what he'd just said—and what he'd just asked. Tenner was going to have to believe. He was going to have to commit.

I'm good for it. Tell me later.

Will do. Keep us posted. Ross paused, his heart beating in his throat, because this was in print, and this moment—the sick ex-wife, sick kid, plans for the future—was as real as anything he'd ever done. *Love you,* he typed next. *Tell Piper I love her too.*

Love you back. Another pause, with the little thought bubbles, and Ross wondered how many things Tenner typed and erased and typed again. *And I will. Later.*

Later.

Ross sighed and turned to Nina. "Piper's getting fluids and fever meds. Tenner said they'll probably release her in the morning, and you two can get better watching cartoons together. How's that?"

"Sounds better," Nina said. "I… all my friends live a thousand miles away. I never realized how alone we were, you know?"

"Oh, honey," Desi said, taking her hand, "you're not alone. You've got Tenner, Tenner's got us. We've got you."

Nina nodded weakly. "Thanks, Des. Can I talk to Ross for a minute?"

"Sure, honey. I'll be camping out on the sofa. Ross can take the guest room, right?"

Nina looked Ross in the eyes and twisted her mouth. "Yeah. Here, he can have the guest room."

Desi left, and Ross took her place by the side of the bed. He started rubbing her back, like Desi had, and Nina closed her eyes again.

"You have to understand," she said softly. "He was all I ever wanted when I was in college."

"I get that," Ross said. "He's all I ever wanted, period." And it was true. He'd never had a lover that could be his everything, until Tenner had yielded to him on a warm spring night, and Ross had fallen in love.

She nodded. "Yeah. My parents… they didn't even come to our wedding, you know? And they've seen Piper maybe once, right after she was born. And… and it was okay, because I had a husband and a daughter who loved me. I had friends at work, even if they lived in New York. But then he told me he was gay, and that felt like… like all that security had been a lie. And I was so mad. And then, he asked for the divorce, and… and it was… it was like a chance to hurt him back. I knew it was wrong, putting that thing in the settlement. But I… I didn't know how else to show him how much he'd hurt me. And I missed him. This whole time, that friend I fell for in college, he's been right there, picking Piper up, making sure I was okay, anticipating my every need—and I never saw him." Her voice broke. "And now, I'm so grateful to have him in my life... in any way." She started to sob. "And you're being so *nice*."

"Shh... shh... it's okay," Ross said, leaning over and sheltering her with his shoulders. "It's okay, honey. I'm gonna have to leave sometimes. You can keep him safe until I'm back. He's still yours that way. And you still have Piper together. You're friends now, just like you've always been friends. And you can be my friend too."

"Thank—" Hiccup. "—thank—" Hiccup. "—thank-thank-thank *you!*"

And that was the last thing she managed to say until the storm of weeping passed and she fell asleep.

Ross waited a couple of minutes, looking at her little oval of a face, seeing her in Piper, seeing her appeal to Ten. In a remarkably short time, she'd gone from being the evil ex to being a vulnerable woman—but then, she'd never been the evil ex to Tenner. She'd been someone he cared about and had let down, just by being human.

Ross and Nina, they were going to be fine.

Finally he turned off the light and went downstairs, to where Desi had helped herself to some microwave popcorn and was watching her favorite rom-com on Nina's Netflix.

Ross had to laugh. "Made yourself at home?"

"Well, tea delivery is a thankless job. You gotta take your perks where you can." Desi grinned at him. "Want some popcorn?"

Ross's stomach grumbled, and he remembered the takeout boxes in the car. "How would you like pork medallions in cranberry glaze?" he asked seriously. "With a sweet potato cake cooked in brown sugar and balsamic vinegar?"

Desi's eyes got big—she'd always had a soft spot for somebody else's cooking. "Is there a dessert in this magic lamp? Because Nina is apparently scrupulous on the sugar thing, and I could use some cookies."

"Individually portioned chocolate mousse pies," he said, pulling out his phone. "Give me a sec and I'll go get them from the car."

"You," she said soberly, "are my favorite little brother."

Ross grinned. "I'm your only brother, but I'll take it." He pulled out his phone and texted, *Bad news, Ten—my sister's eating your dinner.*

That's fine. I owe you another one anyway. Maybe someplace less fancy, with steak.

Done. The future was looking pretty good, Ross decided on the way out to the car. He'd have to make sure it stayed bright.

WEARING SHADES

TENNER BROUGHT Piper home the next morning and tucked her into her own bed for some much-needed rest.

"Is Mommy okay? She was feeling icky too," Piper murmured.

"She's fine. I told you, Ross took good care of her."

"Are you going to stay, Daddy?"

"Me and Ross were going to go practice with the team," he said with a yawn. "I think we'll come back tonight, though, and bring you guys some soup."

She laughed and snuggled down, obviously grateful to be in her own bed. She hadn't slept well in the hospital, but her color sure was better, and her fever had fallen to below 101. It would be a long week of recovery for her, like it had been for him and Ross, but she was over the worst of it.

"I'll have Mommy come snuggle," he said and kissed her on the forehead. "I know she was worried."

"Tell her I had juice," Piper said practically, and then her eyes fluttered closed, and she hugged her favorite bunny close.

Tenner met Nina on his way out the door. "You're up," he said kindly, and she smiled.

"I'm mostly dead," she said, and *The Princess Bride* worked its magic and they both laughed a little. "It'll take me a while before I storm the castle."

"Well, fine. I'm sure the castle will wait."

Unexpectedly she hugged him, and he held her in surprise. "You and Ross were so great last night—so great."

"Oh, honey. Did you think we'd leave you alone?"

"I probably deserved it," she muttered, and he kissed her temple. "No."

She shook her head. "I've missed you. As a friend. Do you think… you, me, Piper—we could be that kind of family? The kind you see on TV and go, 'Oh, hey, they have history, but they're doing okay'?"

"Can Ross be included?" he asked. God, it was all he'd ever wanted for himself.

"Well, after the last two weeks, I think the only guest room he's going to sleep in is mine," she said practically, and he knew he was grinning and couldn't seem to stop.

"Go," she said, shoving him away with a yawn. "Apparently you two idiots are going to play softball today, which is insanity because all I want to do is sleep."

"We'll come back with soup," he promised, but she shook her head.

"Desi's coming over later with soup. But if you guys want to drop by, that's fine." Her eyes grew sober. "And that goes for... you know. Anytime. When he's gone, and you want family—anytime. Okay."

Tenner nodded. "You too. Now go sleep and cuddle and get better. See you soon."

She climbed into bed with Piper, who curled into her chest with a happy little sigh. "Mommy!"

"Sweetiepants!"

And he left them together and went to give Desi the biggest hug in the world.

"This was so kind of you—seriously. She was so alone and—"

Desi waved his thanks away. "No worries, and by the way, you missed out. Your dinner last night was *amazing*."

Tenner sent Ross a dry look. "Food is always a good reward," he said, and the statement was punctuated with his stomach gurgling.

Ross, who seemed to have had a decent night's sleep, rolled his eyes. "You haven't eaten since yesterday? Jesus, Tenner, it's eleven in the morning!"

Tenner's stomach gurgled again, and he said, "We have practice in an hour, and I need to go home and feed the cat!"

"Gah! Joe will be fine. But you! Piper says I take care of you, baby, and I'm falling down on the job!"

Tenner shook his head. "We have got to go change and go to practice—"

Desi rolled her eyes. "You'll be gone for two months, you say?"

Ross nodded. "Yeah."

"It's a good thing Patrick takes him out to lunch twice a week, that's all I'm saying."

Ross cocked his head. "Twice a week? And you can't put any meat on your ass? Oh my God. Hurry up and let's go so I can feed you."

Tenner scowled. "Look, I know what you told Piper, but—"

Ross silenced him with a kiss, hard and hungry and needy, and Tenner responded, so relieved to feel Ross's arms around him that he couldn't even pretend. He melted, that reassurance, that strength bleeding into him and leaving some of the long, anxious night behind them.

"Bye, guys," Desi said on her way out the door. "I'll see you here, tonight, while we make sure our girls are okay."

Ross raised his hand to wave, but he didn't, not once, take his mouth from Tenner's, and Tenner was grateful.

The kiss was pure comfort, and finally, finally, when they separated, panting for breath, Ross said, "So, breakfast first, feed the cat, and text Hanford to tell him we'll be late. Deal?"

"I don't know what I'm getting out of that—"

Ross kissed him again, short and hard, and pulled back. "Don't fuck with me here. You were gone, the kid was sick, I was worried, and your ex-wife broke my heart. I need you to do what I'm saying here, and don't give me any shit, okay?"

Tenner swallowed and nodded, realizing that this was what made partners, just as much as the "You do this and I'll do that" dynamic. "Yeah," he said meekly. "Let's go feed the cat."

"And the *human*!" Ross muttered, exasperated. "No, don't answer that. I don't want to hear it. You look exhausted, and it's making me stabby, and we need to leave and let them sleep. Now go. I'm driving. We'll grab an Egg McSomething on the way."

TENNER WAS tired and out of sorts at practice, and when Ross told the team why, they told him to go home.

"You should have called me," Hanford said after the team scattered to practice fielding. His eyes went back and forth between Ross and Tenner as if they weren't about to dash his hopes. "I'm great with kids."

"Ross took care of us," Tenner said with meaning. "He's really good at it."

Hanford looked at Ross, who was nodding with the same meaning, and his face fell. "Oh. Oh, I didn't realize…. I'm sorry. I, you know…."

Tenner shrugged and hoped he could help the young man save face. "We were quiet about it," he said, not even wanting to think about what his neighbors had heard that Tuesday when they'd stayed home an extra day to have sex.

"Yeah." Hanford sighed and looked out at the rest of the guys. "Well, Kipper asked me to pizza next week," he said, a little bit of hope in his voice. "Maybe I should go."

"Definitely," Ross said, and Tenner sent him a dirty look.

And then yawned.

Which meant it was *their* signal to go, so he could nap before dinner.

PIPER AND Nina got slowly better that week, much like Ross and Tenner had, and Ross gave up any pretense of sleeping at Pat and Desi's. And that was a good thing, because, as it turned out, they had less time than they thought.

The Monday after their abortive date, Ross texted Patrick and Tenner that he'd pick them up for lunch. At first Tenner was just happy to see him in the middle of the day, but when they got out to his SUV, he looked grim-faced and upset.

"What's wrong?" Patrick asked.

Ross let out a breath, wearing a face Tenner had never seen before—angry and frustrated and almost tearful. "I... the territory we'd kept from burning before I came up here is in danger again. They start deforestation next week. So I... I leave on Saturday."

Saturday?

"That's... that's really soon," Tenner stated, trying not to lose it. "When are you coming back?"

Ross had his foot on the brake and turned that heartbroken face to Tenner. "I don't know," he said, voice pitching. "I... I've got to do this. The company that's running the deforestation will only negotiate with me, and all the people who've been trying to replant the area are people I recruited. I can't leave them like this, baby. I—" He glanced into the back seat where Patrick sat, looking sad but resigned. "I'm so sorry."

"You're coming back," Pat said, waving his hand like it wasn't even a thing. "We'll be okay."

Tenner swallowed hard, and Ross turned back to him. "Will *you* be okay?" Ross said, and then, without even a glance at his brother-in-law, he said, "Will *we* be okay?"

Tenner stared at him, looking unhappy and worried and… and so, so dear. "I can't imagine being more in love with you in two weeks than I am right now," he said with a shrug.

Ross let out a strangled laugh and held his hand to his heart. "Wow! Right when I thought you had no game."

Tenner rolled his eyes. "I have great game," he said with dignity. "Just not… you know. When I'm super depressed." He'd been planning on two more "date weeks." Two more chances to make amazing love with Ross McTierney.

You trust me so beautifully in bed. Can't you trust me enough to hope?

He didn't have a choice—time had apparently forced his hand. He had to hope. He wasn't going to function without it.

"Yeah," Ross said, lowering his voice. "Saturday is going to suck."

They shared a look, complicated and painful. Finally, Pat spoke up from behind them, saving the moment from becoming too fraught.

"But Friday night isn't gonna," he said with decision. "Party after the games. My place. Barbecue to send Ross off and make him want to come back. Who's with me!"

"We can invite Piper since it's Friday," Ross said wistfully. "She'll still be recovering, but I can see her Friday night, right?"

"Yeah," Tenner said, thinking about how warm the nights were now in May. "I think she'll be so excited."

And Ross would be sleeping with Tenner that night—because they had no time left, and Tenner wasn't going to waste a second.

But it wasn't enough, just making that resolve, sending Ross off with that "I love you, come back" in his ears.

Tenner needed more—a sign. A signal. He remembered Ross "marking his room" that first night, and after lunch that afternoon, as he sat in his cubicle and stared sightlessly at his computer, he had an idea, like a bolt of lightning.

He got online and ordered Ross's surprise. It showed up Thursday morning.

THE LAST game of the season was Ross's last Friday in town. After Tenner's team lost its game heinously—but not so heinously they didn't at least get two at bats—Ross met him to go get Piper as the field lights were going down.

"Patrick just reminded me about the barbecue tonight," he said. "In honor of me getting the fuck out of Dodge. You, Piper, Nina—they want the whole nine yards. You can even invite the Sunspots, if you want. Hanford and Kipp might make out behind something and give us a thrill."

Tenner rolled his eyes. "You know what would give me a thrill? If Hanford could catch the damned ball. That would thrill me no end. That would be an instant orgasm where I stood, oh yes it would."

Ross laughed softly. "So you *do* love softball more than you love me."

Tenner looked at him sourly. "No, but I might love it more than I love your brother-in-law. I was supposed to join his team when you left, do you know that?"

"I do," Ross said.

"But I can't. I *can't*. Because these guys still suck on ice, and they keep looking at me, with their big eyes, going, 'You're going to be our captain again in the summer season, right, Tanner?' They don't even know my *name*, Ross. And you know what the worst part is?"

They neared the cinderblock bathrooms—*the* cinderblock bathrooms—and Ross touched his arm so he'd stand still. "You're going to do it?" Ross told him, like he wasn't surprised at all.

"Yeah, I'm gonna do it. I'd feel like some asshole who kicked puppies if I—" The lights clicked off, and they were left alone in the warm dark of the early summer night. "—didn't," Tenner finished weakly.

And Ross was there, his heat, his smell—and he was familiar now, he was Tenner's, but it was no less of a thrill because they'd had each other, spent nights in each other's arms, had promised a future together.

"You're not a guy who kicks puppies," Ross said, running tender fingertips along Tenner's jaw.

"No," Tenner murmured.

Their kiss wasn't urgent or electric. They weren't going to jump behind the bathrooms and bang each other like strangers this time, because they weren't strangers, and they had better places to make love.

But the kiss was an affirmation, a reminder, of all that they had become in the past month and a half, and all they had yet to be. Tenner moaned slightly and clenched Ross so tight it was probably hard to breathe.

"Hey," Ross murmured. "It's okay."

"You promised," Tenner reminded him.

"So did you."

"Your home is with me," Tenner said, because Ross had been a wanderer, and now he wasn't anymore, and Tenner had done that.

"And I'll be home to take care of you," Ross said softly. And God, Tenner hadn't thought he'd needed that, but he'd been so wrong. He needed Ross. Not to pay the rent or to feed the cat but to care for Tenner's soul.

Tenner nodded, eyes still burning, and then pulled back and dropped his equipment bag so he could fumble in the pocket. He came back with a small box that had been delivered the day before but that he hadn't wanted to leave in the house.

"Here," he mumbled. "This isn't very romantic, but here."

He pulled out the two rings, both of them gray silicone, plain and serviceable, and sturdy. "They're not wedding rings or engagement rings, but… but I don't want you a thousand miles away without anything but memories." He slid the ring onto Ross's finger, glad his guess about the size had worked. "There. I bought two extras, so if it rips or whatever, you can replace it. It's just—"

"Perfect," Ross said, pulling out his phone so he could look at the ring in the flashlight. "Perfect, Tenner. Where's yours?"

Tenner smiled a little, glad he understood, and pulled out the plain silicone band for himself. Ross took it and slid it on.

"It's not a wedding ring yet," he said, kissing Tenner's knuckles. "But it will be. I promise."

Tenner's eyes burned some more. "Come back," he muttered. "It's the only promise I need."

Ross took his mouth then and sealed the deal, and after a moment of their hearts beating in the humid quiet, they turned for the parking lot so they could go get their girl.

THE BARBECUE was great, because Patrick and Desi didn't know how to do a gathering badly, and everybody said goodbye and good luck to Ross, but only a few people noticed the rings.

Nina was one of them. "Nice," she murmured, nodding at Tenner's finger.

"Yeah?" And God, he really wanted her blessing.

"Invite me to the ceremony," she said pertly, but she smiled, and it was genuine, and he smiled back.

"I'll make you a groomsperson," he said, and her eyes widened in horror.

And then humor.

"That way, I'll have been in *both* of your weddings." Suddenly she giggled. "Your parents would have kittens."

Tenner laughed too. "We should invite them."

And they both clung to each other for a moment, like friends.

Ross said goodbye to his family that night and slept where he belonged—in Tenner's bed. It was funny, that, because he'd ramped the moment up into such a milestone, something so tremendous it would change his world with his daughter forever. But it was really so simple.

When he went to kiss Piper good night, she asked for Ross too.

"You want Ross to kiss you?" he asked, that little knife of "he's leaving us" twisting in his chest. "You know he's going away tomorrow."

"Yeah," she said sadly, "but he'll come back. He's got to. He needs to take care of you when I'm not here, and sleep in your bedroom when you have bad dreams."

Tenner stared at her. "In the bedroom?" he said, feeling a little off-kilter. This was supposed to be a big deal.

"Not the guest room," she told him. "He's not a guest. He lives here now. So he'll come back after his trip." She smiled at him, with that perfect confidence that adults would figure things out eventually. "Now get him to come in here and kiss me good night!"

"Sure. Ross!" he called, still surprised.

But Ross's footsteps up the stairs didn't sound surprised at all. "You rang?"

Piper laughed and held out her arms and got her kiss, and they went back downstairs for some grown-up time.

"Can you believe that?" Tenner asked, bemused. "She's got the whole thing planned. You have to sleep with me so you know this is your home, so you'll come back."

"She's brilliant," Ross said smugly. "Must get it from Nina."

"Shut up!" Tenner smacked him with a throw pillow, and Ross laughed and pinned him against the couch, tickling him until he was breathless.

And then kissed him until he was needy, and the two of them made it back up the stairs and closed the door and turned out the lights and had very quiet, very ordinary, *very* satisfying sex before they fell asleep.

"Ross?" Tenner murmured as they were closing their eyes.

"Yeah?"

"You *are* coming back here, right?"

"Yeah, Ten. Nothing could stop me."

"This will be your home, right?"

"Yeah. I promised in front of your kid, Ten. I wouldn't break that." He took his left hand, the one with the ring, and laced his fingers with Tenner's. "See? You had the right of it."

Rings. Joining. Family. "I believe," Tenner murmured.

"I promise."

Ross kissed the back of his neck, and Tenner closed his eyes. Ross's word was good enough. Tenner would believe in him until death did they part.

It was the only way he could get out of bed the next morning.

Because the next morning, bright and early, they loaded Ross and his luggage and Piper into the car, to take him to the airport.

Tenner put the car in Park and got out to help Ross with his luggage, and then turned to hug him and was ambushed by a kiss.

A hard, needy kiss, with Ross's hot face up against his, tears he hadn't expected stinging both their cheeks.

"I'll be back," Ross promised.

"I'll be home," Tenner promised in return, and then one more brief press of lips, and Ross saluted Piper in the car, shouldered his duffel, grabbed his suitcase, and left, not looking behind him.

Tenner envied him. He could go deal with the whole travel routine, but Tenner had to get in the front seat of the car and wipe his face until he could drive.

"Don't cry, Daddy," Piper said behind him.

"No?" God, this was miserable. He wiped his eyes on his palms and looked at the ring there, finding a little comfort, but still missing Ross like he hadn't guessed he could.

"He'll come back. He promised. It's all good."

Tenner snorted, blowing tears over the steering wheel. "You say that, but you'll be asking me every weekend if this is the one where he's home."

"No," she said, eyes sober. "Mommy helped me set up a calendar. We're counting the weeks with little X-es. He said at least ten X-es, so I won't start to worry until after that."

"Mommy's pretty smart," Tenner told her. And it didn't hurt to say, which was nice.

"She is. She says you're going to have a wedding, and I'm gonna get a new dress. I like dresses, Daddy, just not when we get all sweaty."

Tenner laughed again. "I know, sweetheart." He wiped his eyes on his shoulder one more time. "You look great in dresses too."

"Yeah, so Ross has to come back so I can wear a dress and Mommy can be pretty and meet a man."

Tenner laughed. "Your Mommy might be fine without a man," he said, putting the car into Drive and negotiating out of SMF without a problem. It was the world's smallest airport. He sort of loved it, right down to the two bird sculptures on the parking building, and the giant jackrabbit in B Terminal. It was funny what you grew to love with a little familiarity.

"You weren't," Piper said. "You were sad, Daddy. Mommy said so, and I think she's right."

"Well, I was lonely," Tenner admitted. "But your mom has friends that she visits when she goes out of town. We'll have to let her find her own person, okay?"

"Okay. But first Ross has to come home."

"Yeah. He will."

They didn't go to gymnastics that morning. Tenner took Piper to Nina's, and they went out to breakfast. They'd just gotten their food when Tenner's phone buzzed.

Boarding. Love you.

Eating at Denny's. Love you too. He took a picture of Piper and Nina, who waved.

Tell them to take care of my boyfriend while I'm gone.

Tell my boyfriend to take care of himself.

Will do.

"Ross?" Nina asked gently from across the table.

"Boarding. He told you two to take care of me while he's gone."

"We will," Nina said firmly. "But make sure he knows we miss him too. We want him to come home to be part of the family."

Piper nodded, and Tenner ruffled her hair.

"He will," he said. "And we'll be an amazingly happy family."
And wonder of wonders, he believed it.

TWO AND a half months later, Tenner was running around with a bunch
of little girls on a soccer field, grateful for the breeze off the lake to help
mitigate the blistering heat of the late August afternoon.

Behind him, Desi was giving their keeper—her daughter Polly—
lessons on how to stop the ball without using her face. Tenner watched the
kids playing sharks and minnows, the classic practice game, and despaired.

Watching these kids play, he got the same feeling he'd had with
two seasons with the CompuCo Sunspots. There was a lot of heart here,
and a lot of joy of the game, but not a smidge of talent anywhere. And
someone had wet their pants.

He watched as Piper tried diligently to win the ball from her
opponent, and then, when Marcie got upset, cheerfully kick it back.
That's when he called time.

"Everybody get a drink of water," he called, "and relax in the
shade." Fortunately their practice field was very Folsom—lots of shade
trees, lots of water fountains for the girls who hadn't brought bottles, and
lots of benches, although the parents had brought their own camp chairs.
Desi came up next to him, and they shared a long-suffering look.

"This is gonna be a riot of a season," she said with a deep breath.
"You heard from my brother lately? He's promised to share the misery."

Tenner shook his head. "I got a text three days ago saying he was
going to be out of touch this week, but that's been it. He said I'd hear from
him next week at the earliest." Tenner texted him a diary every night, just
because he missed him so badly. Ross had told him to please, *please* keep
that up. *It makes me happy to imagine you home,* he'd texted. But the nature
of his work wouldn't allow him to do the same. He'd tried, he texted at least
every two to three days, but he was so busy. Some of his texts had carried
pictures—heartbreaking devastation, workers with smudges on their faces
and exhaustion in their eyes. Tenner had missed him most at night, when
he'd gone home and thought of something he'd wanted to say to his other
half, and then remembered that Ross might not have slept in days.

Piper and Tenner had crossed off every day he'd been missing with
a red X, seven weeks, eight weeks, nine weeks—this next one would be
the tenth. And with every X, each day stretched longer without him.

Tenner had never missed anybody so badly in his life. But with the missing, came the peace. Every moment of their time together was like another thread binding their future to his hopes. This thing Tenner felt, it was real. And Ross loved him in return. Faith—that thing that had deserted him so long ago, seemed to have come back with a vengeance, and it was what kept Tenner functioning while Ross was away.

He'd never had so much faith in another person in his life.

"Next week?" Desi asked, her voice far away. "Are you sure?"

Tenner turned to look at her and saw her eyes were focused on the parking lot, where what looked like an Uber was pulling up to the curb.

A tall, lanky blond guy got out, his curly hair almost to his shoulders, his duffel and his suitcase by his side.

Tenner knew that duffel and suitcase.

He knew that bright blond hair.

"Oh. My God," he said, at the same time Desi said, "Oh my God!" next to him.

"Oh wow. Oh *wow*!" Tenner stood, frozen with surprise, until Desi jabbed him unceremoniously in the side.

"Don't just stand there—go get him! Do you think he's here to see *me*?"

Tenner took off like a sprinter at the mark, dodging around the other practice field where a bunch of seven-year-old boys screamed like an invading army, through the playground and up the hill to where Ross was scanning the chaos below the parking lot.

He saw Tenner as he approached, though, because he dropped his duffel bag and opened his arms.

His mouth on Tenner's made the last two and a half months, miserable as they had been, seem like shadows.

Oh God. He was here. He'd come back. He was *here*.

"Hi," Ross said, smiling softly as they pulled away.

"Hi. You're here."

Ross kissed his forehead. "I had to come here," he said. "You were here. And I'm home."

Tenner kissed him on the lips again, and the kiss was still going when Piper came and tugged on his arm. "Daddy! Daddy! Let me hug Ross! Ross! We missed you so much!"

Ross grinned and picked her up, and Tenner grabbed his luggage so Ross could listen to her chatter. As he walked behind the two of them, Ross looked back and caught his eye and winked.

They would have time. Time to kiss, time to talk, time to make love.

Time to plan—their wedding, watching Pat and Desi's kids while they took a vacation, all the things Ross had wanted to do with him and Piper, family things that had needed time and planning because that's how grown-ups worked.

They would have time.

All the time in the world.

Because Ross had meant it. He was home.

Choose your Lane to love!

Yellow

Amy's Light Contemporary Romance

AMY LANE is a mother of two grown kids, two half-grown kids, two small dogs, and half-a-clowder of cats. A compulsive knitter who writes because she can't silence the voices in her head, she adores fur-babies, knitting socks, and hawt menz, and she dislikes moths, cat boxes, and knuckleheaded macspazzmatrons. She is rarely found cooking, cleaning, or doing domestic chores, but she has been known to knit up an emergency hat/blanket/pair of socks for any occasion whatsoever or sometimes for no reason at all. Her award-winning writing has three flavors: twisty-purple alternative universe, angsty-orange contemporary, and sunshine-yellow happy. By necessity, she has learned to type like the wind. She's been married for twenty-five-plus years to her beloved Mate and still believes in Twu Wuv, with a capital Twu and a capital Wuv, and she doesn't see any reason at all for that to change.

Website: www.greenshill.com
Blog: www.writerslane.blogspot.com
Email: amylane@greenshill.com
Facebook: www.facebook.com/amy.lane.167
Twitter: @amymaclane

FRECKLES
Amy Lane

Small dogs can make big changes… if you open your heart.

Carter Embree always hoped someone might rescue him from his productive, tragically boring, and (slightly) ethically compromised life. But when an urchin at a grocery store shoves a bundle of fluff into his hands, Carter goes from rescuee to rescuer—and he needs a little help.

Sandy Corrigan, the vet tech who eases Carter into the world of dog ownership, first assumes Carter is a crazy-pants client who just needs to relax. But as Sandy gets a glimpse of the funny, kind, sexy man under Carter's mild-mannered exterior, he sees that with a little care and feeding, Carter might be "Super Pet Owner"—and decent boyfriend material to boot.

But Carter needs to see himself as a hero first. As he says goodbye to his pristine house and hello to carpet treatments and dog walkers, he finds there really is more to himself than a researching drudge without a backbone. A Carter Embree can rate a Sandy Corrigan. He can be supportive. He can be a man who stands up for his principles!

He can be the owner of a small dog.

www.dreamspinnerpress.com

A Candy Man Book

Adam Macias has been thrown a few curve balls in his life, but losing his VA grant because his car broke down and he missed a class was the one that struck him out. One relative away from homelessness, he's taking the bus to Sacramento, where his cousin has offered a house-sitting job and a new start. He has one goal, and that's to get his life back on track. Friends, pets, lovers? Need not apply.

Finn Stewart takes one look at Adam as he's applying to Candy Heaven and decides he's much too fascinating to leave alone. Finn is bright and shiny—and has never been hurt. Adam is wary of his attention from the very beginning—Finn is dangerous to every sort of peace Adam is forging, and Adam may just be too damaged to let him in at all.

But Finn is tenacious, and Adam's new boss, Darrin, doesn't take bullshit for an answer. Adam is going to have to ask himself which is harder—letting Finn in or living without him? With the holidays approaching it seems like an easy question, but Adam knows from experience that life is seldom simple, and the world seldom cooperates with hope, faith, or the plans of cats and men.

www.dreamspinnerpress.com

Christmas Kitsch

Amy Lane

Sometimes the best Christmas gift is knowing what you really want.

Rusty Baker is a rich, entitled, oblivious jock, and he might have stayed that way if he hadn't become friends with out-and-proud Oliver Campbell from the wrong side of the tracks. When Oliver kisses him goodbye before Rusty leaves for college, Rusty is forced to rethink everything he knows about himself.

But nothing can help Rusty survive a semester at Stanford, and he returns home for Thanksgiving break clinging to the one thing he knows to be true: Oliver is the best thing that's ever happened to him.

Rusty's parents disagree, and Rusty finds himself homeless for the holidays. But with Oliver's love and the help of Oliver's amazing family, Rusty realizes that failing college doesn't mean he can't pass real life with flying rainbow colors.

www.dreamspinnerpress.com